Circus Shoes

They bumped over the rough grass. The king-poles stood out against the pale blue of the sky. The men's mess-tent was up; from it came a lovely smell of frying eggs and bacon. A man was standing on the top of the steps of the advance wagon; he called out 'Good morning' to Gus. The Kenet's caravan was in place. The car was being detached and backed into position. A stream of caravans, each painted green and white, was towed in. There was much talking and laughing. People said Gus and the Kenets could not have been to bed or they would not have been there first. Gus gave Santa the kettle. She stood a moment looking round.

It's just like Thursday at Bridlington,' she whispered to Peter.

Peter forgot that he had a grievance. It was all so gay it was difficult to feel cross. He took a big sniff of circus smell.

'Only this time we belong.'

Also by Noel Streatfield:

Dancing Shoes

CIRCUS
SHOES

NOEL STREATFEILD

*Hodder
Children's
Books*

a division of Hodder Headline plc

Copyright © Noel Streatfield 1938, 1956

First published in Great Britain as
The Circus is Coming in 1938 by Dent

Published in Great Britain as *The Circus is Coming*
in revised edition in 1956 by Penguin Books

This edition published by Hodder Childrens Books in 1998

The right of Noel Streatfield to be identified as the Author
of the Work has been asserted by her in accordance with the
Copyright, Designs and Patents Act 1988.

10 9 8 7 6 5 4 3

A Catalogue record for this book is
available from the British Library

ISBN 0 340 70445 4

Typeset by Hewer Text Ltd, Edinburgh
Printed and bound in Great Britain by Clays Ltd, St Ives plc

Hodder Children's Books
A Division of Hodder Headline plc
338 Euston Road
London NW1 3BH

Contents

1

Aunt Rebecca

Peter and Santa were orphans. When they were babies their father and mother were killed in a railway accident, so they came and lived with their aunt. The aunt's name was Rebecca Possit, but of course they called her Aunt Rebecca. The aunt had been lady's maid to a duchess. This was a good thing, because when the duchess died she left her an annuity, and, as Aunt Rebecca had no money and neither had the children, it was important. In other ways it was not so good. Being lady's maid to a duchess had made Aunt Rebecca suppose that only dukes and duchesses, and perhaps kings and queens, could be right. She never did or said anything without first thinking how 'Her Grace' would have said or done it. As the duchess's sayings and doings had been rather a bore, Aunt Rebecca's were too.

What Aunt Rebecca said and did would not have mattered much to Peter and Santa because, of course, they were interested in their own things, but most unluckily the duchess had a great many grandchildren who had often been to stay at Plyst (pronounced 'Pleat'), where the duchess had spent most of her time. How Peter and Santa suffered from the duchess's grand-children!

'I don't believe anything nice ever happened to that awful Lady Marigold or Lady Moira or those horrible Manliston children,' Santa grumbled.

Peter said: 'It's all very well for you to make a fuss, but you don't have that dreadful Lord Bronedin pushed down your throat all day.'

Santa had fair hair which hung right down to her waist. It curled a little bit, but not enough, so it had to be what Aunt Rebecca called 'helped'. Santa hated her hair. She wanted it cut short, or at least put in plaits, but instead she was made to wear it loose, because the duchess had said: 'A woman's glory is her hair.' She had also said: 'How hair looks depends on the brushing it gets. Six hundred strokes a night. That's my rule.' Which from Santa's point of view was a very annoying statement.

Though Peter did not realize it, the worst thing Lord Bronedin did to him was over education. Lord Bronedin went to a preparatory school and to Eton. Aunt Rebecca could not possibly afford either, but she would not send Peter to an ordinary school. Instead she sent him to be taught privately. Of course, the annuity would not pay for a proper tutor, but it paid bits to various people who knew a little. There was Mr Stibbings. He was a retired parson. He knew a lot of Latin but could not teach it. Peter went to him for an hour after tea twice a week. Then there was Madame Tranchot. Both Peter and Santa went to her. She gave French lessons at two shillings a lesson. For the ordinary subjects, like reading and arithmetic, there was a friend of Aunt Rebecca's, called Mrs Ford, whose husband had been a schoolmaster. Mrs Ford did not know much herself, but she had her husband's books and taught from them.

Santa, besides going to Madame Tranchot, shared Mrs Ford with Peter and did music as well. She learnt the violin, not because she was musical, but, of all silly reasons, because Lady Marigold had learnt to play a fiddle. Aunt Rebecca being poor, those violin lessons were a shocking waste of money. Santa was taught by a Miss Lucy Fane, the violin was bought on the hire-purchase. Somebody had once told Miss Fane that she looked like a Rossetti picture, and she had never forgotten it. She dressed to look Rossetti-ish, but as she nearly always had a cold she put a red shawl round her shoulders, which spoilt the effect. Partly because Miss Fane always had colds and was too sniffy to teach, and partly because she could not teach anyway, Santa never learnt much, and would not have learnt much even if she had had an aptitude for playing the violin, which she certainly had not. Miss Fane liked pieces which she described as 'that dear little slumber song', and she liked hymns. Santa could never remember how her fingers went in the 'dear little slumber songs', so she took to hymns, or rather to one hymn. It was called 'Art thou weary, art thou languid?' It was easy fingering and expressed so exactly how she felt about violins that in the end she knew that tune quite well.

Of course all these lessons from people who did not know much, or if they knew anything could not teach, meant that Peter and Santa grew up most ignorant children. They were even more ignorant than you would expect from their dreadful education, and that was because they had no friends and no relations. Of course, many friends and relations might just as well not be there for all the good they do anybody, but most people have some nice ones as well. Peter and Santa had nobody. At least nobody they had ever seen. They knew that somewhere they had an uncle. They knew this because each Christmas he sent Aunt Rebecca a Christmas card. But they never knew what was on the card or anything about him, for the moment it arrived Aunt Rebecca turned very red and, making clicking disapproving noises with her tongue against her teeth, hurried upstairs and stuck it in the mirror on her dressing-table, where it stayed until the new one arrived the next

Christmas. Peter and Santa thought it odd that she stuck it up at all, seeing she was not pleased to get it, but she got very few cards and they guessed it was vanity. After all, a card is a card, whoever it comes from.

Because they had no friends and no relations, Peter and Santa did none of the things most children do. They never went to parties, or even out to tea, because Aunt Rebecca did not think anybody in the neighbourhood fit to know one, or the nephew and niece of one, who had been maid to a duchess. They had no aunts or uncles who said: 'What about a pantomime?' or: 'I'd like to take the children to see *A Midsummer Night's Dream*.' They had no cousins to go and stay with in the country or by the sea. They knew nobody but their aunt, Mr Stibbings, Madame Tranchot, Mrs Ford, and Miss Fane, and a very dull lot they were.

Their aunt and the people who taught them being no companions for Peter and Santa, they were tremendous friends with each other. Naturally they quarrelled now and then, but really they both hated the other one to be out of sight.

Aunt Rebecca's house was in London, on the south side of the river in a little street not far from Battersea Bridge. A nice place to live, as it is near the park. Battersea Park is in many ways the best park in London, because of the river. But it was not as much use as it might have been, to

Peter and Santa, as one of the worst things the duchess had said was that children did not walk about alone in London. As Aunt Rebecca had the cooking and housework to do she could not get out much, so it really meant that they stopped indoors most of the time, and got pale and thin like bulbs grown in a cupboard.

The worst part of Peter's and Santa's lives, which was a part they did not know themselves, was that Aunt Rebecca's foolish ways of thinking were catching. It is almost impossible to live with somebody who thinks you are too grand to know anybody and not get a bit that way yourself. Peter would have liked to go to school like other boys, but he supposed Aunt Rebecca was right not to let him. Santa would have liked to go to the girls' school, but she never suggested it because she felt it was not suitable for her. This feeling of being rather superior was added to by the clothes they wore. The duchess had often said to Aunt Rebecca:

'Whatever you do, buy the best, Possit. Cheap stuff never pays.'

Of course Aunt Rebecca could not buy the best, but what she bought was good. The duchess's grandchildren had lived in riding things at Plyst, but were well dressed when in London. Aunt Rebecca took the idea of smart clothes in London very seriously, and dressed Santa as well as she could in nicely tailored coats, a matching hat, and, what Santa hated, always gloves. The same London dressing happened to Peter. Lord Bronedin had looked a perfect disgrace in the country, but he had good clothes for London. Poor Peter was never allowed to wear old clothes, but always well-brushed suits, and in winter a good overcoat. So neither of them ever knew the glory of putting on the sort of clothes which you can do anything in because it does not matter what happens to them. Their clothes, of course, affected everything they did, including the games they played. You cannot play anything but quiet games, in clothes that have to be thought about all the time.

What with one thing and another Peter and Santa were becoming rather odd children; then one day at the end of March, when Peter was twelve and Santa just eleven, Aunt Rebecca died, and, as is the way of such things, Aunt Rebecca's annuity died with her.

2

The Christmas Card

Peter and Santa felt miserable. In their way they missed Aunt Rebecca, for odd, funny things, and they both knew how the other was feeling so there was no need to keep talking about it. Inside, though they did not talk about that either, they were both worrying. After all they were not babies, they knew what happened to annuities when people died, and though, of course, they also knew that somebody or other is bound to look after children, they knew too it might not be the sort of looking after they would care for. The worst of it was there had to be a time of hanging about. The moment Aunt Rebecca died Mr Stibbings had written to the duchess's executors, explaining what had happened, and about Peter and Santa, and asking if something could be done until they were old enough to earn their own livings. Meanwhile it was decided, if the executors said no, they were to go to an orphanage.

The letter came a week after Aunt Rebecca died. It arrived at tea-time. Mrs Ford, Madame Tranchot, and Miss Fane were all there, but no one liked to open the letter because it was, of course, addressed to Mr Stibbings. It was put on the mantelpiece and they all stared at it. Peter and Santa could not eat any more tea because they wanted so badly to know what it said, which was a pity because there was some particularly good hot buttered toast.

'Do you think,' Peter suggested, 'that I had better take it round to him?'

Mrs Ford looked at Madame Tranchot, who looked at Miss Fane. All their faces said the same thing. 'Don't let him do that because I want to know what is in it.' But none of them liked to say quite that. Mrs Ford got round the difficulty by starting to cry.

'It does seem hard that what concerns the nephew and niece of my oldest friend . . .' here she gave a big sniff – 'should be discussed behind my back.'

Peter kicked Santa under the table. She saw he was angry and embarrassed about the crying and might be rude. She thought quickly.

'How would it be if Peter and I went round and told him it was here?'

Everybody thought that a good idea. So Peter and Santa, without giving anyone a chance to change their minds, rushed out. Outside Mr

Stibbings's house they stood still for a moment. Santa panted, for they had run all the way:

'I feel awful inside. Do you?'

Peter nodded.

'Like waiting at the dentist's. I wish we knew what it said. Just suppose it's an orphanage.'

Luckily Mr Stibbings was in and said he would come at once. But Mr Stibbing's 'at once' was almost as slow as other people's 'presently'. Although it was April and not a bit cold, it was astounding how he fussed before he would go out. It was nearly five minutes before he found his scarf, though Peter and Santa helped look, as well as Mr Stibbings's housekeeper. In the end the housekeeper remembered he had worn it in bed one night, and she ran upstairs and found it tied in a black wool bow to one of the bed knobs. When all the scarf (and it was a very long one) was wound round Mr Stibbings, Peter held out his overcoat.

'Here you are, sir.'

Mr Stibbings looked over his glasses in a hurt way.

'All right, my boy. All in good time. Speed is the curse of the age.'

Peter looked so much as if he was going to say something which might sound rude, and, anyway, Santa knew that Mr Stibbings was the sort of man whom hurrying made slow, that she broke in. She asked about an ostrich egg on the hall table. It did

11

what she wanted, in that it stopped Peter speaking or Mr Stibbings feeling annoyed at being rushed, but it took six minutes before they got away from ostriches, and Mr Stibbings dressed and out of the front door.

'You are a fool,' Peter whispered. 'Fancy asking about that then.'

Santa did not answer, because she knew Peter knew why she had done it, and that, in a way, he thought it a good idea. It came natural to him to answer back and it never helped in the end.

When they got back to the house Mr Stibbings opened the letter. He opened it very slowly, because whatever he did he was slow at. Then he put his spectacles straight. Then he did what the children thought an awfully mean thing. He read the letter to himself. Peter turned red and looked so angry that Santa slipped round to him and whispered: 'Don't ask what's in it, because they will.' She jerked her head at the three women at the table.

She was quite right; even before the letter was finished Mrs Ford was crying. Directly Mr Stibbings stopped reading she said in a choked voice:

'That I should live to see the day when what concerns the welfare of the nephew and niece of my oldest friend was kept from me!'

Luckily Mr Stibbings hated crying as much as Peter and Santa did. He made the sort of cough people make when they are looking for the right words. Then he turned to the children.

'My dear young people, I fear it is not good news. It seems that all the money the duchess left is held in trust for a grandson who is a minor. He is . . .' He opened the letter again and started to look through it; but before he found the name Peter broke in:

'I know. It's that Lord Bronedin.'

Mr Stibbings looked up surprised.

'That's quite right. The name is Lord Bronedin. You know of him?'

Peter and Santa made each other a very understanding face. Then Peter said:

'I'd just about say we do.'

Mr Stibbings was too interested in other things to ask them what they meant; instead he sat down in the arm-chair and looked as people look when they know nobody is going to like what they have to say. He rearranged his spectacles to a better position on his nose, put the tips of his fingers together, then looked at the children.

'I was afraid that this was the reply we should receive. But thanks to those whom I may call your good friends . . .' he turned to the three women – 'other arrangements are in train. We have arranged for you, Peter, dear boy, at Saint Bernard's Home for Boys. You Santa, are going to Saint Winifred's Orphanage.'

'What!' Santa was so startled that the word came out in a shout. 'We aren't going together?'

Mrs Ford made clicking sounds with her tongue.

'Don't shout, dear. There are different homes for boys and girls.'

Santa turned to her.

'Not always there aren't.'

'Grammar! Grammar!' Mrs Ford wagged her finger at her. Then she took out her handkerchief and wiped her eyes. 'This is not the arrangement I wished for . . .'

Santa was so upset she felt she would scream if she had to hear about being the niece and nephew of her oldest friend again. So she interrupted.

'If you don't like the arrangement, don't let it happen. It needn't. There must be somewhere we could go together if only you looked for it.' She came to Mrs Ford and shook her arm to be sure she was listening. 'Peter and I couldn't live in two different places, you must see that.'

Miss Fane leant across the table. She held out her hand, palm upwards, as if she expected Santa to put her hand into it.

'I understand how you feel, little one. Separation is terribly hard. But, believe me, your violin will help.'

Santa stamped her foot. She sobbed while she spoke:

'How can you say that? Why should it make it better if I played "Art thou weary?" six hundred times a day?' She turned desperately to them all. 'You must find a place for us. Here you sit, and all you say is it can't be helped. But it's got to be helped. I won't live somewhere else than Peter. And he wouldn't either. Would you, Peter?'

They all looked at Peter. He was leaning against the mantelpiece. His hands were in his pockets and he was staring at the floor, not seeming interested in what was going on. Santa could not see him clearly because she was crying so hard that everything was out of focus. But she felt a cold feeling inside. Peter was not going to fight. Ordinarily he was so much more quickly angry than she was that if he were going to be angry he would have been by now. Mr Stibbings looked at him with approval.

'Peter is sensible, Santa. He knows what must be must be.'

Peter looked up, then he came over to the table and stood beside Santa.

'That's right, sir.' As he spoke he dug his elbow into Santa's side. If ever a dig in the ribs meant 'Don't be a fool, trust me', that one did. He turned to Mrs Ford: 'I shouldn't worry. I expect it won't be bad at Saint Bernard's Home for Boys and Santa will get used to Saint Winifred's Orphanage. Won't you, Santa?'

After the dig in the ribs Santa felt better, and she knew, from the way he said that, she would not mind when she understood, that he had a plan, and she guessed it would help if she seemed to cheer up. She dried her eyes.

'No. I suppose it will be all right. It was just I was so surprised. I had never thought of us not going together.' As she said this she could not help a wobble in her voice. She was sure Peter meant to do something, but after all they were only children, and probably police and people like that would be on the side of Mr Stibbings, Mrs Ford, Madame Tranchot, Miss Fane, Saint Bernard's and Saint Winifred's. She tried to look brave, but she did not feel it.

Peter pulled two chairs up to the table. He pushed Santa into one and he sat on the other.

'There's just one or two things, sir. When do we go?'

Mr Stibbings looked at Mrs Ford, Mrs Ford looked at Madame Tranchot, Madame Tranchot looked at Miss Fane. They all looked embarrassed. Mr Stibbings cleared his throat.

'I'm afraid, dear boy, it will have to be tomorrow. Your lamented aunt only left a few pounds in ready money. That is exhausted. We are all poor people or . . .'

'I know,' Peter broke in. 'You've all been awfully kind.' He paused a moment. Then he said firmly: 'My aunt left some jewellery and stuff. If we are going tomorrow Santa and I would like it tonight.'

Mr Stibbings was a stupid man in a lot of ways,

16

but he meant to be kind. He was very worried at what Peter asked. The duchess had given Aunt Rebecca quite a lot of bits of jewellery, many of them not very beautiful, but all of them good in their way. But should the children be trusted with them? Except for the money that would be raised by selling the furniture, the little bits of jewellery were all the children had. Having appointed himself guardian he had to do what he could to look after them. Allowing them their jewellery was hardly doing that.

'I am afraid, my boy, that would not be wise. I think it should be kept for you until you are out in the world.'

Peter shook his head.

'No, thank you, sir. We'll take it with us.'

Santa was amazed. It did not sound a bit like Peter talking. Such a grand, quiet, that-is-my-last-word-I-don't-want-to-be-argued-with kind of voice, just like a grown-up person.

Mrs Ford began to cry again.

'What a man he sounds. Brave little boy. When I first knew you, Peter, you were such a baby. Let them have their dear aunt's things, Mr Stibbings. It will be a comfort to them, poor pets.'

At the thought of how much the children would need comfort, Miss Fane clasped her hands and looked at the roof, and Madame Tranchot gave so deep a sigh that it nearly blew over a teacup. Mr Stibbings made up his mind.

'There are several little trinkets, dear boy, few of which would be any good to you. But there is a watch which you may have and Santa shall choose something as a keepsake. The rest I will deposit in my bank until you are older.'

Aunt Rebecca's jewel-case had been locked in the corner cupboard when she died. Mr Stibbings had the key. He went now and unlocked it. While he was doing this Peter leaned down as if he had dropped something and whispered to Santa:

'Choose the one I tell you.'

During the last years of her life the duchess had made it a practice to give her faithful maid a piece of jewellery every Christmas. They were an odd-looking collection. There was a gold watch and chain for Peter. Aunt Rebecca had thought it very handsome, but she had never worn it because she was afraid of losing it. There were several heavy brooches, and there was one bracelet. It was plain gold, very dull and solid-looking.

Santa liked a brooch with turquoises, and hoped Peter remembered that she liked it. She had often said so when Aunt Rebecca wore it.

Peter fingered all the things in turn. He looked at Mr Stibbings.

'I don't suppose they are worth much, are they, sir?'

Mr Stibbings shook his head.

'No actual value, no. In sentiment, yes.'

18

Mrs Ford sniffed.

'Yes, indeed.'

'What I mean is,' Peter explained, 'if some day we wanted to sell them, would we get much money?'

'Sell them!' Mrs Ford's voice showed she was going to cry again.

'Well, we might have to. I mean, we might need the money for food.'

Mr Stibbings smiled.

'I hope not, dear boy. I think we can trust Saint Bernard's and Saint Winifred's to fit you for careers that will keep you from want.'

Peter nodded.

'Of course, sir. But I only said "supposing". You see, I want to know.'

Mr Stibbings looked vaguely at the jewels. But Madame Tranchot, who understood money, was turning them over.

'If it should be that you 'ad to sell them, Peter, it will be just the weight of the gold you would get. No more.'

'Well, Santa?' Mr Stibbings smiled at her. 'What do you choose?'

Santa looked at Peter.

'What would you have if you were me?'

Peter was still fingering the things. Suddenly he picked up the bracelet.

'This. You'll be less likely to lose it.'

Santa tried not to show what she felt, but the

bracelet really was very ugly. She took it and held it out to Mr Stibbings.

'I'll have this.'

It seemed ages before bedtime, when Santa could be alone with Peter. Mr Stibbings stayed on and on in order to make last arrangements with Mrs Ford, and it was clear he would be there until quite late. But at half past eight Mrs Ford looked at the clock, and before she could say 'Bedtime' Santa had jumped up. Peter got up, too.

'I think I'll start my packing.'

Mrs Ford gave a knowing glance at Mr Stibbings as much as to say: 'Want to be together their last night, poor little things.' Then she kissed them both.

'Run along. Happy dreams.'

Peter and Santa went upstairs. At the top Peter said in a very loud voice:

'Good night, Santa.' He opened and banged shut her bed-room door. Then he opened his and dragged her inside. He shut the door and beckoned her over to the bed. They sat side by side and talked in whispers.

Santa began.

'Have you a plan?'

'Yes. We're going to run away.'

'Where to?'

'Our uncle. The one Aunt Rebecca had the card from every Christmas. We might stay with him.'

'We don't know where he is, and we haven't any money.'

'That's what the watch and bracelet are for. We'll sell them. And perhaps the card says where he is. I'll get it.'

Santa looked doubtful.

'Don't want them to hear you creeping about.'

Peter got up.

'They won't.'

Luckily the door handle turned very quietly. Peter stood in the passage and listened. Mr Stibbings and Mrs Ford were talking hard. Aunt Rebecca's room was at the end of the passage. Very quietly he opened the door. Would Mrs Ford have moved the card? He hoped not. Softly he crept across the room and felt round the mirror. There it was in the top left-hand corner. In a moment he had shut the door and was back in his room. Without a word he sat down beside Santa and they read the card.

It was a Christmas postcard with a picture of a church covered in snow on it. On the back it said:

COB'S CIRCUS

Just a line, old dear, for the festive season. Hoping this finds you in the pink. Doing a four weeks' season with above and tenting with same April.

Love,
Gus

Peter and Santa stared at each other. They hardly knew what the word 'circus' meant. At some time or other they had seen a poster advertising one, and some vision of that had remained in the back of their heads.

'That's where people stand on horses,' Santa said.

'And a man sits on a lion,' Peter added.

Santa studied the card.

'Do you suppose our uncle's called Gus? What an awful name.'

'I don't see how it can be our uncle,' Peter objected. 'What would he be doing with a circus?'

Santa read what was written again.

'I wonder what "tenting" means. That's what he's doing now. It says April.'

Peter leant over her shoulder.

'So it does. I hadn't thought of that.' He got up. 'Look. Go to your room. Pack as much as you can in your case. Get into bed with all your things on except your shoes. Whatever you do, don't go to sleep. As soon as Mrs Ford's asleep, and she snores so loud I'll be sure to hear if I listen in the passage, I'll come and fetch you.'

Santa crept to the door.

'You'll bring my bracelet?' Peter nodded. 'Where'll we go to?'

He shrugged his shoulders.

'I don't know where we'll go tonight. Tomorrow we'll find Cob's Circus.'

3

Escape

Santa would have sworn that with an important thing like running away hanging over her she would not have felt a bit like going to sleep. But she was wrong. She had never been to bed in her clothes before, so she had no idea how hot she would be. In spite of what Peter had said, she did not keep on all her clothes. She took off her frock. It was, after all, the only frock she was taking, and she had to go on wearing it at least until she found her Uncle Gus, and perhaps much longer, and her aunt's training had made her much too fussy to be seen about all over creases. In any case, it was the last sort of frock to go to bed in. It was green to match her coat and hat, and had pleats. Even with her frock off she was stifling. In a terrific fug she went to sleep.

She woke up to find Peter's hand over her mouth.

'Ssh. Get up. Come on.'

Santa sat up and rubbed her eyes. Then she thought of Mrs Ford.

'Is she asleep?'

'Yes, hours. It's half past three. Come on.'

Santa got out of bed and put on her frock.

'Why is it so late? I thought we were going directly she was asleep.'

'I'll tell you when we get outside. Hurry.'

Santa tied her shoes and pulled on her coat. She could not comb her hair because, of course, she had packed her comb, but she pushed it back and shoved on her hat. Then she put on her gloves and picked up her attaché-case.

'All right. I'm ready.'

It's queer how a house, which seems quite quiet during the day, gets full of noises at night. Santa's door gave a little groan when she touched it. There was no need to have touched the door, as it was open already, but it never made noises in the daytime so she had not expected it to do so now, and felt the annoyed pinch Peter gave her a bit mean. After the groan they both stood still a second to see if Mrs Ford woke up. They held their breaths. Her snores stopped. They could imagine her sitting up in bed, turning on the light, looking round for a weapon with which to hit a burglar. Then suddenly there was a sound. At first a gentle purr, then deep-throated snores. Mrs Ford had gone to sleep again.

After such a devastating start, the opening and

shutting of the front door, which Peter had thought would be the worst part, was as easy as anything. In half a minute they were outside and running up the road.

Perhaps it was relief at getting out safely, but before they had run far they began to giggle, then the giggles turned to laughs, and in the end the laughs took away all their breath, so that they had to lean against a wall simply doubled up.

'Fancy her never waking!' Santa gasped.

'And fancy you being asleep when I came to fetch you!'

This annoyed Santa.

'I like that! What were you doing? You said you'd come for me directly she went to sleep. I bet she went to sleep before half past three.'

Peter took a deep breath to stop the last quivers of his laughter. He held his diaphragm.

'Oh, I do ache! Matter of fact, I thought of something after you'd gone. We didn't want to get away too soon. One thing, we've nowhere to go, and another, a policeman might ask us what we were doing if he saw us hanging about at night. Now it's getting light and it won't matter.'

Santa was surprised. If anything, she would have said she was the more sensible of the two. At least she did not get angry and rude so quickly. But ever since they had heard about Saint Bernard's and Saint Winifred's Peter had seemed different. The way he had just listened to the talk about the orphanages without saying a word, and all the time making a scheme to run away. The way he had insisted on them having some of Aunt Rebecca's jewellery. And, while she was asleep, remembering about it being dark and policemen. She put her attaché-case on the ground.

'You've had a lot of good ideas.'

Peter moved angrily.

'We had to do something. I wouldn't have minded so much if I thought they'd tried to put us somewhere together, but they hadn't.

Santa lolled against the wall. She counted on her fingers:

'Four to five. Five to six. Six to seven. In three hours and a bit Mrs Ford will get up. I wonder what she'll do when she finds we aren't there.'

'I left a letter.' Peter tried not to sound proud. 'I said we'd always wanted to see London and, as we were going away, I'd taken you, and we'd be back about twelve o'clock in time for lunch.'

'Goodness!' Santa's voice was full of admiration. 'You have got clever all of a sudden.'

Peter said: 'Shut up,' but he said it in a pleased way. He fingered his watch.

'Does seem a pity we have to sell this.'

Santa felt sorry. After all, a watch was the sort of thing every person wanted to have. To get one and have to sell it at once would make anybody miserable. It was then she had her good idea.

'Oh! I've thought of something!'

'What?'

'You can pawn it.'

'Pawn!' Peter was shocked. 'We couldn't go into a pawn-shop.'

'I don't see why not,' Santa argued. 'They're quite honest. Madame Tranchot told me about them. She said in England it was called "a visit to your uncle". She said there were always three golden balls hung outside to show they'd give you money for things.'

'Would we get as much as selling them?'

Santa put her hands under her armpits because they were getting cold.

'As long as we get enough it won't matter. How do we find out where the circus is?' Before he could answer she clutched his arm. 'Somebody's coming!'

They listened. There were footsteps a long way off; slow and rather heavy footsteps.

'It's a policeman,' Peter whispered.

Santa's heart began to thump.

'Shall we run?'

'No. Pick up your case and just walk ordinarily. If he stops us leave explaining to me.'

They picked up their cases and started up the road. Santa's knees wobbled. With every step the policeman's feet sounded louder. Presently they saw him. He had a torch and was stopping at doors and looking at them. Peter started a rather breathless conversation:

'An ostrich has no true nest. The eggs are deposited in a shallow excavation. The male bird incubates the egg during the night and . . .'

They were level with the policeman and right under the street lamp, so he could not help seeing them. The policeman paused.

'Up early, aren't you?'

'Yes,' Santa agreed. Peter trod on her foot to remind her that he had said he would answer questions.

'Where are you off to?' asked the policeman.

'Covent Garden,' Peter said firmly. 'We're going to see the flowers.'

'Oh! Your family know where you've gone?'

'Yes,' said Peter.

'Well, hope you enjoy yourselves.'

The policeman walked on and so did Peter and Santa.

When the policeman was quite out of hearing, Santa whispered:

'That was two lies. We aren't going to Covent Garden, and our family don't know.'

Peter was so angry his whisper was a hiss.

'I like that! It was a jolly good answer, and all you do is to say it was lies.'

'Well, so it was.'

'It needn't be. We can go to Covent Garden. It's where the flowers and vegetables come from. It's open all night, I think.'

'Where is it?'

'I don't know. But we can ask, can't we? The policeman seemed to think it was an ordinary place to go to.'

Santa walked on in silence. Then she said:

'Even if we go to Covent Garden it's a lie about our family knowing. They don't.'

Peter stood still.

'Will you stop grumbling! We haven't got a family, so how can they know? If Aunt Rebecca wasn't dead it would be different; but she is, so now we haven't a family.'

'You mean Mrs Ford and Mr Stibbings and Madame Tranchot and Miss Fane aren't?'

'Of course not.'

Santa cheered up.

'Well, that's different.' Suddenly she giggled. 'What made you say that about ostriches? The policeman must have thought it queer.'

Peter nodded.

'I bet he did. But it was all I could think of. It's what Mr Stibbings told you yesterday when you asked about the egg in his hall. Come on. If we're going to Covent Garden I expect we'd better hurry. It may be miles.'

By the time Peter and Santa got to Covent Garden the sun was rising. They were tired, but in spite of that they loved it. They liked the porters with piles of baskets on their heads. It was all so bustling and smelt so good. But after wandering round for about three-quarters of an hour their legs began to give out. They looked round for somewhere to sit. Near them was a fruit merchant. He was selling tomatoes. Piled up outside his stall were some empty wooden boxes. Peter went up to a man who looked like the owner.

'Would you allow my sister and me to rest for a bit on those boxes?'

'You won't hurt me,' said the man.

'You mean we may?'

The man pushed back his hat and scratched his head.

'I don't know what they teach you kids nowadays. Don't you understand a bit of plain English? I said: "You won't hurt me." Well, then, sit and get on with it.'

Santa saw by Peter's back that he was cross. By Aunt Rebecca's training he had been polite and his feelings were hurt. But she could see that, oddly enough, the man did not admire Peter in spite of his politeness. She stepped forward.

'Thank you so much. I hope you've done well today?'

'Not so bad. Like tomatoes?'

Santa nodded.

'Very much.'

The man took two big ones out of the cork shavings in which they were packed. One he wiped on his coat and gave to Santa, the other he threw to Peter.

Peter was not expecting a tomato. Nor, seeing

he had played no games, was he much of a catch. The tomato hit him on the chest and fell on the pavement, where it burst open. The man gave a faint, scornful jerk of his head and turned away.

'Sorry, Lord Marmaduke. If I'd known your lordship was coming I'd 'ave 'ad a silver tray here to pass it on.'

Santa flushed.

'He didn't know you were going to throw it.'

'Know! I'd like to see my kid, who's just three, miss a catch like that!'

Santa was furious.

'Peter can do other things.'

The man looked over his shoulder.

'What things?'

'Well . . .'

Peter caught her arm.

'Come on.'

Santa hesitated. She hated leaving the conversation like that with a vague slur on Peter's abilities. But the awful thing was that she had not got an answer. What could Peter do? If it came to that, what could she, except play 'Art thou weary?' on the violin?

'Come on,' Peter urged.

Santa decided to retire with dignity.

'Good morning, and thank you for the tomato.'

They went round the corner and leant against the wall. Santa started to pull the tomato in half, but Peter stopped her.

'I won't have any, thank you.'

Santa went on dividing.

'Don't be silly. No good being hungry.'

'I'd much rather be hungry than eat anything of that horrible man's.'

Santa had split the tomato fairly, if messily.

'I expect he just got out of bed the wrong side.' She took a bite of tomato. 'I wouldn't bother about him.' She held out his half. 'Eat that, then let's go and find a pawnshop.'

Neither Peter nor Santa knew that part of London and they walked a very long way before they found a pawnbroker's. They walked down Long Acre and through Leicester Square, getting more and more tired. Then suddenly in a side street Santa gripped Peter's arm.

'Look!'

He looked. Just across the road was a shop closed in with dark green shutters. Over it was written 'Samuel Aronson. Jeweller.' Above the door hung three golden balls. On the glass of the door it said: 'Pledge Office'.

Peter put down his attaché-case.

'What shall we do till it opens?'

'Sit somewhere,' said Santa.

'Sit!' Peter sounded scornful. 'Where?'

Santa looked up and down the street. It was the most shut-up looking road, all shops with shutters. Nobody was about except a black cat and, a long way off, a paper boy.

'I don't see why we shouldn't sit on a step,' she suggested. 'There's nobody to mind.'

Peter looked amazed.

'A step! People don't sit on steps.'

Santa settled herself on the step, her attaché-case beside her. Peter looked at her. She did look most awfully comfortable, but he felt self-conscious for he had never sat on a step; on the other hand, at present there was only the cat to see them. He sat down beside her.

'I could never have believed a step could feel so lovely,' Santa sighed.

Peter had his head resting against the door. His eyes were shut.

'All suitcases are made that way,' he murmured.

Santa opened one eye. Such an idiotic reply could only mean one thing. Peter was going to sleep. In another three minutes she had followed his example.

They were awakened by a man. He was leaning over them. He gave Peter a shake.

'If it's all the same to you, young man.'

Peter started, sat up, stretched, and suddenly remembered where he was. He looked ashamed and jumped to his feet.

'Oh, I say! I am sorry. You must think it very odd our being here.' He gave Santa a push with his foot. 'Get up, Santa.'

Santa opened her eyes. She smiled at the man.

'Is this your step?'

He nodded.

'I'm sorry we chose it, but we were waiting to go in there.' She nodded towards the pawnbroker's.

The man looked sympathetic.

'Mother short?'

Peter and Santa were surprised. Why should somebody who found you sitting on his doorstep care how tall your mother was? However, although he had only seen a photograph of his mother, Peter thought it polite to answer.

'I don't think so. Do you, Santa?'

Santa mentally considered the photograph. Her mother in a wedding dress. She was certainly taller than the bridesmaids.

'No, not short. Tall, I should think.'

The man gave a quick laugh.

'Don't you know what "short" means?' He had opened the door and was in his passage. He spoke over his shoulder. 'Being short means not 'aving enough money. Wherever was you brought up that you 'aven't learnt that?'

Santa picked up her attaché-case.

'It's funny we never did. For we've never had any money at all.'

Peter disliked this public discussion of their affairs. One of the things the duchess had said more often than any other, and therefore Aunt Rebecca had repeated more often than any other,

34

was that ladies and gentlemen never mentioned money.

'Come on, Santa. We mustn't take any more of this gentleman's time.'

The man laughed.

'You are a caution.' He turned to Santa. 'Aronson's won't open for a bit yet. If your brother can bring himself to drink out of a cup without a handle bring him in and you can 'ave a cuppa tea.'

They had a very nice meal with the man. He gave them not only tea but bread and butter. Only people who have got up at half past three and had nothing but half a tomato know how good the bread and butter tasted and how the tea warmed their insides. Even Peter, who was hurt at the man thinking he minded the cup not having a handle, enjoyed every mouthful.

When they had finished, the man, who said his name was Bill, leant back in his chair. He gave a nod in the direction of Aronson's.

'How much money do you want?'

'Well, that depends . . .' Santa began.

Peter gave her a kick under the table.

'Perhaps you'd take a look at the things and say what they are worth?' He took his watch from his pocket and got up and fetched the bracelet from his attaché-case. He put them in front of Bill.

Bill picked the things up and ran his eyes over them. Then he nodded.

'Both gold. Good for a bit. Didn't your mother say what she wanted for them?'

Peter swallowed.

'They weren't given to our mother. They were given to our aunt.'

'Well, didn't auntie say?'

'No.' Peter hesitated. 'You see, they're for railway fares, and it depends what they cost.'

'Well, where to?'

'I don't know.'

Bill leant back in his chair.

'I'm not throwing no insults, but it strikes me you kids aren't speaking the truth.'

Peter turned red.

'You've no right to say that.'

Santa was prepared to leave everything to Peter as long as he kept his temper, but if he was going to lose it he would be no good to anybody. She leant across to Bill.

'As a matter of fact, we are speaking the truth only we've left an important bit out. Our aunt is dead.'

'Dead!' Bill looked at the bracelet and watch. 'Then who do these belong to?'

Santa and Peter spoke in one breath.

'Us.'

After that Bill had to hear everything. Peter unpacked Uncle Gus's postcard. Between them they told him all about Mr Stibbings, Mrs Ford, Madame Tranchot, Miss Fane, Saint Bernard's Home for Boys, and Saint Winifred's Orphanage. It took quite a long time telling and he never interrupted once. At the end he said:

'Where's Cob's Circus?'

Peter took a gulp of tea, for talking had made him thirsty.

'We don't know. We're going to find out.'

'Where?'

Peter pointed to the address on the postcard, which was Birmingham.

'He was there at Christmas. I thought someone there would know.'

Bill shook his head.

'That's no good. Can't have you two wandering all over the country.' He felt in his pocket and brought out sixpence. 'There's a newsagent down the street. Hop along, Peter, and ask for a circus paper. I expect that'll tell us what we want to know.'

While Peter was gone Santa and Bill cleared the table. Santa wanted to wash up, but Bill said it could wait. In about five minutes Peter was back; he had a newspaper in his hand.

'The man didn't know if this was the one, but he said it was for circus people.' He laid the paper on the table. It was called *World's Fair*.

They pulled it to pieces and each searched a few pages. It did not seem at all an easy paper to find things in. It had photographs of circus acts, but it did not say where they were doing them. Then suddenly Bill thumped the table.

'Here it is! Listen. "Judging from the splendid attendance at Whitby these last three days and from what I hear of the advance bookings at Bridlington, I should not wonder if this proved a record opening month for Cob's Circus!"' Bill looked at the top of the paper. 'Published last Saturday.' He gave the paper a cheerful slap. 'We have it! Uncle Gus is at Bridlington.'

Bill went to Aronson's to pawn the bracelet and the watch. Before he went to get the money he made Peter and Santa give him a promise.

'I'm taking a risk on you two. Maybe I did ought to hand you to the police, but you do seem to have an uncle and I reckon this watch and the bracelet's your own, so I'll give you a chance. But you've got to do something for me. You won't be in Bridlington till evening and maybe the circus is some way from the post office. But first thing tomorrow I'm expecting a telegram. If I don't get that telegram by eleven I'll go to the police. Promise?'

Peter and Santa nodded.

'Promise.'

'Right.' Bill opened a drawer which was full of odds and ends and brought out a greasy card. It had his name and address on it and said he was a tailor. 'Pack that in your case, Peter, beside

Uncle Gus's, and remember, telegram first thing, or you're for it.'

It seemed odd to get as fond of anybody in a short time as Santa had got of Bill. He saw them on to a bus for King's Cross, and as the bus moved off she had a lump in her throat as if she was saying goodbye to an old friend.

The journey to Bridlington was long, but neither Peter nor Santa noticed much of it. They had one meal of ham sandwiches and lemonade but most of the time they were asleep. Sometimes one of them opened an eye and saw a station or a house whiz by, but almost at once they shut them again.

It was Santa who noticed they had arrived. Somebody got out of the train and brushed her foot. She opened her eyes and saw it was dark outside. Then by a station lamp she read: 'BRID . . .' so she opened her eyes wider and read 'LINGTON'. She leant across the carriage and shook Peter.

'Wake up, Peter. We're there.'

What with having slept and Bridlington being much farther north than they were used to being, the station seemed very cold. They shivered and yawned and stumbled up the platform with legs still working badly from having been in a sitting position for so long. At the barrier Peter stopped. He felt in his pocket. Santa had one sickening moment when she thought he had lost the tickets, but it was all right, they had only got caught in his handkerchief.

Outside the station they stood looking round.

'Where do we find out?' Santa asked.

Peter looked up the street.

'There's a policeman, how about him?'

The policeman was a nice, good-tempered-looking man. He smiled at Peter and Santa.

'Well?'

Peter smiled back.

'Could you please tell us the way to the circus?'

'The circus!' The policeman laughed. 'You're a bit early, sorry. The circus won't be here till tomorrow.'

4

The Build-up

Santa cried. She was dreadfully ashamed about it afterwards, but that was what she did. Not in front of the policeman, but the moment her back was to him. Peter looked at her in surprise, because she was not a person who cried much. He opened his mouth to ask her what was the matter, but shut it again, deciding it would be no good. She was not crying quietly, but loud hiccuping sobs which made people turn and stare. He took her arm and hurried her up the road and into a teashop, and sat her down at a table in the corner.

There was a nice, cheerful waitress behind a glass counter full of chocolates. She came over at once. She looked sympathetically at Santa.

'Poor little thing. What is it?'

Peter shrugged his shoulders.

'I don't know.'

Santa put her head down on her arms and

howled. The waitress stopped being a waitress and became very friendly.

'Aye, that's a shocking noise and all. Is summat oop?'

She had a soft voice with a funny accent. Santa heard that even through the noise she was making. She choked back her sobs.

'That's a good girl. That's fine.' The waitress knelt down by her. 'Dry tha tears and tell what's t'matter.'

Santa sat up and found her handkerchief. She leant against the waitress as if she had known her always.

'I'm so tired.'

'Is that all? Well, if it's nowt worse nor that.'

'It is worse.' Santa scrubbed her eyes. 'We've come all the way from London to see our uncle and he won't be here till tomorrow.'

'What's keeping the man?'

Peter looked in a worried way at Santa. She did look tired. Her face, where it was not red from crying and black from the train, was greenish white.

'He's with Cob's Circus,' he explained.

'Cob's Circus, is it?' The waitress gave Santa a friendly shake. 'That's funny like to cry at. Why, it'll be here early in the morning, lovey.'

'Will it?' Santa blinked at her. 'How do you know?'

The waitress got up.

'My brother has a milk round. He doest' milk for the circus. "You be here early", that's what the gentleman in the advance wagon said to him.'

'I can't think why it isn't here now.' Peter was puzzled. 'We spent threepence on a paper called *World's Fair*, and it said that Cob's Circus was in Whitby last week and was coming here this week.'

The waitress nodded.

'Aye, that's reet. Whitby Thursday, Friday, and Saturday of last week. Then it moved over to Thirsk. Now tonight they'll move from Thirsk here. They're doing three days in each town, you see, lovely.'

Peter did not see, but he tried to look intelligent. The waitress did not seem to care if they understand or not. She rested her hands on the table.

'I expect food's what you need. Got any money?'

'Oh, yes.' Peter could not help sounding proud. 'Nearly ten shillings.'

The waitress shook her head at Santa.

'Lot of crying for nothing you've been doing. Got enough to fix up beds and all. Come on oop to mother. She'll see you reet.'

It was a lovely morning. Very few people were about in the streets because it was early, but those who were sounded gay. A newsboy whistled, a policeman hummed, a milkman rattling by with a cart-load of milk sang at the top of his voice, two women cleaning doorsteps told each other funny stories and roared with laughter. The animals, too, showed it was a good morning. A black cat danced across the street, the milkman's horse whinnied to the one belonging to the butcher, and a very old fox-terrier who had crept about all the winter scampered up the road, suddenly feeling young again.

Peter and Santa did not need a good morning to make them happy. They had slept well, eaten an enormous breakfast and had almost got to their uncle. It was Santa who saw how near to Uncle Gus they were. She stood still and pointed at a hoarding.

'Look!'

There was a large poster which said: THE CIRCUS IS COMING, and across that was another one which said: FOLLOW THE GREEN STARS FOR COB'S CIRCUS.

'Green stars!' said Santa. 'Where?'

They had not far to look. At intervals all up the street green stars painted on a white background had been hung from the lamp-posts. It was ridiculously easy to find the way, and made the walk into a game. Both of them tried to be the first to spot the stars. The stars did not go straight on but turned corners. Because they were looking at the stars and not at where they were going the sea came to them as a surprise. They had turned a corner and there it was.

The first time you see the sea must be exciting

for anybody. When you have got as old as eleven and twelve and a half before it happens it is as startling as if somebody had knocked all the breath out of you.

'I never knew it would look like that,' Peter said at last.

Santa was so impressed her voice was a whisper.

'Fancy there being so much water anywhere.'

They went on, but more slowly. They had to keep stopping to stare at the waves. The stars led them right along the front up a hill, then suddenly they came to an end.

In front of them was a large stretch of rough grass. The only things on it were two caravans and two immense masts stuck into the ground.

Santa nudged Peter.

'Do you think that's it?' She nodded at the caravans.

Peter shook his head.

'A circus has lions and things.'

At that moment the door of one of the caravans opened A man came out. He looked round and saw the children.

'Hallo.'

'Hallo, sir,' Peter said politely. 'Can you tell me if you are Cob's Circus?'

The man laughed.

'Not all of it. I'm with the advance.'

'Oh.' Santa looked pleased at having struck

something she knew. 'It was you who told the milkman to come early.'

'That's right. The men'll want their breakfast.'

'What men?'

The man took her by the shoulders and spun her round.

'See those?'

Santa looked at the two great masts.

'Yes.'

'Those are the king-poles. The first thing to come off the train will be the big top. That's the circus tent, and with it will come the men to put it up.'

'And they want breakfast?'

The man laughed again.

'I should say so. I don't suppose they got off the ground at Thirsk till well after midnight. Then they have to get to the station. They'll be unloading now. Not much of a night Wouldn't you want your breakfast?'

Santa was just going to answer that she certainly would when they heard a rumble behind them. A large wagon was coming towards them. It was painted white and green. When it turned they saw COB'S CIRCUS painted in great letters across its side.

'Here they come,' said the man. 'You can watch the build-up, but don't get in the way.' He went back into his caravan and shut the door.

From that moment it was as if magic were

possible. It seemed to the children a whole town grew under their eyes. The wagon was followed by a stream of lorries, all painted green and white, all mysteriously knowing exactly where they ought to go. All over the lorries men were sitting who, the moment they arrived, tumbled off like leaves blowing from a tree. In what seemed only a few minutes a great mess-tent was put up beside the wagon which had just arrived. All the men helped to put up the tent. Then out of the lorry they pulled trestle-tables and benches which they erected inside the tent. While they worked a glorious smell of frying bacon came from the wagon.

Even though Peter and Santa had eaten enormous breakfasts, they could not help wishing the bacon was for them.

Meanwhile more wagons and lorries were arriving every minute. The lorries bundled across the grass dropping men off them all the way, but seeming to know where they wanted to be and why. The wagons were attached to caterpillar tractors which manoeuvred them at enormous speed and with great accuracy to exactly where they were to stand.

By now the sun was right up. The sea below was getting more and more blue. There had been a little mist hanging about the grass and hedges, but it was fading away. An air of bustle and gaiety was everywhere.

There was a tap of water outside the mess-tent. A man came out with a cake of soap and a towel to have a wash. He grinned at Peter and Santa.

'Come to see the build-up?'

They agreed. Then Peter asked:

'Could you tell me if Mr Possit is here yet?'

The man soaped behind his ears.

'Gus!' He looked round the ground. 'No. None of the artistes are here yet. Be along soon now.' He put his head under the tap, washed off the soap, and walked off drying himself.

Peter frowned after him.

'I think it's a bit odd of a man like that to call our uncle "Gus".'

Santa picked a buttercup.

'I wonder why he called him an artist. Artists paint.'

'Whatever he does,' Peter argued, 'he shouldn't call him Gus. It's what Aunt Rebecca called a familiarity.'

Santa held the buttercup under his chin to see whether he liked butter. It was hard on so springlike a day, with the smell of the sea in your nose, to remember dull things that a duchess had said. But a sentence floated back to her.

'Only those who permit familiarities receive them.' She glanced up. Then gripped Peter's arm. 'Look, aren't they pretty?'

A string of caravans had arrived. One by one they climbed the hill and turned on to the ground.

Each caravan was painted green sprinkled with white stars. Each was towed by a car. Each car seemed bursting with people, men, women, and children. As they arrived they called cheerful 'good mornings' to each other and the tent-men.

Like everything else in Cob's Circus the caravans knew just where they had to go. Each car backed its caravan into its proper place, then, first disgorging its passengers, moved off behind to park. In a steady stream caravans kept on arriving. Side by side they stood, a little way off from the big wagons. When they were all in place they looked like a fairy-tale street.

Such a noise and laughing came from the caravan dwellers. The great topic was by which route they had come, and how those that had got there first managed it.

The moment the caravan street was built, cattles were produced and a somebody run for water.

'I wish our uncle would come,' said Satan. 'All this making breakfast is getting me hungry again.'

Peter nodded at the caravans.

'Perhaps he's in one of those.'

'Goodness!' Santa's face lit at the thought. 'I wish he was. Perhaps we'd live in it, too. Wouldn't it be lovely? Do go and ask if he's here.'

But Peter hung back. Asking a passing man was one thing. But going up to those chattering groups, half of whom did not speak proper English, was quite another. He had an awful feeling they might not understand what he said, and perhaps they would laugh when his back was turned.

'Let's wait a minute. Just look what they're doing over there.'

An extraordinary change was coming over the scene. What had looked like a scattered town had suddenly become a focal point.

Round the masts a lorry had deposited bundles of canvas. The children had watched the men throw them down, but at the time it had meant nothing to them; there was so much to wonder at they had not time to puzzle over details. But now they saw what they meant. The men had finished breakfast and like ants they were swarming over the ground. The bundles were unpacked, and proved to be parts of an enormous tent. With rope all these parts were laced together. Peter and Santa gasped.

'My word, it'll be as large as Convent Garden Market when it's up,' said Peter. 'Look at it all.'

Santa stared up at the top of the masts.

'Do you think it's going to go up there?'

Peter nodded.

'Yes. I think those are the things that hold it up. I . . .'

He broke off, hearing laughing.

A boy and a girl were standing by them. There was something unusual about them. The boy was about eight and the girl ten. But they had older faces than their bodies. Both had large brown eyes, high check-bones, and a mass of curly hair. They were wearing heavy coats of a rather queer cut, and wellingtons. They spoke English, but, by putting emphasis on peculiar words and syllables, it sounded wrong.

'Haven't you never seen the big top go up before?' the boy asked Santa.

'No. As a matter of fact we've never seen a circus.'

The boy and girl stared at Peter and Santa as if they had just said they came from Mars.

'Never seen a circus?' As the girl spoke she bent slowly backwards until her hands touched the ground and she stood in a hoop. She went on talking in that position. 'Can you do this?'

'No.' Santa looked at her anxiously. 'Doesn't it hurt?'

'Hurt!' The girl straightened herself.' ' 'Course not. It's only a back-bend. My name's Olga. What's yours?'

'Santa.'

The boy turned a cart-wheel.

'That's like mine. It's Sasha. What's his?'

Peter did not like being talked about as if he were a statue or something.

'Peter.'

Sasha did not seem to realize he had spoken, because he answered Santa.

'We've a brother as big as him. His name is Alexsis. He's going into the act next winter.'

Olga turned a somersault.

'Not if he doesn't work he isn't. Father says he's lazy. We've a big sister called Paula. She works with the Kenets.'

Santa made a face towards the caravans to suggest to Peter this was the moment to ask about Uncle Gus. Peter made an agreeing face back.

'Do you know if Mr Possit has arrived yet?'

Olga and Sasha stood still for a moment. They looked at Peter, then at each other. They giggled.

'He does speak,' Sasha said.

Peter frowned.

'Of course I do! Why did you think I didn't?'

Olga lifted one of her legs above her head.

'We thought you were out of a shop. One of those things they put clothes on in a window.'

Santa saw Peter hated this so she said quickly:

'Do you think Mr Possit's here?'

Olga put down her leg and raised the other one.

'Don't know him.'

Sasha did a hand-stand.

'He means Gus.'

Olga stared up at her foot over her head.

'I never did know that Gus's name was Possit.'

' 'Tis though.' Sasha did the splits. 'He got here before we did.'

Peter found it very difficult to talk to people who were always upside down.

'Could you show us where he is?'

Olga turned a somersault, then took his hand. 'Come on.'

Peter was embarrassed. He could not feel that holding a girl's hand was a suitable way to appear before his uncle.

Sasha put his arm through Santa's.

'Why do you want Gus?'

'Well – you see he's our uncle.'

'What!' Sasha stood still and stared at her. Then he dropped her arm and began to run. He raced to a caravan at the end of the line and beat on it with his fists.

'Gus! Gus!'

A window opened and a man's head looked out.

'What is it?'

Sasha was absolutely dancing with excitement. 'How is it you call it when you are an uncle?'

'Stand still,' Gus growled, 'and tell us what's the trouble. Who's an uncle?'

Olga brought Peter and Santa to the caravan. 'You are.'

'Me! Why?'

Peter lifted his cap politely.

'Good morning, sir. We are Peter and Santa.'

'Kedgeree and rum!' said Uncle Gus. It was plain that he was not speaking of Peter and Santa.

'Kedgeree and rum' was obviously an expression to show surprise. He looked very startled. As he had the kind of face which shows everything the owner is feeling, his was a very startled face indeed. Then he drew in his head. 'Wait there. I'll come down.'

If Uncle Gus brought anything specially to mind, it was a churchwarden. If ever a man looked born to hand round a plate in church, he did. He had sandy hair parted in the middle. Eyebrows that always had a faintly shocked lift to them as if he were about to say: 'What, only a penny again this Sunday! I had hoped you would make it threepence.' He wore a very neat dark suit and a dark tie. In fact, a more respectable-looking man you could not find.

He ran down the steps of his caravan and examined Peter and Santa in silence. Then he said:

'What made Rebecca let you come? She doesn't hold with me.'

Santa stepped forward.

'We don't know that she holds with you now. You see she's dead.'

'Dead!' Uncle Gus raised his right hand to take his hat off. Then he remembered he had not got one on so he saluted instead. 'Dead,' he repeated in a very deep voice. Then he added cheerfully, 'Never speak ill of the dead. But that woman was a fool.' He gazed at the sky for a moment as if remembering what a fool Aunt Rebecca had been.

Then suddenly he looked back at the children. 'What are you doing here?'

Peter knelt down and unpacked his attaché-case. He got out the Christmas card.

'We found this, sir.'

'Don't call me sir. Gus to all, I am.' He turned the card over and looked at the picture. He sighed. 'Very choice. Pity your poor aunt didn't live to enjoy it.' He put the card in his pocket. 'But why come here?'

'Well, you see . . .' Peter and Santa began together.

Gus held up his hand.

'Cabbages and cheese, one at a time.' He nodded at Santa. 'Ladies first. You tell me.'

Santa took a deep breath and began at the beginning. She told everything. About their lessons. About Saint Bernard's and Saint Winifred's, Mr Stibbings, Mrs Ford, Madame Tranchot, and Miss Fane. The watch and the bracelet. Covent Garden and the tomato man, Bill. The pawn ticket. Where they had slept last night. She could not help thinking while she told the story how impressive it sounded. She was glad Olga and Sasha were there, for even though they did keep turning somersaults and things, part of it must have sunk in and been admired. When she finished she felt quite like an actress at the end of a big scene, and almost expected a round of applause.

She did not get it. Olga stopped practising

flip-flaps for a moment. She rested on the steps of Gus's caravan.

'When we were tenting in Sweden,' she said, 'Alexsis and me was lost. I was only five then and Alexsis was eight. We had no watch and no bracelet. We had nothing so Alexsis takes me in a field and we work a little floor act. Then we go to the inn and we make the money for the railway back to the circus.' She got up and did a neat flip-flap. At the end she looked severely at Peter. 'That was a better way. It isn't nice to pawn things.'

The statement seemed to penetrate the almost comatose state in which Santa's story had put Gus.

'Pawn!' he exclaimed. 'Couple of children! Never heard anything like it.'

Peter was hurt. All the time Santa was telling the story he had felt impressed at their cleverness. He had particularly admired the way he himself had figured in it.

'What else could we have done?' he asked angrily.

'You acted very silly from the start,' Gus said severely. 'Mind you,' he added in a kinder voice, 'I'm not altogether blaming you. Brought up by Rebecca nobody could be anything but silly. But all the same, for down-right silliness you two beat the band.'

Santa flushed.

'Why?'

Gus sat down on his step. He held up his finger.

'First, knowing you had an uncle, why not go to this reverend gentleman name of Stibbings and say: "Reverend, we've go an uncle. Will you send him a telegram and he'll decide what's right to be done."'

'But . . .' Peter broke in.

Gus eyed him severely.

'Don't interrupt.' He held up a second finger. 'Second. Why all this fuss about the orphanage? You've never seen Saint Bernard's and Saint Winifred's. You'd no call to make all this commotion previous to finding out what's wrong.'

Santa sat beside him.

'We wouldn't be sent to different places.'

Gus shook his head.

'Them as has the money for the piper calls the tune.'

'But children never have any money,' Peter said angrily.

'Then they can't call a tune.' Gus got up and went into his caravan. He reappeared a moment later wearing a navy blue overcoat and a Homburg hat. He went to his car and got into the driver's seat. He pressed the self-starter.

Santa dashed over to him. She stood in front of the car.

'You shan't arrange to send us back. You can run me over first.'

Gus looked out of the car window. His voice was tired.

'Rebecca brought you up more silly even than I thought. I must telegraph the Reverend Stibbings you're safe. Mr Cob won't like a lot of police turning up here making inquiries.'

'Telegraph!' Santa clasped her hands. 'Oh, will you wait? We've got a telegram to send, too.' She went to Peter's suitcase and rummaged through it till she found Bill's card. She brought it over to Gus. 'Will you send him a telegram, too? We said we would before eleven.'

Gus opened the door of his car.

'What's stopping you sending it yourselves?'

'Oh, may we?' Peter and Santa jumped in. 'You know,' Santa explained, 'we've never ridden in a motor car before.'

Gus let out his clutch. He drove a moment in silence. Then he said:

'Strikes me there are so many silly things you have learnt to do and so many sensible things you haven't that I don't know where we'll start.'

5

Settling In

When a circus is being built up, every minute the
scene changes. The post office was not far from
the ground, yet when Gus, Peter, and Santa came
back everything looked different. The big top had
been laced together and hauled up the kingpoles.
The children had not noticed them, but a ring of
staples had been driven into the ground before
the circus arrived. Now guy-ropes were hitched to
the top and a gang of men hammered the staples
into place. Others attached the side curtains. Still
more placed wooden props in position inside to
keep the whole tent taut. In fact, since the first
wagon had appeared over the hill a great theater
big enough to hold over two thousand people
had gone up.

'Goodness!' said Peter. 'They've finished making
it while we were away.'

Gus gave a disapproving snort.

'Can't you get your words right? You build it.

Build-up, that's what we call it. If you're coming tenting, may as well get your words right.'

Santa hung over from the back of the car.

'Are we coming tenting? Oh, dear Gus, do let us.'

Gus drove his car across the ground to its original parking place.

'I don't know yet. All depends on what the reverend says.'

'But you're our uncle, not him,' Santa pointed out.

Gus nodded.

'I'm not forgetting. Maybe him and me'll meet and have a little talk. We'll see. Now out you get and you can go and have a look at what's going on. But don't get in the way, mind.'

It's very difficult not to get in the way when everybody is busy except you. Peter and Santa did just look in the big top where one of the side flaps was not yet in place. But at once they heard behind them:

'If you don't mind.'

They jumped hurriedly out of the way. They were just in time. A man shot past them balancing an immense pole across his shoulder.

'Do let's stop outside,' said Santa, 'until it's done. Somebody's sure to be angry with us in a minute.'

They moved on and, avoiding the staples and guy-ropes, came to the other side of the great tent. There, to their surprise, they found another tent of quite a different shape. It was lower than the big top, and long like a passage. Peter looked in. He beckoned to Santa.

'There's nobody there. Let's go inside.'

The tent was a stables. Even though Peter and Santa had never been in one, they guessed what it was at once.

On their right were twenty stalls. Each stall was divided from the next by a wooden partition. Each was spread with deep, clean straw. On their left was a space. Farther down there were ten more stalls. Here the tent really came to an end, but another was laced on to it, which made a bend and helped give the passage effect.

The second half of the tent was full of men. One group on the left was busy building some more stalls. Others were erecting a wooden platform at the far end. Santa, who had never visualized there being more than one lion, one horse, and perhaps an elephant in the circus, was most impressed at all these preparations.

'There must be an awful lot of animals,' she whispered to Peter.

An old man was leaning against a tent prop near them. He had a face like an apple that has been put away too long. It was brown and wrinkled by dozens of tiny lines. He was wearing a black coat, check breeches, and black gaiters and boots. A straw was sticking out of the corner of his mouth. His voice was slow and quiet. He spoke as if his life through he had been careful not to speak roughly or quickly for fear he should startle anything.

'Well – what are you two up to? If you've come to see the menagerie you're too soon.'

'We haven't, sir,' Peter explained politely. 'We're just looking round, if you don't mind.'

The old man laughed.

'Me? I don't mind. But don't you let Mr Cob catch you. He's a mild man but he's fair roused when folk come round too soon on a build-up mornin'.'

Peter felt it was time they asserted themselves.

'We've not come round.'

'No,' Santa added. 'As a matter of fact we're staying here.'

The old man looked surprised.

'Are you now! Who do you belong to?'

Peter, in spite of what Gus had said, could not feel that just a Christian name, and only a bit of one at that, was enough for an uncle of his.

'Mr Gus Possit. We're his nephew and niece.'

The old man looked more surprised.

'Gus! Nephey and niece. Didn't know 'e 'ad any.'

Santa leant against the nearest tent pole.

'He hadn't seen us till today. What does he do

in the circus? A man said he was an artist. But that means painting.'

The old man chuckled.

'Can't see Gus painting. Does a bit of everything like. Very useful artiste. Auguste 'e is really. Then 'e does a trapeze act.'

Santa tried not to show that she did not understand a word. She changed the subject.

'Are you an artist?'

'Me!' A gust of laughing shook the old man. 'No. I been with Mr Cob and 'is dad before him. Ben's my name. Nearest I ever got to being an artiste was when I was a nipper and stood on the ring fence to blow a 'unting' orn. Never much of a hand at it, I wasn't, so I soon give it up.'

'What do you do then?' Peter asked.

Ben spat his straw out thoughtfully.

'Everything. Groom. Bereiter, that's what we call an assistant breaker. Coachman. Second head of the stables. Then two years back I come to head. "Ben," Mr Cob says to me, "I'm makin" you Master of the "Oss." That's the high-falutin' way they calls me on the programme. "And from now on all the hands'll call you Mr Willis." That's me name, see?'

'And do they?'

Ben stooped, chose another straw, and put it in his mouth.

'Men and 'osses they're all the same. Teach a 'oss something and that's the way he'll always do it. Can't make him no different. Same with men. I been Ben since I was borned. And Ben I'll die. Can't expect people to take to a lot of Mr Willis-ing sudden like. 'Tain't natural.'

'Shall we call you Mr Willis?' Santa suggested.

Ben shook his head.

'No. Jus' Ben. I don't like new ways. The old ones have done me for seventy-five years. They'll do me a bit longer yet.' He straightened up and looked down the tent. 'Time we was getting going.'

Peter looked round to see why.

'Where to?'

'Station. Fetch my 'osses.' He gave the children a friendly nod and went off.

The big top had changed again. The seating was going up. Circular wooden platforms had been erected and the seats stood on these. Santa was puzzled why, but Peter grasped the system in a moment and explained it to her.

'Don't you see, the lions and things are going to show on that earth they're digging up. They stay on the ground, but everybody else is raised up so they can see.'

Santa looked at the place where he pointed. A large circular piece of ground had been dug up. Several men were at work raking it.

'I wonder if we dare go and look,' she whispered.

A man above her who was putting up seating heard what she said. He smiled cheerfully.

'They won't eat you. The worst they'll do is turn you out. You go and have a look-see.'

The man was in rather an awkward position to talk to. The children were standing on the ground at the entrance to the tent, and he was fixing some seats high up on their left. He looked down at them and only his head showed over some boarding. It meant talking with your chin right up in the air, which was not comfortable, but he had a friendly face, the sort which might answer questions without being annoyed. Santa smiled at it.

'Do you mind telling me if that' – she pointed to the ring of earth – 'is where the lions and things will be?'

'That's right.' The man's head nodded. 'That's the ring. They're making it now.'

'Making it?' Santa looked at him in surprise. 'Our uncle, Mr Gus Possit, said "build" was the right word. Don't you belong to the circus, either?'

'Me!' The man finished fixing a seat. 'I'm a tent hand. That's right though, what Gus said. We call it build-up for the big top. But you "make" the ring.'

'How?' Peter and Santa asked at once.

The man made a face at them

'You'll have the tent master after me. You go down and have a look for yourselves.'

'Won't anybody mind?' Santa asked anxiously.

The man looked towards the ring. The ring-side seats were already up. Quite a lot of people were sitting in them. He looked at their heads.

'See that little fellow with the red hair?' There was one head of unmistakably flaming red, so they both nodded. 'That's Alexsis Petoff.' The man looked down at Peter. 'He'll be about your age. You ask him what you want to know.'

'Alexsis!' Santa hopped because she was so pleased to hear somebody talked about that she knew. 'The one that's going into the act next winter?'

The man turned away to see to another row of seats.

'Maybe he will, maybe he won't. But you sit alongside him. Born in the ring young Alexsis was. He'll tell you all you want to know.'

Luckily there were two empty seats next to Alexsis. Peter and Santa sat in them. They sat rather nervously like people who are not sure they have come to the right party, because although they were very conscious of being Gus's nephew and niece they were not a bit certain they would not be turned out. Santa dug her elbow into Peter.

'Speak to him. Tell him we know Olga and Sasha.'

Peter cleared his throat like a person who is going to make a speech, but is not a bit sure what he is going to say. Luckily he did not have to bother. Alexsis turned and looked at them. Then beamed.

'It will be Peter and Santa who was the nephew and niece of Gus.'

Santa was so interested in his English being so bad she could not even shape her own words properly.

'It will be. But why do you talk so much worse English than Olga and Sasha?'

Alexsis had a face that easily looked worried. It looked worried now.

'When we was in England,' he explained carefully, 'it is that every child must go to school. But when I was little we was not in England. I have German, French, Russian, and a little Italian, but I have not much English. My father say it is because I am lazy.'

Santa looked at him with interest, remembering this was exactly what Olga had said her father said about him.

'Are you?'

'No.' A queer far-away look came into Alexsis's eyes. 'It is that I may not do what I can do.'

'Oh!' Santa looked at Peter. They both felt embarrassed. Alexsis had such a desperate way of speaking. Santa changed the subject.

'Why is it "building" the big top, and "making" the ring? Somebody told us it was. Is that right?'

Alexsis looked surprised at such ignorance.

'But of course a ring must be made. A field is hard. Yes? How could the artistes work?'

Peter was a little vague as to what he meant. Work as he understood it meant bookwork, or housework, or something like that. He knew the animals would appear in the ring, but he could not see why it wanted 'making' so carefully.

'But they've dug it up now. Why are all those men working on it?'

Alexsis suddenly grasped that they were completely ignorant.

His face looked more worried than ever, as he fumbled for the right words.

'A ring he must always be the same size and soft to the foots.'

Santa shook her head.

'Not foots. Feet.'

'So!' Alexsis nodded. 'It is that I forget. First the men come and dig up the ground. But ground he is hard. He is rough. He have stones. Sometimes he slope. Then you put more good earth to make a ring.'

Peter was interested.

'Where do you get the earth from?'

'You buy him. Some town it is only seven ton. One town it is twenty.'

Peter nodded at the men who were working.

'What are they doing now?'

'They rake him smooth. They maybe water him. Presently the elephants come to tread him down.

Then when all is done they put sawdust. Very pretty the sawdust. They pattern it.'

Santa sighed at what seemed to her a shocking waste of labour.

'Well, of course, we've never seen a circus. But we've seen pictures of them. It all seems a lot of fuss to me.'

A party of men came down one of the gang-ways. They carried between them some portions of curved wood with plush tops. They put the bits all round the ring, screwing them together. At the side where the children had come in leading to the stables there was a hinged piece which made a door.

Peter got up and examined it. He looked over his shoulder at Alexis.

'Is that an edge to keep the animals behind?'

Alexsis got up.

'That is the ring fence. Inside that is the circus. You understand? No?'

'Yes.' Santa was sorry to see he was going. 'Must you go?'

'Yes. The horses will have come. My father wish me to work one of them.' He ran off in the direction of the stables.

Santa looked after him.

'Pity he couldn't stay. Even though he does speak so funnily he told us a lot of things. Look, there's Uncle Gus. Gus I mean.'

Gus had come into the big top from the opposite

entrance. Both Peter and Santa got up supposing he had come to look for them. After all one does not meet nephews and nieces for the first time every day, it was only natural that he should want to come and talk to them. But not a bit of it. He came in with another man. The two of them unstrapped a large wooden box. Gus never even looked round to see if the children were there. After a minute or two the children sat down again, feeling as stupid as people do feel who have expected to be wanted and then found they were not. However, they had not very long to feel stupid in, for Gus and the other man began to do the most exciting things.

Out of the box came a steel bar, some rolls of wire, and a rope ladder. Gus had clogs over what looked like dancing pumps. He kicked the clogs off and put them on the ring fence, seized a bundle of wire, and like a monkey climbed up a ladder attached to one of the king-poles. While he was up there his friend was fixing the other ends of the wires to staples on the ground. They were both very busy and hardly spoke. Sometimes Gus said 'Now', or 'Coming', and the man on the ground caught an end of wire and replied 'O.K.' or 'Easy does it'. When they had their bar fixed up in the roof, it looked like an ordinary garden swing.

All the while Gus was working, various tent hands who had finished their work for the moment stood round the ring smoking and watching. This disgusted Peter.

'If I were Gus,' he whispered to Santa, 'I'd make those fellows put the things up for me.'

Santa nodded. She, too, was puzzled why her uncle had to do what appeared a menial job. If their uncle was an artist he must be important even if everybody did call him Gus.

'So'd I,' she whispered back. 'But perhaps they don't know how to.'

At this moment Gus seemed to have got everything finished to his satisfaction. He came sliding down a rope into the ring. He fetched his clogs and beckoned to his friend.

'Ted. Come and meet my nephew and niece.'

Ted was younger than Uncle Gus, with black curly hair. He raised his eyebrows.

'Nephew and niece. Never knew you had any.'

'Kedgeree and rum – I'd nearly forgot it myself.' Gus took his arm. 'Peter and Santa. Meet Mister Ted Kenet.'

'Pleased,' said Ted. He felt in his pocket and produced a small paper bag. He held it out. 'Have one. Sweets, with a little sulphur for the blood. Nothing like sulphur in the spring.'

Santa looked in the bag. The sweets were yellow, rather like pieces of Edinburgh rock. She took one and bit it gingerly, as she did not like the sound of sulphur. However, it did not taste bad. She made an encouraging face at Peter to tell him so, for he was much more fussy about eating things he did not like than she was. Peter took a small piece. He looked at Gus.

'What's that you've put up?'

Gus gave an apologetic glance at Ted.

'Brought up by my poor sister Rebecca. Mustn't speak ill of the dead, but the woman was a fool.' He turned to Peter. 'That's a trapeze.'

'Oh.' Peter did not like to ask what a trapeze was; instead he turned to the question of why people like his uncle and Ted should work with all these workmen standing about. 'Why do you have to put it up? Why not them?' He nodded in the direction of the tent hands.

Gus's face looked ashamed all over.

'You hear that, Ted? He'd let somebody else put his stuff up for him. The boy's a fool.' He pointed dramatically at the roof. 'When Ted and me go up there to do our act, there's nothing between us and the ring. If something went wrong we'd break our necks most like.'

Ted nodded gloomily.

'Or worse. That's why I take sulphur sweets. That and a nice drink of sarsaparilla keeps the blood cool.'

Gus held Peter by his coat sleeve.

'Every artiste in the circus puts up and takes down his own stuff. Pork and beans, where'd he be if he didn't!'

'Dead,' said Ted. He looked at his watch. 'Dinner-time. So long.'

'So long,' Gus replied. Then he jerked his head towards the tent exit. 'Dinner-time for us, too. Come on.'

Gus's caravan looked quite small from the outside but inside it had a surprising lot of room. It was divided in half by a partition which made two rooms. In the first half, which was the one the door opened into, there was a stove, various shelves and cupboards, a flap table which let down from the wall, and seats which did the same. It was in fact a dining-room kitchen. On the stove a pot was standing from which came a very good-smelling steam.

The other room was a bedroom. There were two bunks in it. One had bedclothes and was obviously Gus's bed. Peter and Santa tried not to stare too obviously at the second bunk, but they could not help wondering where the one who did not have it would sleep.

Gus did not give them long to look around.

'Table wants laying, Santa.' He showed her where the table-cloth lived, and the knives and forks and things. Santa thought he must be a very neat man, for everything was clean and lived in a special place. Gus seemed to guess what she was thinking.

'Must be shipshape in a caravan. No room for a mess. Besides, my old mother, your grandmother, brought us up right.' He passed a jug to Peter. 'Fetch some water. Tap's by the men's mess-tent.'

While Peter was gone, and Santa laid the table, Gus stirred what was in the pot. He took a deep sniff.

'Beautiful. Always have a stew of a Sunday, and a Thursday.'

Santa took some forks out of their drawer.

'Why Sundays and Thursdays specially?'

Gus took three plates to warm on the rack of the stove.

'On account of the build-up. Cut up my meat. Slice my veg. Fix my stew. Put it on a low heat to simmer. Fix my stuff in the big top. Come back and dinner's ready.'

Santa found the salt cellar and the pepper and mustard pots in the cupboard.

'Fancy you being able to cook. I never knew men could. But then of course I've only known one man and that was Mr Stibbings.'

Gus gave the stew a final stir.

'The reverend may not have had the chances to learn I've had. You never knew your grandma. Proper termagant she was, bless her. "Them as can't work can't eat," she always said.'

Santa looked at the table carefully to see if she'd forgotten anything.

'What, even when you were little?'

'Time I was four. Not cooking I wasn't, not then. But doing my bit towards preparing the

74

dinner. And she was right. Many's the time I've blessed her since.'

Peter came back with the water. Gus held out the kettle.

'Fill that ready for the washing-up, then stand the rest outside. We'll set the kettle on now, then it'll have boiled time we want it.' He took a large spoon and put helpings of stew on each plate. 'There you are, sit down and eat hearty. Oughtn't to be a bit of carrot to scrape out of the pot in this lovely air.'

Peter filled the kettle and put it on the stove, stood the jug outside, and came and sat at the table. He turned to Santa.

'When I was getting the water I met Olga and Sasha and a whole lot more children. D'you know, they'd been to school.'

Gus tasted a mouthful of stew; he nodded at his plate approvingly.

'Beautiful!'

'Fancy them going to school,' said Santa. 'They only got here this morning.'

Gus raised shocked eyebrows.

'How long you've been in a place has nothing to do with education. Don't you two know the laws of the country? Every child must go to be educated.'

Considering that how they were educated had been one of Aunt Rebecca's pet subjects of conversation, both Peter and Santa were

a bit hurt at Gus's assumption of their ignorance.

'Of course we know that,' Peter said. 'Only it
seems odd to find a school you like the minute
you arrive, that's all.'

'Like!' Gus looked puzzled. 'Schools are all
much the same, unless you take a scholarship,
that is. You'll find out what the one here's like
yourselves tomorrow.'

'Will we?' Santa was startled. 'What school are
you sending us to?'

Gus looked rather as though he were afraid
his nephew and niece were weak in the head.

'What school! Wherever it is, of course. There'll
be one up the street, I dare say.'

Peter flushed scarlet. He felt sure he would be
a fool in a school.

'But I mean to say – I've never been . . . ! You
see I was taught at home.'

Gus thumped his fist on the table.

'Taught at home! School's what you need.
What was good enough for your grandfather,
your father, and for me, if it comes to that, I
reckon is good enough for you.'

'But . . .' Peter stammered. 'I thought – I mean
to say . . . I mean, Aunt Rebecca told us . . .'

Gus gave his head a despairing shake. Then
he went on with his dinner. He spoke between
mouthfuls.

'Mustn't speak ill of the dead, but it seems to

me your poor aunt stuffed you two up with a pack of nonsense. I wonder now what Rebecca told you. Do you know what your grandfather was, for a start?' The children shook their heads. 'He was a gardener.'

Aunt Rebecca had never defined her position in the duchess's household. Peter and Santa had never asked. They had heard the duchess continually quoted and had come to think of her as perhaps a distant relation. They were surprised and sounded it.

'A gardener!'

Gus gave them a funny look.

'No need to take that tone. We'll be lucky if you turn out anything half as useful. Very good gardener your grandfather. Became head at Plyst. You'll have heard your aunt speak of the place.' Peter and Santa nodded. They had indeed heard of Plyst till the name made them yawn. 'Your grandmother was in the kitchen there till she married.'

'In the kitchen!'

Gus nodded.

'I was telling you, Santa, that she was a good cook.'

Peter and Santa went on eating in silence. It is a very funny feeling to have your world turned upside down. They had after all spent a good many years being told they were too grand to mix with their neighbours. Now they found not only that they came from quite simple people, but that Gus was proud of it. It was muddling.

'What did our father do?' Santa asked at last.

'Tom? He fancied horses. He went as groom to the duke. You see, my old dad, your grandfather, he always said: "Put your feet under another man's table and you'll be all right!"'

Santa looked puzzled.

'What did he mean?'

Gus jerked his thumb at the table.

'What's usually on it?'

Santa looked round.

'Food?'

'That's right. That's what he meant. Go into service and you know where your food's coming from. That's what your dad did. They had everything found.'

Peter looked up.

'Then why didn't you go into service?'

'Me!' Gus laughed. 'I started all right. I was always turning somersaults and flip-flaps and practising hand-stands, and though my old dad walloped me it didn't cure me. So when I was just turned twelve he spoke for a place for me under him in the garden.' He gave another chuckle. 'Nice gardener's boy I was. Standing on my head all day among the flower-pots. Then one day along comes his grace and sees me.'

'Goodness,' said Santa, 'what did he do to you?'

Gus helped himself to some more stew.

'I didn't see him. So he stood there watching me for quite a time saying nothing. Getting a bit lame he was then, and always carried a stout stick to help him round. Suddenly he ups with this and lands me a wallop. My word, I was right side up in no time. "Is this the way you garden?" he says to me. Then he lands me another. Then he looks round. "Fetch Possit," he says.'

'Grandfather?' asked Peter.

'That's right. Gus finished his stew thoughtfully. 'Wonderful old chap, his grace. They don't make them better. He had me up to the house that evening. Made me show him all I could do. And in spite of my dad, who was dead against it, had me apprenticed to Mr Cob.'

Santa collected the dirty plates.

'Was he against it because your feet wouldn't be under somebody else's table?'

'Partly it was. Mostly it was me being in the theatrical line. Never been anything like that in our family.'

Peter leaned forward.

'Have you been with Mr Cob ever since?'

'Off and on. Then war came and I joined up, and Mr Cob closed down.'

'Why?' Santa asked.

Gus got up and went to the cupboard. He took out bread, butter, and cheese.

'On account of the feed mostly. You can't keep

six elephants and about forty horses and a lot of lions going when there's a war on. So he pays everybody off, and stores most of his stuff.'

Santa looked, worried.

'But what happened to the animals?'

Gus cut bread for them all.

'They weren't Mr Cob's. He'd an interest in the horses but the rest were just acts he'd engaged.'

Peter took the piece of bread Gus handed him.

'What happened when the war was over?'

Gus cut himself a bit of cheese.

'I was all right. Travelled all over the place. Then one day I ran into Mr Cob. Leicester Square it was, just after Christmas. "What are you doing, Gus?" he says to me. Well, it just happened at that moment I wasn't fixed, so I told him. "Right," he says. "Come and sign on tomorrow. I'm tenting again." You should have heard the way he said it. You see, he was born in the circus, and those war years when he wasn't on the road hit him hard. "I'm tenting again." He said it like a kid who finds what he wants in its stocking of a Christmas morning.'

Gus seemed to sink into memories of that day when he had met Mr Cob again, for he sat saying nothing. Santa wanted to hear the rest, so she said:

'And did you sign on?'

Gus took a mouthful of bread and cheese.

'Yes, and been with him ever since.'

Peter was still puzzling over their family history.

'Who was our mother?'

Gus cut another bit of cheese.

'Funny woman your Aunt Rebecca, never telling you anything about yourselves. Your mother was sort of nursery governess. An orphan she was.' He spread some butter on his bread. 'Funny how life turns out. There's me doing the trapeze act, running risks all the time, you might say, and here I am enjoying my dinner. There was your mum and dad with a little home and living all safe and secure, and they go for a halfday's shopping to the next town; something goes wrong with the train signal, and where are they? Gone.'

Santa helped herself to some more cheese.

'And that's when we came to Aunt Rebecca.'

'That's right. You see, there were five of us. Rebecca she was the eldest, and she works up to be personal maid to the old duchess,' Gus went on. 'Then there was me. Then there was Tom, your father. Then Sydney and Bert, they were killed in the war. Your dad going seemed to break my old father up. Then about two years later my old mother, your grandmother, went. The old duchess was dead by then, and she'd left your Aunt Rebecca a little annuity, so she said she'd take you two. Mind you, it was good of her for she hadn't much. I wrote and offered to put up so much a week but she turned me down flat. She said she had learnt what was what while she had been with the duchess and she should bring you up how she thought right, and would I keep out of it. She didn't want you to know there was anything so common in the family as a clown in a circus.'

Santa nodded at the kettle.

'It's boiling. Shall I start to wash up?'

Gus nodded.

'The basin's in the corner. You do it outside, it's less messy. Peter can dry.'

Santa poured some water into the basin.

'It hasn't made much difference in the end. Aunt Rebecca not wanting us to know you, I mean. Because here we are.'

Gus sighed.

'Poor Rebecca!' Once more he raised his right hand to take off his hat, then remembering he had not one on put it down again. 'What she'd say if she could see us now.' There was a knock at the door. Gus got up. 'Like as not that's the reply from the reverend. You stay here.'

It was the reply. The children heard Gus go down the caravan steps. The noise of a tearing envelope. Then, 'No answer.' In the pause before he came back Santa whispered:

'Do you want to stay here? I mean now you know about school and everything?'

Peter nodded.

'Yes. I just feel muddled. Don't you?'

Gus came back. The telegram was in his hand. He laid it on the table and smoothed it out.

'The reverend says' – then he read slowly: "Greatly relieved naturally decision as to future rests with you Stibbings."' He folded the telegram and put it back in his pocket. 'Very right and proper.'

Santa came over to Gus. She carried the bowl of water.

'Mr Stibbings is always right and proper, Gus dear. But what are you going to do with us?'

Gus looked first at her and then at Peter.

'Would you like to stay with me for the rest of the tenting time?'

Peter looked at Santa.

'You would, wouldn't you?'

'I think it would be heavenly.'

Gus gave a quick glance at Peter.

'And you.'

'I'd like it.'

'Right.' Gus put the telegram in his pocket. 'That's settled. Now we must get a move on. I've another bed to fix, Mr Cob to see. When you've done the washing-up you must write to the reverend to thank him, and to Mrs Ford to send on your things. We must hurry or we'll never be through by five-thirty.'

'Five-thirty?' Peter stopped in the doorway. 'What happens then?'

Gus looked shocked.

'What happens! The show of course. What we're here for, and the only thing that matters. And don't you two forget it.'

6

In The Stables

It was wretchedly dull writing letters with so much
going on outside. Peter and Santa simply could
not give their minds to it. Every few minutes one
of them would go to the caravan door and have
a look out. All sorts of things were going on.
Scattered groups came up from the town and paid
sixpence to look at the animals. People brought
the most exciting-looking clothes out from their
caravans and hung them up to give them a brush.
A smart-looking woman, with a very alive skin and
black hair cut in a fringe, came and sat on the steps
of her caravan and covered a small wooden ring
with artificial roses. While she worked she talked
to somebody inside the caravan. Santa, who was
the first to hear her speak, looked very surprised
and beckoned to Peter.

'French! My goodness, doesn't she do it well!'
Peter listened.
'Perhaps she is French.'

Santa sat down again. Grudgingly she took up her pen. She gave the end of it an angry bite.

'Why must we write letters? I'd like to watch her make that ring of roses. I wonder what it's for? It's too small to wear.' She sighed and looked down at her letter. 'You know I don't know what to ask Mrs Ford to send. Gus said only useful things. I've written down "mackintosh". That must be useful. But I can't think of anything else. What have you put?'

Peter turned his page over.

'I've said: "Please send all my pyjamas, even the old ones. Any pants and vests and socks you can find. My shirts and my ties. All my handkerchiefs. My other suit, and the old one that wants mending on the elbows.'

Santa began to write furiously.

'What a fool I am. Of course those are what we want. Pyjamas. All my vests and things. All my socks. As a matter of fact I've only got three good pairs, and one I've got on and one is in my case. Still, she may as well look, she might find some old ones. What next?'

Peter looked back at his list.

'Shirts and ties. You don't wear those. There's your shoes and all your handkerchiefs.'

Santa nodded.

'And my frock and coat and things. And my summer frocks, only they'll be too short. And that's all.' She wrote quickly across the bottom,

'Much love, Santa,' then got up and went back to the door. 'Oh, Peter, come and look. There's a man climbing about on the top of the big top.'

Peter jumped up. It was perfectly true. There was a man right up at the top of one of the king-poles. They watched with enormous interest, wondering what on earth he could be doing. Suddenly they saw. He was fixing up a chain of coloured electric lights. They came back to the table again. Santa addressed an envelope to Mrs Ford and pushed it across to Peter to put his letter in. Peter drew a picture of a caravan on the blotting-paper.

'I was wondering. Do you think we ought to write to Bill?'

Santa tried to think fairly. Of course they ought to write to Bill. He had been kinder than almost any one they had ever known. All the same the thought of writing yet another letter gave her a sinking feeling inside. Nobody could want to write three letters the first day they came to live in a circus. She made a 'must we?' face.

'We'd have more to tell him tomorrow.'

Peter was just as glad of an excuse as she was.

'That's true.' He threw an envelope across to Santa. 'Shove yours to Mr Stibbings in there, and lick it up. I'll do Mrs Ford's.' Suddenly he stopped with his tongue out ready to lick. 'Doesn't it seem funny how important they seemed. They don't matter a bit now.'

Santa was licking so she could only say 'Um'. But now she came to think, it was very odd. Mr Stibbings with his slowness and fussiness. Mrs Ford and her tears. Madame Tranchot with her black-bordered handkerchief and her hands thrown into the air. Miss Fane and her violin. All suddenly just gone away. It was as though they had been packed up and put in a box like the old ivory set of spillikins that had belonged to the duchess.

Peter had pushed Mrs Ford's envelope into the middle of the table. Suddenly he pounced on it.

'I say, we are fools. We never said where the things are to be sent to.'

Santa looked blank. Circuses seemed very come-and-go affairs, not at all the sort of places to have luggage sent to.

'Well, where shall she send it? We'd better wait and ask Gus.'

Peter had managed to reopen the envelope without tearing it. He frowned at it.

'I'd much rather not ask him. I think it's the sort of thing he'd think we ought to know. I'd much rather find out for myself.'

'How?' said Santa.

Peter got up and went to the door. He was not exactly cross, but somehow since they had run away people were making him feel that they thought him stupid. Nobody ever had before. In fact Aunt Rebecca, Mr Stibbings, Mrs Ford, and

Madame Tranchot had all in their way given him the idea he was rather bright. He knew that he was not stupid really. All the same, the way Gus said things made him feel a fool, which was just as bad as being one. If possible he did not mean to give him the chance to make him feel like that again.

Santa looked at him anxiously. She knew just what he meant about Gus. He was the sort of man who expected you to know everything straight off without being told. She joined Peter at the door.

'I can't think why we didn't tell Mr Stibbings we had an uncle.'

Peter gave an angry jerk of his shoulders.

'You thought it was a good idea to run away. You said so.'

Santa sat on the caravan step.

'Of course I did. What I mean is, it's funny we both thought running away was the only thing to do. It would have been more sensible to say we had an uncle.'

Peter kicked at the caravan door.

'I can't think why Aunt Rebecca never told us about Gus, and why didn't she say she was just maid to the duchess?'

Santa puzzled the question over in her mind.

'As a matter of fact she never said she wasn't. I mean she never said why she knew that awful duchess. Anyhow I'm quite glad. I always hated

Lady Moira, Lady Marigold, and the Manliston girls. Now I needn't be like them any more.'

Peter felt surprised and pleased.

'And I needn't do things like Lord Bronedin.' Santa stretched out her legs.

'We needn't do anything like anybody. We're just us.' Suddenly she leant forward and gripped her knees excitedly. 'I can cut off my hair.'

Peter was doubtful. Of course he knew Santa's hair was a beast of a nuisance to her. All the same he was not sure he thought it a good idea to cut it off. It looked rather nice sometimes.

'I shouldn't. You'd probably look awful with it short.' He stepped through the door on to the step on which Santa was sitting. 'Look, there's Alexsis. Let's ask him about how luggage comes.'

Alexsis came and sat on the steps with them. It took him quite a time to grasp what it was they wanted to know. Peter and Santa kept prompting each other, and they spoke too fast for his bad English. When he did grasp what they were talking about he got up and ran down the steps.

'I will ask my father. He understands this things.' He turned and held up a finger. 'You wait? Yes?'

Alexsis's father, Maxim Petoff, was only in his caravan. Alexsis brought him back with him. He made a formal introduction.

'This is my father, Maxim Petoff. He is equestrian director. He trains the horses. You understand? Yes?'

Neither Peter nor Santa did understand much. They had never seen a performing horse, so had no idea what training them meant. But they smiled politely as if they understood perfectly.

Maxim Petoff was the sort of man everyone smiled at. He was tall with brown curly hair like Olga's and Sasha's. He had eyes that turned up a bit at the corners as if crinkled with laughing. He had even higher cheek-bones than his children. He had lovely teeth which showed when he smiled. He held out his hand, first to Santa, then to Peter.

'So this is the nephew and niece of Gus. And there is trouble with a box. Let us go and sit inside and you will tell me.' He came into the caravan and sat down at the table. There was something so big about him, not so much in the way he was made, as in himself, that the caravan which had seemed quite roomy was suddenly very small. 'Well?' He smiled at Peter.

Peter explained what they wanted to know. When he had finished Maxim talked the problem over with himself.

'That letter is for London?'

Santa and Peter nodded.

'They get him tomorrow. That is Friday. They must pack the box. Then they must send it to the station. That maybe will be Monday. It costs much money to send by passenger train, so it will be sent by goods. Next week is three days Carlisle. Three days Whitehaven. It is the week before Easter.' He stopped and took on the proud voice of somebody who has worked out a difficult puzzle. 'The box must go to White-haven.'

Santa had been enthralled at his casual mention of towns. After all, going to Bridlington had been a great adventure to them, and here was Mr Petoff making long journeys sound no more than walking to Miss Fane for a violin lesson.

'And where do we go after that?' She had to accentuate the 'we' a little. It was such fun to be able to say it about yourself and a circus.

Maxim laughed.

'That's right. Always say "we". You are already part of us. We' – he beamed at her – 'go to Blackpool. We stay all the week.' He got up. 'I must go. I am a busy man when there is a build-up.' He patted Santa's head and smiled at Peter. 'We shall be good friends.'

Gus came back just as Mrs Ford's letter was stuck down for the second time. He nodded approvingly at the two envelopes.

'That's right. Two letters in one envelope. Save the pennies. That's always been my motto.' He picked up the letter to Mrs Ford. 'Where are you having your stuff sent?'

Peter and Santa answered at the same time. They both tried not to sound pleased with themselves.

'Whitehaven.'

But it was evidently no good expecting admiration from Gus. He thought a moment. Then he nodded.

'Yes. Whitehaven's best. Week before Easter. Might miss us at Carlisle. Besides, there's no show on Good Friday. Give us nice time to fix your stuff.' He looked at his watch. 'Tea's at four. I'm going to have a lay down. You two go and have a look round. I've told Mr Cob you're here so you'll be all right.'

Peter and Santa jumped down the steps. There was no question where they were going. All the animals would have come from the station and they had not seen them. They set off running.

Although they had seen the stables being built, the sight of them full came as a complete surprise. They walked right the way through them awed into silence.

There were horses in the twenty stalls on the right. Ten chestnuts and ten greys. On their left, where before there had been a space, two huge barred cages had been placed. Looking through the bars with sleepy disinterested eyes were lions. Farther down below the lions' cages, in the ten stalls were more horses. Four were cream-coloured. Over every horse a name was hung. The ten chestnuts were called after things in the kitchen: Pepper, Salt, Vinegar, Mustard, Tapioca, Coffee, Cocoa, Rice, Soda, and Clove. The greys' names had no connexion with each other: Allah, Juniper, Ferdinand, Biscuit, Half-penny, Robin, Pennybun, Masterman, Lorenzo, and Canada. The lions' individual names were not given, but right across the two cages was written: 'Satan's Lions'. The four white horses had grand names: King, Emperor, Rajah, and President. The other six were called Rainbow, Whisky, Forrest, Magician, Pie-crust, and Wisher.

They came into the other half of the stables. In the space on the right a great wagon had been placed. On it was written: 'Schmidt's Sea-lions.' From the inside of the wagon there came splashing and queer hoarse barks. Next to the sea-lions a space had been fenced in. There were kennels at the back of it. Playing about outside in the enclosure were four French poodles. They glanced up as the children stopped to look at them. Their eyes were humorous, but behind the humour they seemed a little blasé. On the roofs of the kennels was painted: 'Lucille's French Poodles.' Facing the sea-lions' wagon and the French poodles were six great heavy horses and ten Shetland ponies. The horses were called sensible names to fit their size: Mack, Fred, Carter, Mike, Paul, and Joseph. The ponies were Prissy, Diamond, Alice, Nixie, Cinderella, Nimbo, Poppy, Fanny, Lucy, and Lassie.

At the end of the tent where the wooden platform had been put up were six elephants. They were fastened to the ground with ropes but seemed quite unmoved by them. They swayed to and fro with almost a dancing movement. When anyone came near them they held out hopeful trunks which said far better than any beggar's bowl: 'Can't you spare a little something?'

Peter and Santa, having watched the elephants in silence for a minute or two, suddenly let out great sighs as if they had been holding their breaths.

'Do you realize,' said Peter, 'that there are forty-six horses?'

Santa nodded.

'Um. That's counting the little ones. What do you like best?'

Peter needed no time to think.

'The horses. Don't you?'

They heard a chuckle behind them, and there was old Ben. He had his usual straw in his mouth. He nodded in an approving way at Peter.

'That's sense, that is. Elephants are all right. This lot are clever as paint. But when you've trained them no matter what they do they're always kind of funny. Now 'osses, they're beautiful.'

'There's the poodles,' Santa put in. 'You like them, don't you?'

Ben chewed thoughtfully at his straw.

'Very pretty little act,' he said at last. 'But, you know, to me those dogs aren't dogs, if you follow. Myself I always fancy a fox-terrier. But clever!' He spat out his straw and stooped to choose another. 'Almost indecent clever those French dogs are.

D'you know if those dogs spoke English instead of what they do, which is French, I'd mind what I said in front of them. 'Tis my belief they'd understand every word.'

Peter and Santa looked at him carefully to see if he was being funny. But he was not. His face was quite serious. He saw what they were thinking.

'No, I'm not joking. If you'd seen as much of circus animals as I have you'd know what I mean. There's some so clever 'tain't natural.'

Peter picked up a straw and chewed it too. He did not like it much but it seemed the right thing to do in a stable.

'Do you like the sea-lions?'

Ben grinned.

'Yes. I'm always glad when we have them out with us.

'You know, to me those dogs aren't dogs . . . But clever!' Does you good to hear the children laugh when they come in the ring.'

Santa leant against a tent pole.

'Are they clever?'

Ben looked across at the sea-lions' wagon. He smiled at it affectionately.

'Never made up me mind. You know how 'tis with some children. Sharp as needles. They don't know they're clever. Just born that way. Sometimes I think that's how 'tis with sea- lions. Born for the job.' He paused and broke a piece off his straw.

'Great artistes are like that. That's how 'tis with the best of my 'osses.'

Peter moved away out of reach of one of the elephants who was blowing down his ear.

'Which are the best of the horses?'

Ben jerked his head to show them they were to come with him. He went past the ponies and over to Mack, Fred, Carter, Mike, Paul, and Joseph. He felt in his pocket and got out some sugar. He gave half to Peter and half to Santa.

'You go up and give them a bit. Gentle as babies they are!' He gave Fred a friendly slap to make him move so that Santa could get into his stall. 'Get over, Fred.'

Peter looked round from giving a lump of sugar to Carter.

'They look much bigger than the other horses.'

Ben spat out his straw.

'So they are, too. We use 'm for what we call "jockey acts". You'll see when you've watched the show. These six are Suffolk punches. Can't beat 'm for rosin-backs.'

'Rosin-backs?' Santa came out of Paul's stall. 'What's that?'

Ben found another straw. He cleaned it on his coat.

'It's hard tellin' you two things. Gus was saying you've never seen a show. But maybe he'll get Mr Cob to pass you in tonight. Well, you watch "The Arizonas". That's what they call them on the

bar

97

programme. It's a trick-riding act. The Kenets do it. There's four brothers, Ted, Jo, Willy, and George, and they've Paula Petoff in with them.'

Santa gave her last lump of sugar to Joseph. She came back to Ben.

'We've met Mr Ted Kenet, and we almost know Paula Petoff. At least we've met Mr Petoff, and Alexsis, and Olga, and Sasha.'

Ben finished cleaning his straw and put it in his mouth.

'Well, when you see this jockey act the Arizonas do you have a look at the 'osses' coats.' He ran his hand over Mike's back. 'You'll see a grey look on them. That's rosin. Keeps the artistes' feet from slipping.'

Peter moved to one side to get out of the way of some people who had come from the town to see the animals.

'Can anybody come in?' he asked in a whisper.

Ben shook his head.

'Pay sixpence. And half the time they give as much trouble as if they'd paid a pound. Mr Cob he sticks up great notices to say "No smoking". But half of them don't seem able to read. You would think a baby if two would know you can't get throwing cigarettes about in a stable. But they don't. I've my boys watchin' all the time. Even then we had a fire once.'

'Goodness!' Santa leant against the wall of Mike's stall. 'What happened?'

'Well' – Ben moved his straw to the other side of his mouth – 'it wasn't in this Mr Cob's time. It was in his dad's. 'Course in those days tenting wasn't what 'tis now. We 'adn't the staff of grooms and that we carry now. What's more we 'adn't water laid on to the ground. Well, after the show the folks could pay same as they do now to see the menagerie. Dirty night it was, with a bit of a wind. Some fool, we never knew who, must have thrown an old end of cigarette in the straw of one of the stalls. Well, maybe the straw was damp. Anyways it doesn't catch at once. We was all dossed down for the night. The grooms' bunk house – that's what we call the men's sleeping tent – was away at the other end of the ground. I was sleeping in the forage tent which was where it is now just behind the elephants. Suddenly I sits up. You ever smelt fire?'

'No'. Peter shook his head. 'Was the tent on fire?'

Ben chewed his straw a moment. His eyes looked far away as if he were seeing that night all those years ago.

'Funny smartin' was all I felt at first. Then suddenly there came a puff of wind, and one of the horses screamed'. He shook his head at Peter and Santa. 'We was out of that forage tent before you could say the word fire. Somebody was sent running to call up the men. The stables weren't as big as they are now. It was more all in one like. Though that's sixty years ago, for I was only just turned fifteen at the time, I'll never forget the noise in that tent. We'd eighteen 'osses and they was all screaming. We'd a mixed wild animal act. One lion, two panthers, three polar bears, and a monkey. The lion was trying to tear down the bars of his cage, and it seemed like the panthers and the polar bears was gone crazy.'

'What was happening to the monkey?' Santa asked.

'I didn't see the monkey myself, I was busy with the 'osses. But a groom told me later he was actin' just like a child. Sittin' in the corner of his cage with great tears runnin' down his cheeks. Pitiful to see, they said it was. As well we had five elephants all trying to stampede at once. Well, of course, the first thing to do was to get our 'osses out, and meanwhile somebody was running for the men who trained the wild animals and the elephants. Then all the ring boys came along and they started a chain of buckets. Then before we knew where we was there was the fire engine up from the town. The wind had got up and was ragin' round and blowing the flames towards the big top.'

He stopped. Santa tried not to hurry him but she did so want to know what happened.

'And did the big top catch fire?'

'No. They saved it.'

'And how about the animals?' asked Peter. 'Did you get them out all right?'

Ben's face was sad.

'All except the 'oss in whose stall the fire started. Brandy-ball his name was. Been a hunter. We used him in a high-school act. He was burned to death.'

Santa's face was horrified.

'How awful!'

'It was.' Ben began to move slowly up the stables. 'Sometimes today Mr Cob will 'ear me speak a bit rough to someone I catch smokin'. Mind you, I never speak rough the first time. But if they don't put it out quick I may speak a bit sharp. But I always say to Mr Cob: "You'd speak sharp if you could remember old Brandy-ball"'

Santa and Peter got on either side of him. Peter looked up.

'What's high school?'

Ben chuckled.

'You two want to know too much all in one time. You says to me, "Ben, which is the best of the 'osses?" Well, I doesn't answer that direct. I gets you to meet the rosin-backs. This stable is much like the world outside. There's simple people, and clever people. Well, those Suffolk punches is simple. They're like farmin' folk. Shy maybe, but staunch when you know'm. Well, you get to know'm. You watch them work. When you got them clear you shall meet some of the others. No good gettin' a whole lot of words in your head and not know what any of them mean.'

They were level with the lions' cages. Santa stopped.

'Are they clever?'

Ben looked reflectively at the lions.

'Wonderful what Satan does with them. 'Course he picked 'em as cubs. He wouldn't have one in his troupe that was clumsy like. But for me I never fancy performin' cats, that's what we call 'em. I don't like to see any act that 'as to be done behind bars. All the other animals is loose and enjoys their work.'

'Don't lions?' asked Peter.

Ben shook his head.

'Some say so. But there's many feels with me, and Mr Cob's one of them, it's a pity any circus has a cat act. Same's it's a pity there's so much dangerous stuff, high aerial and that, done without a net.'

Santa propped herself up against the rail which was in front of the lions' cages.

'Well, why does Mr Cob have them?'

Ben took a thoughtful suck at his straw.

'On account of 'uman nature being what it is. There's 'undreds and thousands of people that don't come to a circus on account of the skill and the beauty and that, they come on account of seein' what's dangerous.'

Peter was puzzled.

'Why?'

'Nobody knows. It's one of the things left over from the time we was savages maybe. Lots of people haven't got so far from that now. Anyhow it's a fact, and anyone in the circus business will tell you so, that it's the savage animal, and the dangerous act, that half the time pulls 'em in.'

Santa made a face at him.

'Pulls who in, where?'

Ben spat out his straw.

'That's the way we speak when we mean getting an audience. If we get some specially big attraction Mr Cob'll say to me, "That'll pull them in, Ben." Do you follow?' Peter and Santa nodded. Ben gave them a smile. 'Well, I must be goin' to my tea. Now if Mr Cob passes you in tonight don't forget to watch out for my rosin-backs. And you watch how Paula and the Kenets work.'

Peter and Santa looked after him. Santa threw her hair back off her shoulders.

'I suppose it's our tea-time too. Do you suppose "pass you in" means Mr Cob will let us see the circus?'

Peter spat out his straw as nearly as possible in imitation of Ben.

'Sounds like it. We'll ask Gus.'

'Right.' Santa started to run. 'Don't let's fuss about tearing anything. Let's race. Bet I get there first.'

Peter shot after her.

'Bet you don't.'

7

The Circus

Gus was awake when they got back. Or rather he was just opening his eyes.

'Well,' he said, 'what have you been up to?'

They explained they had been seeing the animals and talking to Ben. Gus yawned. He looked at his watch.

'Tea-time. Fill the kettle, Peter.'

Peter took the kettle outside. Santa got out the cloth and began to lay the table. Gus came in from the other room and looked at her approvingly.

'That's right. I don't always lay the cloth at tea-time seeing I only have a cup of tea, but with a woman about it's different.'

Peter came back with the kettle and put it on the stove. Santa gave him a look to show that Gus seemed in a nice temper and so this seemed a good minute to ask about seeing the circus. Peter cleared his throat.

'If you please – I mean Ben said that perhaps – I mean—'

Gus gave him a pained look.

'Kedgeree and rum, boy, can't you say straight out what you want? "If you please" – and "Ben said" – and – "I mean . . ." Well, what is it?'

Peter turned red. He was looking a fool again. He wished he had left the asking to Santa. However, Gus had his eye fixed on him. He must finish now.

'We wondered' – he paused and Santa held her breath, afraid he was going to hesitate again, but he got it out at last – 'if you would ask Mr Cob if he would pass us in tonight?'

Gus did not answer directly. He went to the glass and straightened his tie. Peter and Santa thought he was thinking if he would or would not. But he was not. He was trying to be fair to Peter. From the first moment he had set eyes on him in his neat blue coat he had annoyed him. He was sure underneath the boy was not as namby-pamby as he looked. Just before he had gone to sleep he had spoken severely to himself for being unfair. After all, he had told himself, what could you expect from somebody brought up by Rebecca? He had decided to be more tolerant. Now the first second Peter spoke he had let him get on his nerves. That was why he tied his tie before answering. He was giving himself time so that he would answer quietly. He turned round, smiling.

'Don't see why not. It'll have to be the first

show because you kids must be in bed early.'

Santa got out the butter and skipped with it to the table.

'Oh, thank you awfully, Gus.'

Gus looked at the table.

'Is that all right for you? What do you generally have for tea?'

Santa put out some jam.

'Just this. Bread and butter and jam. Sometimes cake, but not often, because they take eggs to make and Aunt Rebecca hadn't much money.'

Gus sat down.

'Then you'll have supper, I suppose, before you turn in?'

'Yes.' Santa measured out the tea into the pot. 'Nothing much. The duchess didn't think children needed a heavy meal before they went to bed.'

'Never did care for the old duchess, so what she said doesn't cut no ice with me. Would bread and milk or a milk pudding or something of that sort be about right?'

Santa put the teapot on the table.

'It would be very nice. We often had bread and dripping with Aunt Rebecca.'

Gus poured out the tea. He nodded at the food on the table.

'You get on with that. Never eat anything at tea-time myself. I have a big supper later. I've fixed to have it with the Kenets now you two are here. Wake you up if I'm clattering about.'

Peter spread a piece of bread with jam.

'We shan't mind.'

Gus's eyes flashed.

'It isn't what you mind, young man, it's what I arrange.'

Santa saw that even Peter's ears were turning red, a bad sign. She could see rows of angry answers welling up inside him. She gave him a look to ask him to say nothing. They ate for a bit in silence. Then she said: 'Where are we going to sleep?'

Gus sipped his tea. He was furious with himself. Some uncle they must think him. Picking on Peter every time he opened his mouth. He smiled at Santa.

'The Schmidts have a spare camp-bed and bedding. It's coming in here for you. Peter will sleep with me in the other room.'

Santa cut herself another piece of bread.

'Is that the Schmidts who own the sea-lions?'

'That's right.' Gus poured himself out some more tea. 'You'll see them around somewhere. They've a couple of kids about your age. Twins they are. Fritzi and Hans.'

Santa spread her bread with butter.

'Will they come to school with us?'

Gus stirred his tea.

'That's right. There'll be quite a lot of you now.'

Santa finished a mouthful.

'Olga and Sasha Petoff, and Peter and I, and Hans and Fritzi Schmidt. Six.'

Gus paused to drink.

'No. There's seven of you. The Moulins have a kid.'

Peter let his mental eye go up and down the stables. He looked in a puzzled way at Gus.

'The Moulins haven't any of the animals, have they?'

Gus leant back in his chair and lit a cigarette.

'Yes. French poodles.'

'Oh!' Santa raised her eyebrows. 'On them was written "Lucille's French poodles".'

'That's right. That's what they call them. That's Madame Moulin. Her name's Lucille. They've one girl. Fifi they call her. She's very smart.'

Santa was surprised. Although Gus was such a neat man himself he did not seem the sort of person who would like smart clothes on children.

'Are they very rich?'

Gus looked puzzled. Then he laughed.

'I don't mean what you mean. When I say smart I mean clever. She's a very neat little acrobat, though she can't be more than ten.'

'Is she?' Santa was surprised. 'Will we see her in the circus?'

'No.' Gus blew a smoke ring up to the roof. 'She can't go in the ring in England. That's on account of the law. Twelve is the earliest you can get a licence, and then there's a lot of trouble. The kids don't go in the ring in England not till they're fourteen.'

Peter finished eating. He lolled back in his seat.

'What about Alexsis? Doesn't he go to school?'
Santa thought that a silly question.

'You know he doesn't. He was sitting in the big top with us this morning.'

Gus got up.

'Alexis had his fifteenth birthday round Christmas.'

Peter and Santa got up too. They began to clear the table.

'Funny he isn't in the act now,' Santa said. 'Olga and Sasha said he was going in next winter if he worked.'

Gus stood in the doorway.

'He would be working now if Maxim had his way. But Mr Cob wouldn't give him a contract. He's got sense, Mr Cob has.'

Santa folded the tablecloth.

'Why? Isn't Alexis any good?'

Gus threw away the butt of his cigarette.

'All depends.' He came back to the table. 'I'll get Alexsis to take you in tonight. He'll be along by the time you've washed up. I'll go and fetch that bed.'

The washing-up basin stood on a Tate's sugar box at the side of the caravan. Peter brought out the kettle of water and filled it. Santa washed up while he dried. While they worked they looked around them. The circus was changing again. All the afternoon it had had a sleepy look. Nobody seemed in a hurry. Nobody much had been about except Ben and the grooms who were watching the stables while the townspeople saw the menagerie. But now there was an air of bustle. It was not so much that anything was happening as a kind of excitement in the air, like you feel sometimes just before a storm.

Peter, who was drying a plate, moved to the other side of the caravan. He came back in a moment.

'Come and look. There's hundreds of people waiting outside to come in.'

Santa took her hands out of the bowl, and, holding them away from her so she did not wet her coat, went to look.

It was quite true. The ticket wagon was pulled forward. A long queue was formed ready to buy tickets as soon as the pay windows opened. Peter and Santa stood staring at the people with interest. Then suddenly they felt embarrassed. It is an odd feeling to be stared at by about a hundred and fifty people at once, and that was what was happening to them. They hurried back to the washing-up bowl. Santa giggled as she put a cup in the water.

'I think they must have thought we belonged.'

Peter picked up the other plate to dry it.

'Well, so we do.'

Santa stopped washing and stared at him.

'Do we?'

Peter nodded.

They both looked round them. At the big top.

At the line of caravans. At the wagons. At the tents. They heard all down the line of caravans talk and laughter in perhaps five different languages. They heard a short hoarse bark. They heard deep roars.

Santa looked at Peter. They both began to laugh. It was so unlike any world they had ever dreamed of. But it was true they did belong. The situation was so queer that the only thing you could do about it was to laugh.

Gus came along with two fair-haired children. Between them they were carrying a camp-bed, some blankets, and two pillows. Gus put down the bed and leant it against the caravan.

'Here's my nephew and niece. These are Hans and Fritzi Schmidt.'

Peter and Santa grinned, and the Schmidt children grinned back.

They were rather a nice-looking pair. They had hair nearly as fair as Santa's. Hans's was cut so short he hardly looked as if he had any. Fritzi's was worn in two plaits; the plaits were turned up and tied close to her head with check bows.

'What do you think, Santa?' said Gus. 'Mrs Schmidt wanted to come over and make up the bed for you. She said she didn't think you'd know how to.'

Santa washed the last knife.

"Course I can make a bed.' She did not add that the duchess had insisted on Lady Moira, Lady

Marigold, and the Manliston girls learning all the domestic things. She had said: 'Every woman must be able to do the work herself, or how can she direct others?' Although Aunt Rebecca had never seen much possibility of Santa having any others to direct, she had trained her carefully. She had in fact trained Peter too. After all she was not as young as she had been, and she had worked all her life. She was glad of help in the house. In fact, training in housewifery was probably one of the few things that Aunt Rebecca would have insisted on, even if the duchess had never said anything about it.

'My mother makes the joke,' Hans explained solemnly.

Fritzi climbed the caravan steps.

'Santa and I the bed will make. My mother thinks that in England no woman the things of the house is taught.'

Gus and Peter pulled the bed up the steps. When there were four of them inside, as well as Hans looking through the door, there did not seem much room for a camp-bed, but somehow it went in.

'Come on, Peter,' said Gus. 'We'll leave the rest to the women. I'm going to buy a bit of a tent tomorrow. That's where we'll put the bed in the day time. And in the summer you can sleep in it, Santa. You'll find sheets in the drawer under my bed.'

Santa and Fritzi went into the other room. There was a large drawer running the full length of Gus's bed. Inside were quite a lot of sheets, pillow-cases, towels, and kitchen cloths. Everything was neatly folded and marked in the corner, 'G. Possit'. Fritzi was overcome with admiration. She clasped her hands and gasped.

'Kolossal! Such a man is he. It as neat as my mother's is.'

They took two sheets and two pillow-cases and went back into the other room. Used as she was to making beds, Santa noticed that Fritzi was quicker and more thorough than she was. She would not allow a crease. Santa was quite glad when the bed was finished. Fritzi was so severe that she was afraid they might start to make it all over again. As Mrs Schmidt had lent the bed, blankets, and pillows, she would not have liked to refuse. But in her own mind she marked Fritzi down as terribly fussy. When they had finished they came out and found Peter and Hans sitting on the steps. Peter looked up at Santa.

'I was asking about the sea-lions. The ones they use come from California. Mr and Mrs Schmidt bought them when they were quite little.'

'That is so.' Fritzi sat down on the top step and patted the place beside her to ask Santa to sit too. 'My grandfather he does not sea-lions show. He has the wild beast.'

Hans nodded.

'He in all Germany the best wild animals had.'

Peter stretched out his legs.

'Well, why doesn't your father have them?'

Hans looked up at Fritzi. They both made gestures to show they did not know.

'My father he with some bears works,' Hans explained; 'and in Hamburg he my mother meets.'

Fritzi patted Santa's knee to be sure she was attending.

'She two sea-lions has. They work well.'

Hans nodded to Peter.

'You see?'

'No.' Peter shook his head. 'Why didn't your father go on with his bears?'

Hans looked at Fritzi. Fritzi nodded and took up the story. She spoke slowly, as if she were dealing with subnormal intelligences.

'The bears my grandfather's was.'

Peter turned round.

'I've got it. The sea-lions belonged to your mother.'

Fritzi and Hans looked pleased.

'That is so,' Hans agreed gravely.

Santa rested on her elbows.

'But how did your father know how to train sea-lions? They are quite different from bears.'

'No.' Hans's face was very serious. Obviously, both to him and Fritzi, training animals was not a subject you spoke of casually. You discussed it properly or not at all. 'All animals are as little children. First they must to speak learn.'

Santa sat up.

'What language does a sea-lion speak?'

'With us,' Hans explained, 'it is German. With you it would English be.'

'But they don't speak any language,' Peter argued. 'I mean no animals do.'

Fritzi's voice showed that she was amazed at his ignorance.

'All animals to speak learn. How else do they obey? First each a name must have. Each day he will the more easily when he is called come.'

'So,' Hans agreed. 'Then he must his trick learn. You speak German?' Santa and Peter shook their heads. 'Well, one sea-lion, the best, he is Siegfried called. Mine father he say in German, "Siegfried, come." One day, two days, three days he does not come. Then one day he come.'

Fritzi broke in.

'Then he have a fish.'

Hans went on.

'Siegfried he go back in the tank. He thinks, "Why did I that fish have?" The next day my father say to him, "Come," and Siegfried remember. He come. He have his fish. He has his first lesson learned.'

Peter and Santa had been so interested in hearing about the sea-lions that they had not been noticing what was going on outside. Now they were startled to hear a band. They looked up. A band was playing in front of the big top. All the bandsmen wore green with a white star on their coats and a white band on their caps. The conductor wore a green coat and white trousers with a green stripe down them.

'What's that band doing?' Santa asked.

Hans and Fritzi did not know what she meant. They were incapable of grasping that there were children in the world who did not know that all circuses have bands.

'They "pull them in",' Fritzi said at last.

It was Peter and Santa's turn to look at each other. Ben had said: 'That's the way we speak when we mean getting an audience.' Was the band Mr Cob's? Was it playing to get an audience?

'Is it Mr Cob's band?' Santa asked Fritzi cautiously. Fritzi nodded. 'Do they play like that to let people know there's going to be a circus,' Santa went on, 'and to make them buy tickets?'

'So,' Hans agreed.

Santa gave a pleased look at Peter. Evidently they had got that right. One more expression they understood.

Alexsis came out of the Petoff caravan. He beckoned to Peter and Santa. They got up.

'Tomorrow,' said Fritzi, 'we for you will come. We take you to the school.'

The first time you go to a circus must be exciting to anybody. To Peter and Santa, who had reached eleven and twelve and a half without even seeing a film, it seemed as if for over two hours they had stepped out of the world they knew and into a fairy story. Somehow, in spite of what Ben and Hans and Fritzi had told them, they had not expected the animals to be so clever. They had known people would ride on the horses. They had thought the dogs would beg. They did not know what they thought the elephants would do. And they had no idea what sea-lions looked like, and even in a dream could not have imagined them so clever.

Mr Cob was standing in the entrance to the big top. He wore a red coat and a top hat. He carried a long whip.

'Mr Cob,' said Alexsis, 'this is the nephew and niece of Gus.'

Mr Cob shook hands with Santa and Peter. He was a tall man with greying hair, a mouth that looked as if it had given a lot of orders in its time, and eyes that seemed to take in the whole of you in one quick flashing look.

'Never seen a circus before, I hear.'

'No, sir,' said Peter.

'Well' – Mr Cob looked round – 'there's a box empty round the other side.' He turned to Alexsis. 'Tell the girl to put you in there.' He nodded to the children. 'That's because it's your first visit. Next time you want to see the show you ask me and I'll put you in at the back somewhere.'

Peter still had their money on them so he bought

a programme. The girl who put them in the box seemed very unwilling to sell it to them.

'Alexsis can tell you what's on,' she objected. 'Don't go wasting your money.'

Alexsis too disapproved.

'There is no need. I tell you all the acts.'

But Peter and Santa were firm. This was their first circus and they intended to know exactly what was happening. They paid their threepence and pored over the programme together. There were eighteen acts:

1. THE MOSCOW COURIER.

2. THE TWO FRASCONIS. In their daring trampoline act.

3. MAXIM PETOFF'S PONIES.

4. LUCILLE AND HER FRENCH POODLES.

5. THE ARIZONAS. In their sensational equestrian display.

6. PEEKABOO. The comedy horse.

7. MAXIM PETOFF'S LIBERTY HORSES.

8. THE ELGINS. In their remarkable acrobatic novelty.

9. MADEMOISELLE PAULA PETOFF. In her graceful bareback riding act.

10. SATAN'S LIONS.

11. FOLLOW AND LEADER. In their unique clowning novelty.

12. SCHMIDT'S SEA-LIONS.

13. THE KENETS. In an exposition of Haute École.

14. THE MARTINI FAMILY. In their world-famous Risley act.

15. CLOWNS AND AUGUSTES. They have more uses than one for water.

16. KUNDRA'S ELEPHANTS

17. THE DANCING BUTTERFLIES. Sixteen girls in an exceptionally pretty dancing and acrobatic display.

18. THE WHIRLWINDS. In their hair-raising trapeze novelty.

By the time they had finished reading the programme the band had come in from outside and were sitting in a balcony over the artistes' entrance. Alexsis pointed to them.

'You watch the leader of the band. When he raise his baton then the circus it will begin.'

Peter looked back at the programme.

'The first is the Moscow Courier.'

Alexsis made a gesture with his hand as if wiping all the words off the programme.

'That will be Paula, my sister. But she may not be first.'

Peter hated to think his programme was wrong. He spoke quickly and angrily.

'Well, it says so. I suppose they wouldn't print the programme wrong.'

Alexsis looked hurt.

'You must not be angry. All programme for a circus says what you will see, but it cannot say how you will see it.'

Peter was still annoyed.

'Then they shouldn't charge threepence.'

Alcxsis spoke to Santa.

'A circus it shows two times on each day. The acts they change, so the most difficult to set up is put at the end of one show and he is ready for another.'

Santa poked Peter in the side.

'Don't you see? It's all there. But they won't be in that order.'

Alexsis showed her an indicator over the orchestra and another over the entrance.

'The number he will come there.'

'It's a very silly system,' said Peter.

Santa gave him a kick.

'Shut up. What's the matter with you?'

Peter kicked her back.

'Who howled in the road yesterday?'

Having started to argue they would have gone on for ages, but at that moment the conductor raised his baton. Alexsis leant back in his seat.

'Now we begin.'

In one moment Peter and Santa had forgotten there was such a thing as an argument in the world. The band played. A blaze of light shone down on the sawdust of the ring. The ring-men threw open the gate in the ring fence. An enthralling smell of animals and earth and sawdust swept over the big top. Mr Cob took up his place on one side of the artistes' entrance. Two ring-men held back the tent flaps. A mass of colour was grouped against the canvas. The circus had begun.

The parade went by. Neither Peter nor Santa could take in much of it. There was so much to see and it was so new. There were clowns in all imaginable garments. Gus was dressed as a sailor and was striding along on immense stilts. There were the horses. They wore the gayest harness. The ponies pulled a little coach with a girl standing up in it dressed as a butterfly. Then came the four French poodles. They were dragging a tiny brightly painted wagon. The six elephants were magnificent with golden cloths on their backs. They held each other by the tail. On the front one, dressed all in gold, with a golden turban, sat a man whom the children guessed must be Kundra. There were groups of people walking in fantastic clothes. Velvets, tinsels, and tarlatan. All chosen with an eye to gaiety. A lovely procession of motley. While it passed it was like living in a dream. When it had gone it was quite odd to see the ring was still sprinkled with sawdust. It would not have been surprising to see it had turned to gold.

There was not much time to think of miracles, for in a second 'One' flashed up on the indicator.

'This is Paula,' Alexsis whispered.

Paula had the same red hair as Alexsis. She was wearing a jade-green velvet tunic and cap. From her cap blew an ostrich feather. She was standing on the backs of two of the greys, one foot on each. She rode round the ring. Then, just as she passed the entrance, in bounded a third grey. He passed under her legs and as he went she caught a silk rein looped on his back, and drove him before her. Round the three horses went until they were again past the entrance; then a fourth grey cantered in, passed under her legs and was again caught and driven in front of her. Santa was terrified.

'Oh, goodness, won't she fall off?'

Alexsis laughed.

'No. She have rode this since she is little.'

'How many horses is she going to drive in the end?' asked Peter.

'Seven,' Alexsis explained. 'Then there are the two she stand on. That makes nine.'

The children began to count. Five. Six. They were terribly afraid she would miss the ribbon on the seventh. But no, she caught it, and drove her team out amidst roars of applause. In a minute she was back standing in the ring bowing and smiling.

There was a shout of laughter and suddenly the place was full of clowns. Peter grabbed the programme.

'What's this? No number's up.'

'No. It is the clowns and augustes. A reprisal.'

'A what?' said Santa.

Alexsis screwed up his face to try to explain.

'Always when the clowns and auguses come on that is not an act, that is a reprisal.'

'That can't be right,' Peter argued. 'Numbers eleven and fifteen are clowns and auguses. They're on the programme.'

'Then that is not a reprisal,' Alexsis explained patiently. 'That is a specialty. It is different. Look, the Frasconis.'

They looked. While the clowns had been playing about in the ring and on the ring fence, the ring hands had fixed up a trampoline. An old man dressed rather like a ring hand had stood by and supervised. Now he moved to the entrance and stood by Mr Cob.

'Who's that?' Santa whispered to Alexsis.

'That is Mr Frasconi. He is a very great artiste of the trampoline. These are his two sons. He teach them and build the act.'

The two Frasconi sons were dressed in pink fleshings and a piece of velvet made like leopard skin. The things they did when on the trampoline were breath-taking. The trampoline might only look rather like a mattress raised off the ground, but it was anything but a mattress to the two brothers. The smaller of the two bounded up and down on it, shooting up as if he would hit the roof, then coming down in amazing twists and somersaults. No matter how he came down the bigger brother, who was the bearer, never missed catching him.

'I can't believe they're real,' Santa sighed, when at last they finished leaping about and stood bowing on the ground.

After another reprisal from the clowns and augustes, the ponies trotted in. Alexsis leant forward and watched intently.

'I think,' he said in a worried voice, 'Prissy is not quite well.'

Peter and Santa gave each other a look. To them the ten ponies looked exactly alike. They suspected Alexsis was showing off.

Maxim Petoff looked grand in the ring. He wore riding things and carried a whip. He never used the whip. He just murmured orders to his ponies and they all obeyed. They had difficult things for a pony to do. They had to divide and trot round in opposite directions. They had to walk round with their forelegs on the ring fence and their hind ones in the ring. They had to stand for a moment on their hind legs begging like dogs. When they had finished Maxim stood by the exit and gave each of them something from his pocket as a reward.

Lucille's French poodles were so clever it was almost ridiculous. Three of them did really difficult acrobatic feats. The fourth, who had an enormous sense of humour, was the clown. She tried to do what all the others did and just did it a little wrong. She made the audience rock with laughter. Peter nudged Santa.

'Do you remember Ben said they were almost

indecently clever? I think they are, too. That one that always does everything wrong. She knows she's making us laugh.'

Santa nodded, then she gripped his arm.

'Look. That's the little ring of roses we saw being made this afternoon. I believe that must have been Lucille we saw making it. She was talking French.'

Peter looked at Lucille with his head on one side.

'But this lady has got yellow hair.'

Santa said nothing. She wished she was as observant as Peter. She had quite forgotten the hair. But of course, now she came to think of it, it had been black, with a fringe.

The rose ring was for the clown dog. She stood some way from Lucille looking at her over her shoulder with her tongue hanging out and the sauciest expression on her face. The band, which had been playing a march, suddenly broke into a waltz. The dog stuck out her tail. Lucille threw her rose ring. It was caught on the tail. There was a pause, then the ring began to swing. In perfect rhythm the dog spun it.

If ever a dog knew she was clever that one did. She had no sooner finished her act than she began to show off. She was just like a small child who gets above herself at too much praise. She raced round the ring fence while Lucille tried to catch her. She chewed up a ball. She walked on her hind legs without being asked to. And finally, when Lucille had sent all the dogs away and was bowing in the ring, she came shooting back and bowed too. Lucille was rather fat, with a good deal of her both behind and in front. The dog had evidently noticed this, and how it made her give rather clumsy bows. You would not think a dog could imitate a fat woman bowing, but that one did. How everybody laughed!

During the reprisal number eight was shown on the indicator. Alexsis smiled.

'This will be the Elgins. It is very, very beautiful. It is a floor act.' He saw they looked puzzled so he added: 'Their foots are on the floor.'

Santa was watching the artistes' entrance with one eye, and a clown who had water coming out of his hat with the other, but she really could not let Alexsis go on making the same mistakes over and over again.

'Feet,' she said. 'You know I told you that before.'

'So,' Alexsis agreed. But he was not really attending. His eyes were glued to the entrance.

The Elgins were a beautiful act. There were three men and two girls. They wore very little, but what there was of it was made of red velvet. The idea at the back of the act was that they should keep on forming pictures grouped quite perfectly. To get into these groups the three men hurled the girls at each other. They might have

127

been pieces of wood they were chucking about, they did it so casually. And the two girls might have had no bones to break, from the nonchalant way they shot through the air. Peter and Santa thought it very pretty, but they did not like it as much as the other acts. But it was quite different with Alexsis. He was pale with pleasure when they had finished.

'They are grand artistes,' he said.

Peter was watching a clown and an auguste throwing balls to the audience. He was hoping one would not fall on them. It would be awful if everybody stared, but it was quite likely it would be thrown at them with Alexsis sitting with them. All the circus people must know him.

'I don't think,' he argued, 'they are half as great artistes as Paula. I bet none of them could ride nine horses at once.'

Alexsis looked at him pityingly.

'You do not understand what you say.'

Santa sighed. Peter was being tiresomely argumentative, but Alexsis's last answer would have annoyed anyone. She expected Peter would answer back, and so he would have, but at that moment the clowns' ball hit him, on the head. Peter had forgotten the ball. His mind was racing round with retorts for Alexsis. Instead of using one, he worked off what he was feeling by giving the ball a great thump. It was a fine punch. The ball missed the clown and bounded away into the middle of the ring. At that moment 'Five' came up on the indicator.

'That was a good smack,' Alexsis said carefully, fumbling for the words.

Peter pulled Santa's sleeve.

'It's the Arizonas.'

Somehow, having fed the rosin-backs that afternoon, both Peter and Santa felt possessive about the Arizonas, perhaps because this was the first moment that they did know a little in a world where everybody else was well informed. If anybody sitting near them had criticized the act they would have been furious. But nobody dreamed of it. The Kenets were all beautiful riders. They and Paula were dressed in cow-punching out-fits. One Kenet had a lasso with which he caught not only the horses but his brothers. The act went at a terrific speed, accompanied by shouts from everybody in the ring. They all leapt from the ground on to the horses and on to each other's shoulders. They turned somersaults and arrived right way up on the horses' backs. They formed pyramids. They jumped from one horse to another. They all rode one horse at the same time. It was terribly exciting to watch. Peter and Santa were quite exhausted by the time the horses had cantered out and Paula and the Kenets were bowing in the ring.

They had no time to be exhausted, for into the ring tumbled the clowns. They had seen Gus in various clothes playing various jokes, but this time he came on with a lasso just like the Kenet brother had used. He seemed just as clever with it as the Kenet brother had been, only he used it funnily. He caught the other clowns and augustes round the neck, and then caught himself in the lasso. He skipped with it. He did it beautifully, but he looked so pleased each time he got through the rope safely that you felt it was only by luck he had done it, and you could not help laughing. Finally he lassoed three clowns at once, caught them all, then got his own foot tangled in the end of the rope, and was dragged out of the ring on his back.

Alexis was delighted that they found their uncle so funny.

'He is a very good artiste,' he said admiringly.

Number seventeen came next. It was a pretty dancing act. The girls wore blue dresses and blue wings. They waltzed to the music of *The Blue Danube*. Then suddenly they pulled off their dresses and wings, and with nothing on but some trunks and a little bit of blue stuff round their chests, threw each other round as the Elgins had done.

After this came number six. Most people have seen a comedy horse. They know just how silly it can be. Peter and Santa had of course never seen one before. They hurt inside, they laughed so much.

Just as Peekaboo trotted out of the ring, Gus

and Ted Kenet appeared. They wore fleshings and spangled trunks. Number eighteen came up on the indicator. Peter turned in great surprise to Alexsis.

'Is Gus "The Whirlwinds"?'

Alexsis had no time to answer, for Santa wriggled excitedly in her chair.

'Don't you see, it's what we saw them put up this morning.'

It was. Gus and Ted climbed up to their trapeze. Of course Santa and Peter knew nothing at all about trapeze work, so they did not see what a technically beautiful display they were looking at. Santa in fact saw very little, for she was so afraid Gus would fall that she sat with her eyes shut half the time. Peter watched, but he felt the palms of his hands get all wet. Ted Kenet had said he needed sulphur sweets and sarsaparilla to keep his blood cool. They looked a poor protection against that terrifying way he and Gus were behaving on the trapeze. They seemed to forget that there was nothing between them and the ground, and swung round and round holding on first by a knee and then by an ankle. They seemed scarcely ever to hold by their hands.

'Is he down yet? Is he down yet?' Santa kept asking Alexsis. Alexsis understood just how she felt.

'No, not yet. I will tell you.' Just as Santa felt she could not bear it any more, there was a roar of applause. Alexsis, clapping hard, whispered: 'It is finish.'

Santa looked at him out of the corner of her eye. Was it possible that Alexsis, too, was glad when the trapeze act was over?

There was an interval after that. Then number seven. Maxim Petoff's Liberty Horses.

Maxim treated his liberties as he did his Shetland ponies. He whispered orders and the horses seemed to understand. The greys danced. They waltzed in pairs, reared up on their hind legs. The chestnuts did some quite involved manoeuvres. Individual horses reared up and walked right across the ring. Another danced a two-step. There seemed to be nothing they could not do. They even knew their right order behind each other, for after each group every horse pushed himself back into his proper place. After each decapo, as Alexsis told them the individual performances were called, the horses acknowledged the applause by going down on their knees. The audience loved them. They loved Maxim too: he looked so strong, and was obviously such a gentle trainer.

Gus came on again. He was Follow or Leader this time. He and another of the Kenets did some funny but terrifying work on ladders. They had pots of paste and a bundle of bills. They came into the ring looking for somewhere to stick their bills, and then the fun began. They pretended to quarrel. They climbed up their ladders and with them swaying to and fro they had a fight from the top. How covered in paste they got! Peter and Santa laughed till the tears were pouring down their faces. But all the time they kept wondering how, if Gus did this twice a day, he was so clean.

Number nine. Santa thought it the prettiest act of the lot. Paula in a rose-coloured ballet frock on one of the rosin-backs, jumping through a paper hoop held by her father. She looked quite lovely with her flaming hair and frilly skirts. The audience seemed to adore her; they clapped till their hands were sore.

Of course, if you have seen sea-lions perform you know the sort of things they will do. Peter and Santa had not only never seen performing sea-lions, they had never seen any at all. In spite of what Hans and Fritzi had told them, and what Ben had said, they were quite unprepared for the brilliance of the performance. Sea-lions have not really got clever faces. They do not look like artistes. But how clever they can be! Schmidt's sea-lions did all the things performing sea-lions do. They balanced balls on their noses. They juggled. They climbed up a pyramid of blocks and balanced on one flipper. They played instruments. They were enchanted at their own skill and rolled about at the first hint of applause, slapping their flippers together asking for more. They were as clever as Lucille's poodles. Only the poodles were obviously skilled artistes revelling in their own gifts, whereas the sea-lions were like a lot of precocious children. They were rather like Gus with the lasso, desperately clever but apparently surprised and naïvely delighted to get anything right.

The Martini family came next. They were made up of a father, a son, and two daughters. The girls wore sort of rompers made in satin, and they wore socks. Santa thought they were younger than she was. But Alexsis assured her they were quite grown up. Before they came into the ring he tried to explain a Risley act. He told them about the first Risley who had the idea of juggling with a real boy. Of how the idea caught on, and that kind of performance was always known as a 'Risley act'.

'But didn't the boy get hurt?' Peter asked.

Alexsis shrugged his shoulders.

'Maybe. But if a clown he start as a Risley kid, always he is glad. It is the great training.'

Santa was just going to say that she would not be glad at being hurt however great the training might be, when the Martini family ran into the ring.

The Martinis were followed by the elephants. The six beasts marched into the ring holding each other by the tail. Kundra gave a signal and a great table and four chairs were trundled in. Four of the elephants sat down, the other two acted as waiters. It was a very funny act. Peter and Santa enjoyed every minute of it, but Peter felt a little uncomfortable at finding them so funny. They seemed such magnificent creatures, too grand somehow to be laughed at.

The clowns and augustes did a water act. There can be nobody who would not have liked at some time or other to have buckets and buckets of water and slosh it all over people. The next best thing to doing it yourself is to see somebody else do it. There never could be a better opportunity of seeing someone else do it than there was with Cob's Circus. The only concession made to the ordinary laws about not getting wet was a waterproof sheet stretched across the ring before the act began. After that nobody cared at all. In spite of the fact that the augustes were fully dressed, or at least they wore clothes, if unusual ones, they poured entire buckets of water down each other's necks, they threw buckets of water all over each other, they skidded in the water and sat down in it, they lay down in it. It was an orgy of getting wet and everybody in the audience adored it.

By the time the Kenets and Paula came on to show high-school riding Peter and Santa were dazed. They had had a tremendous day, and all this being thrilled and clapping and laughing had about finished them. That any horse could be trained to do what those horses did was unbelievable, but then everything was unbelievable. They were almost past marvelling. Alexsis was disappointed in them.

'You do not like the haute école? That is the most best work in riding.'

'You can't say most best,' Santa reproved him. 'And we did like it.'

Peter nodded.

'I believe it was the most interesting; only we've seen such a lot.'

Alexsis was satisfied.

'That is so. There is just Satan and that is the end.'

During the reprisal an immense iron cage was hooked together. From one side of it a cage tunnel led through the artistes' entrance. Suddenly yellow forms streaked along it. Satan dressed as the devil, pitchfork and all, entered from the other side. The doors clanged shut. He was alone with his lions.

Satan was a superb trainer of wild animals; he was also a great showman. He knew what the public liked was to feel he was in danger. To get this atmosphere he taught his lions to roar, to claw at him as he passed, to look as if at the slightest excuse they would spring. No wild animal act is safe, but Satan loved his lions, whom he had known since they were cubs. Some nights they were difficult to handle, bad-tempered, temperamental; but this was not one of them. But Peter and Santa did not know that. They were frankly terrified. They expected every second to see Satan eaten. They could only dig their fingers into the palms of their hands and wish it was over.

Then suddenly it was over. The band played *God Save the Queen*. They pushed their way out into the cold night. The audience hurried down the hill back to the town. Peter, Santa, and Alexsis went through the wicket gate fencing round the big top. They crossed the rough grass and fumbled their way to Gus's caravan.

'Good night,' said Alexsis. 'Sleep well.'

Gus had left a note on the table.

'Help yourselves to what you want for supper, and go to bed quick.'

Santa blinked.

'I don't believe I want anything. Do you?'

Peter did not really want anything either, but he thought Santa looked as if some supper would be good for her.

'You get on undressing. I'll make us some bread and milk.'

Santa had her bread and milk in bed. Peter sat on the end of it eating his. Suddenly they both looked up. Peter opened the door.

'It's the band. They're beginning again.'

They listened. The band blared. There were voices talking and laughing from the crowd waiting to get in. A horse whinnied. Someone called out something in German. A lion roared. Peter shut the door. He smiled at Santa as he took her empty bowl. It was too queer to be true. Could this really be them?

8

School

Hans and Fritzi called for Peter and Santa. It was a cold damp morning. Hans and Fritzi had on big mackintoshes and wellington-boots. They had large scarves wound round their necks. Hans had no hat but Fritzi had on a queer little blue felt with a pom-pom on the top. They did not look smart but they seemed sensibly dressed.

Fritzi liked worried when she saw that Santa had on the same clothes that she had arrived in.

'You have no other clothes arrive yet?'

'No.' Santa glanced down at herself. 'I've got a mackintosh coming.'

Hans nodded at their feet.

'And you have boots?'

'What, like those?' Peter shook his head. 'No, we never wear them.'

Gus came to the caravan door. He was wearing a pullover and slippers. He was smoking. It was his time for reading the paper and he hated to be disturbed.

'Kedgeree and rum! You kids are making a fuss getting off! What's the trouble?'

Fritzi pointed dramatically at Santa's feet.

'Such shoes for her to wear.'

Hans broke in.

'So it is with Peter. The wet will come through.'

Gus looked at Peter's and Santa's feet.

'Turn your soles up both of you.' Peter and Santa turned them up. Gus nodded at Hans and Fritzi. 'They're no good. I'll have a talk with your mother later. Maybe she'll take them shopping.'

Fritzi moved off.

'That will my mother do.'

Hans beckoned to Peter and Santa.

'Come. We go for Fifi.'

Fifi was sitting on the steps of the Moulin caravan. She was small, olive-skinned, with black, straight hair cut in a fringe. She, too, was dressed for the weather. But she looked quite different. Worn right over her left eye was a blue beret. She had on a smart reefer coat, and over it a dark blue mackintosh cape. She too had gum-boots, but hers were not big and clumsy like Hans and Fritzi's, but well-fitting. She got up as she saw the four of them arriving.

'Good morning, Hans. Good morning, Fritizi.' She came down the steps and politely held out her hand to Santa. 'Good morning.'

Santa was just going to shake hands when the black-haired woman they had seen making the wreath of roses looked out of the caravan door.

'Are the little nephew and niece of Gus there?'

Fifi with a gesture presented Peter and Santa.

'Yes, maman. See!' She turned to Peter and Santa and made another gesture towards her mother. 'This is my mother, Madame Moulin.'

Madame Moulin smiled.

'Fifi is very excited that you have come. It is more for games.'

Santa was so puzzled about the hair she forgot her manners.

'But when you were with the poodles in the circus your hair was fair.'

Peter turned red. He kicked Santa on the ankle.

'Shut up, you fool!'

But Madame Moulin was not a bit angry. She laughed.

'That is a wig. In the ring it is better for hair to be gold.'

Fifi caught at Santa's hand.

'Quickly, quickly. We shall be late.'

'But what about Olga and Sasha?' Santa asked. 'Aren't they coming?'

Fifi gave a magnificent shrug and gesture with her hands. With it she expressed the complete inability of herself or anybody else to say what

141

Olga and Sasha might do. She seemed to consider this unspoken comment quite enough, for she said nothing.

Fritzi was evidently quite used to Fifi's ways, for she answered exactly as if she had spoken:

'That is so. They have no sense of time. Come. We shall be late.' She caught hold of Peter's arm and hustled him along.

Hans hurried after them. He came up on Peter's other side.

'They are Russian. Russians keep not the time.' They walked past the line of caravans and through the wicket gate in the fence round the big top. Hans was just shutting the gate when they heard a shout behind them. Olga and Sasha were dashing after them. They waited. Olga and Sasha panted up.

'Good morning, Olga. Good morning, Sasha,' said Fifi.

Fritzi looked at them reprovingly.

'Such children always to be late!'

Olga skipped along the path.

'It's not late, and if we are it's because Alexsis and my father have a terrible argument and the breakfast is not cooked.'

Santa was interested.

'Doesn't your mother cook the breakfast?'

They were on the pavement by now, and the surface, though wet, was not muddy. Sasha turned a cartwheel.

'But of course. But not when Alexsis and my father have an argument.'

Peter took the opportunity, while speaking to Sasha, to get his arm free of Fritzi's. He hated being hurried along as if he were a naughty small child who would run home if he were not held.

'Why not? Did she argue too?'

Olga shot forward on to her hands, spun over, and came back on her feet.

'How can she cook if there is an argument?'

Fritzi pursed up her mouth.

'Such a show to make, Olga. You should not make the flip-flap in the street when your trousers have not your dress match.'

Olga turned a cartwheel.

'Why should they match?'

Fritzi gave Santa a despairing glance, which Santa returned. They two, at least, knew, if nobody else did, that when a person is wearing fawn knickers under a navy-blue skirt, it is better to remain the right way up.

Fifi caught hold of Sasha.

'Tell me, Sasha, did your father agree about Alexsis?'

Sasha and Olga at once stopped spinning about. Hans and Fritzi looked serious. All of them hung on Sasha's answer.

'No. My father says we have always been with horses and Alexsis must do the same.'

'But there is Paula?' said Fifi.

Olga put her arm round Fifi's shoulder.

'But she is a girl. She may marry.'

'But certainly she will marry,' Fifi agreed. 'But there is Sasha.'

They all looked at Sasha consideringly. Hans shook his head.

'Mine father say how Mr Petoff right is. Alexsis is the eldest son. To him must the horses go.'

Fifi threw up her hands and eyebrows.

'But why? Alexsis is an artiste. But his talent is not with horses. My papa says it is wrong to force him to that which he does not wish.'

Sasha hopped along on one leg.

'But I have talent with riding. Ben says so as well as my father. I am eight. In six years I can go into the act.'

Hans made a face.

'Six years! Your father wish it now.'

'What does Alexsis want to do if he doesn't do the horses?' Santa asked.

The other children looked surprised. Obviously Alexsis and his future was such a common subject for discussion in Cob's Circus that they had not supposed anybody did not know about it.

'He wishes to be an acrobat,' Olga explained. 'He has always said so.'

'He's very good,' Sasha added.

Fifi nodded. She spoke with authority. She evidently knew what she was talking about.

'But superb!'

They were nearing the school. Sasha lowered his voice.

'He works every day with the Elgins.'

Olga held up a finger.

'But it's a secret. My father doesn't know. And Gus mustn't know or he might tell our father.'

'So,' Hans agreed. 'Come, Peter. Here is the school.'

Naturally children who lived in a circus were objects of interest in the schools. The whole place buzzed with excitement when they arrived. Not only were they circus children, but foreign. They had, too, other charms beside being foreign. They could do the most astounding things in the playgrounds. Their handstands and flip-flaps, which were common as the daisies in the circus world, were considered brilliantly clever by the local children in the towns they visited.

If the teachers felt a sinking of their hearts when two Russian, two German, and one French child arrived suddenly, expecting to be taught for three days, they showed no sign of it. The children had cards to show what stage their education had reached, and one glance at them proved that their nationalities were no hindrance to them. They were all ahead of the average English child of their own age.

Peter and Santa had, of course, no cards. They were put as a start to work with children of their own ages. Peter's first lesson was arithmetic,

Santa's geography. It took neither of them five minutes to realize how appallingly backward they were. It was a nasty shock. If there was one thing that they knew for certain it was that they were far better educated than ordinary school children. All the morning, as the subjects for the lessons changed, they said to themselves: 'Well, anyway I'll shine at this.' But they did not. After all, Mrs Ford was not a teacher herself, and the fact that her husband was had not made her able to teach. Even before the recreation break Peter and Santa had sunk to depths of humiliation, taking the exaggerated view that they knew nothing at all. Peter was at least humiliated by himself, but Santa had Fritzi in her standard, and Fritzi had eyes which very easily looked as if they were marvelling at the lack of qualities of people who were not German.

In the recreation ground further shame was waiting for them. The boys, having seen what Hans and Sasha could do, supposed that every boy who lived in a circus was as happy one way up as another. They could not believe Peter could not stand on his hands.

'Then what can tha do?' one of the boys asked. He was a boy in Peter's standard, so he knew a good many things Peter could not do.

Peter felt desperate. After all, he had been brought up as nearly as possible in imitation of Lord Bronedin. Up till now he had thought Lord

Bronedin a bore, but a sense of inferiority turned him into a snob.

'I don't belong to the circus. I've had a tutor at home.'

There was a roar of laughter from the boys in his standard.

'A tutor!'

'Must 'a' been a fine teacher.'

'What did he teach tha?'

'Latin.'

There was a slight pause, then the boys rolled about with laughing.

'He's had a tutor.'

'And he taught him nowt but Latin.'

They fell against each other. Then Hans created a diversion. He leapt in the air, caught his ankles, turned over, and came down again on his feet. Admiringly the boys drew round.

'Did tha see that?'

'Do it again, Hans.'

Peter leant against the wall loathing himself. Why had he made such a silly answer? He might have known they would laugh. Why had he and Santa been brought up like that? It had been all wrong. They knew nothing, and nobody wanted them. Lolling there against the wall he indulged in an orgy of self-pity. The bell rang for school to start again. Hans came up. He felt in his pocket and brought out a sweet. He held it out to Peter.

'For you.'

Peter was not in the mood for sweets. What he wanted was somebody to say: 'Don't mind them. It's just jealousy.' He moved away.

'No, thank you.'

Hans looked after him with a puzzled face. Then he gave a philosophic shrug of his shoulders and ate the sweet himself.

Santa had the same troubles in a minor degree.

'Stand on tha hands, Santa,' somebody said the moment she came out.

Santa looked shy.

'I can't.'

Olga, Fifi, and Fritzi came to her rescue.

'She can't,' Olga explained. 'They have been brought up by an aunt who taught them nothing at all.'

Fifi picked up one leg and held it over her head.

'But nothing. Their uncle says they are like two babies just born.'

Fritzi nodded.

'My mother says to bring up to such ignorance is cruel.'

Santa stood by looking a fool while all this went on. She would have liked to say that at least she knew French. But with Fifi there she could not. It was obvious one sentence from Fifi would floor her. She fell back on something she had never expected to brag about.

'I play the violin.'

Olga, Fifi, and Fritzi were impressed.

'Have you got your violin with you?'

'It a wonderful instrument is.'

Fifi shrugged her shoulders and raised her hands. The gesture said plainly: 'If she can play the violin, what more do you want?'

After that the girls moved away. Fifi gave a small acrobatic display and they gathered round to marvel.

Santa, left alone, inwardly called herself an idiot. What on earth made her mention the violin? They would expect her to play it. She could just imagine their faces when she started *Art thou weary, art thou languid*. Then, just as the bell went, she remembered something that cheered her up. She had not asked Mrs Ford to send her violin. She would not be able to play.

'Early bed tonight,' said Gus. 'We're starting round about six tomorrow.'

Santa was sitting on the steps of the caravan working at some sums.

'Can't we see the pull-down? Hans says it's more exciting than the build-up.'

Gus nodded.

'So 'tis, too. But you've got your schooling just now, and you don't want late nights. It'll be your holidays next week; you can see it then.'

Peter was studying an atlas.

'I don't suppose I'll want to.'

Santa looked up from her sum, then quickly looked back again. What was the matter with Peter? He had been as excited about the circus as she was to begin with. But ever since school yesterday he had sulked. Of course it was sickening for him to be moved down to work with Hans, who was a year and a half younger, especially as Hans was so much more clever than he was. But it was no worse for him than it was for her. She had been moved out of Fritzi's standard into the one with Fifi and Olga in it, which, seeing Fifi and Olga were only ten, wasn't much fun. She thought probably it was much worse for her. Peter did not have to work with someone who curtsied to all the teachers like Fifi did, and so made other people, who, of course, would not dream of doing a showing-off thing like curtsying, look awkward. Then Peter had not to work with Olga, who never seemed to be attending, who made all the class laugh, and then did better than anybody else.

Gus looked at Peter and sighed. What a difficult boy. What was the matter with him now? He had seemed keen enough about the circus the day they arrived, but since yesterday he had been as cross as a bear. He had come back for his midday dinner sulky and silent. He had returned again at tea-time worse than ever. Gus had sent him and Santa off shopping with Mrs Schmidt, and had hoped that would cheer him up; but no, he had reappeared in just as bad a mood, and had hung about the caravan until it was time for bed. Today was just the same. What had bitten him? Gus tried to be fair, but he suspected that the trouble was snobbishness. The boy thought himself too good for his school. If that was so, the sooner he got over it the better. He got up.

'Well, time I was moving across to the dressing-tent, I suppose. Why don't you two go along to the stables? You can see all the animals go into the ring. But don't get in the way.'

Santa got up to let Gus go by. Then she went on with her sum. Of course she was not going to the stables alone, but to suggest to Peter that he came was to be certain he would say 'No'. Perhaps if she left him alone he would suggest it himself.

Peter looked at Santa out of the corner of his eye. He knew he was being hateful, and he wished he was not. But he felt simply miserable. Somehow with Aunt Rebecca he had been the boy, and there had been a sort of understanding that over some things he knew best. Santa had always been admiring. She knew he usually thought of things first. She had been quite happy to let him plan things. Now suddenly he seemed to be nobody. Any tent hand knew more about circuses than he did. All these Germans and Russians and French were better at lessons. Gus considered him a hopeless fool, could not even trust him to buy himself gum-boots and a pullover; he had to send Mrs Schmidt with him. Well, he did not care. They could all think him a fool if they liked. He probably was, so why worry? All the same, he was sorry he was being cross with Santa. It was not really her fault. He comforted his conscience by saying to it: 'Well, she can go to the stables by herself, can't she?' But his conscience would not be comforted. He and Santa had always done things together. It was not likely that she would go off by herself now.

Santa went on struggling with her sum. She looked longingly across at the big top. The people were queueing up to go in. Being Saturday, there had already been a matinée performance. Some of the audience from the matinée were still straggling out from the menagerie. Somewhere a wind instrument was having a few notes blown on it. Evidently the orchestra were collecting to come out and play in front.

Olga and Sasha came and leant against the caravan.

'Why do you sit here?' asked Olga, using the side of the steps as a practice bar and raising her right leg in an arabesque.

Santa was glad to see them. She laid down her book and pencil.

'I'm trying to do those sums.'

Sasha stood on his hands and rested his legs against the caravan.

'Where's Peter?' Santa gave a jerk of her head to show where Peter was. Sasha, still standing on his hands, slowly opened his legs in the splits. 'Why is it that you and Peter work so hard at your lessons? You worked last night and again this morning.'

Santa thought this a mean question. Surely it was perfectly obvious why they would have to work hard.

'We're backward. You know that.'

Sasha slowly closed his legs again.

'Still I don't see.' He gave a slight jerk to his body and landed on his feet. 'When me and Olga first come to England we don't speak English good.'

Olga went on with her bar practice.

'That's right. We don't speak it good at all. We go to school every day, and every day we cried because we couldn't understand what anybody said. So I ask my father: "Must we go?"'

Sasha fell on to his hands again, and walked a few steps on them.

'You see we had German. That's the language that is always spoke in a circus.'

Peter's British spirit was aroused by this statement. He came to the caravan door.

'That's wrong, anyway. English is. Everybody here speaks English.'

Olga picked up her right leg by its ankle and held it over her head.

'That is because we're in England. But among the artistes, no.'

Sasha fell over. He got up on his hands again, and once more tried to walk.

'Mr Cob speaks German to the artistes. That's so with all ring-masters.'

'Well, it's very silly if he does.' Peter went back to his atlas. 'English is a much better language.'

Olga looked down from the foot over her head and made a face at Santa.

'He has a mood. My father's often like that.'

Santa was glad she called it a mood. She would have called it temper.

Sasha fell over again. When he had righted himself and was once more on his hands he said to Santa:

'I was telling you about us and the school. Always we don't want to go. Always we must.' He fell over, so Olga went on:

'Partly in England it's the law, and partly my father wants us to speak. Then one day we understood. It was like that.' She clicked her fingers. 'Then we liked school. So it'll be with you.'

'But Peter and I are English. It can't be that.'

Sasha walked triumphantly six steps before he fell.

'It's the same. Fritzi says so, and Fifi, and Hans. You have been learned differently. One day it'll come.'

Santa hoped very much that they were right, but she had a gloomy suspicion they were not. Even

154

after one day's school she could see there were strange gaps in the things Mrs Ford had taught them. She picked up her book and pencil.

'Goodness, I hope you're right.'

Olga gave a bound in the air and landed on the bottom step of the caravan. She clasped Santa's knees.

'Don't look so sad. Look, the band is coming out. Let's go and suck some pieces of lemon.'

'Lemon!' Santa raised her eyebrows. 'Whatever for?'

Sasha was enchanted with the idea. He turned three rapid cartwheels.

'Yes. Lemons. Come on.'

Santa looked round at Peter.

'Will you come, Peter?' Peter shook his head and went on staring at his atlas. Santa looked helplessly at the others. 'I can't. He doesn't want to come.'

Olga and Sasha made strange noises. They caught hold of Santa by one hand each and pulled her off the steps.

'When anyone has a mood,' Olga said severely, 'even so bad a mood that they say they will shoot themselves, leave them alone, it is better.'

'But,' panted Santa, hurrying after them to the Petoff Caravan, 'Peter never has talked about shooting himself; he never would.'

'With us,' said Sasha, 'there is always talk of shooting.'

Santa was sorry for them.

'How awful. And do they ever?'

'No.' Olga ran up the steps of their caravan. 'Never. But they feel better because they've said that. It is the way with moods.'

Each holding a quarter of lemon, Olga, Sasha, and Santa went over to the big top. The band had just arrived and were striking up.

'Hide your lemon in your hand and don't use it till we tell you,' Olga whispered.

Santa palmed her piece, but she wondered what for.

Olga and Sasha, with Santa following, walked quietly up to the band. They stood directly behind the musical director. Then Olga looked round and gave a faint nod. Simultaneously she and Sasha began to suck their bits of lemon. Santa, though she found it so sour it dried the inside of her mouth, did the same.

The effect on the band was disastrous. First one wind instrument player and then another gave up. The sight of those lemons dried their mouths so that it was impossible to blow. Then the drums and cymbals saw what was happening and they began to laugh. The music tailed off to nothing. The director looked round. He saw the three children. He made a movement. Olga and Sasha dashed off round the other side of the big top. They were laughing so much it was quite difficult to run. Santa, after one scared glance at the musical director, flew after them.

'Goodness!' she said. 'You made the band stop playing. Whatever will happen?'

'Nothing.' Sasha giggled. He looked at Olga. 'Did you see old Ted trying to blow his euphonium?'

The memory seemed to Olga such a glorious joke that regardless of the wet grass she lay down in order to laugh more easily. When she had finished she got up.

'What shall we do now? Shall we make an apple-pie bed for someone?'

Sasha was enchanted.

'Let's make it for mother and put in that fish she bought today.'

'The fish!' Olga clasped her hands at the glory of the idea. 'It will be cold, and she'll scream. Come, Santa, you shall help.'

But Santa had had more than enough of the Petoffs for one evening. They might think all these things fun, but they had not got an Uncle Gus whom they did not know very well, who might change his mind and send a person to an orphanage.

'No. You go. I want to see the horses.'

The stables looked quite different. The sleepy atmosphere was gone. The animals had heard the band, and every one of them was excited. There was the same sort of excitement you can feel behind the scenes in a theatre when the call-boy says: 'Half an hour, please.' The horses were being dressed in their ring finery, and each was throwing about his head as if to say: 'Now let me see. Is that comfortable? I can't work if there's a pull anywhere.'

The sea-lions were in their tank but there was a tremendous noise going on. Mr Schmidt was putting fish into a barrel. He smiled at Santa.

'My childrens are calling.' He patted the wagon. 'Each one to me is trying to say: "The band it plays. Do not be late."'

The poodles were behaving like a lot of ballerinas waiting in the wings for their entrances. Not for one second did they stay still. They wriggled. They stood on their hind legs. They shook themselves. Lucille, in her ring clothes and wig, was in with them. She held out her hand to Santa.

'Good evening.' She looked at her dogs with pride. 'They are great artistes, full of temperament.'

'They're awfully clever,' Santa agreed.

Lucille nodded.

'But difficult! You know how it is with artistes. Great children, all of them. Some little thing is wrong, and they cannot give of their best. So I come down early and look at my dogs. How is it with you today, Simone? And you, Violette? Do you feel happy, Marie? And then I turn to Mis. She is my funny one. A little genius, that. And I say to her: "How are you, Mis?" I would like to say more. I would like to kiss her, but no.' She lowered her voice. 'All artistes are jealous. It is the temperament. If I kiss Mis, I must kiss them all, or they will not work.'

'Do you mean they wouldn't do that jumping and all that?'

Lucille made a gesture with both hands.

'But certainly they would not. Maybe I will pet them and give them sugar, and they will do a little. But by that time Mis is upset. She cannot work. The act is spoilt.'

Santa looked in respect at the poodles. Evidently they went in for what the Petoffs called moods. Of course, they could not say they would shoot themselves, but evidently to Lucille what they did threaten was just as bad. Santa would have liked to ask some more questions, but Mis gave Lucille's foot a small bite. Anyone could see it meant: 'Now, then, that's enough talking to that girl, what about me?' So, afraid of making her jealous, she hurried away.

The ponies were excited. Their grooms were putting on their harness, and the mere feel of it seemed to go straight to their heads. They stamped, they cavorted around, they tossed their heads. The grooms kept up a steady flow of soothing sounds, broken now and again by: 'Quiet now, Diamond.' 'Give over, Lucy.' 'Stand still, Nixie.'

Only the rosin-backs seemed unmoved. Except for the rosin rubbed into their coats, they had no dressing-up to be done. They looked alert. They had heard the band the same as the other animals, but they did not believe in fussing. They were like yokels in a village inn at a time of national excitement. Just as interested as the rest of the world, but seeing no need for a lot of words about it.

The elephants were dressed. Their keepers had put on the last of their velvet coats. They were still swaying from side to side, but with a difference. They carefully lifted first one leg and then another, they swung their trunks, not for begging but for rehearsal. They were like some stage actors and actresses who need to get into their parts well before the cue comes for them to enter.

A voice behind Santa made her jump.

'Where's your brother tonight?'

Santa beamed at Ben. She leant against one of the tent-props.

'He's doing geography. We go to school now and we're very bad at lessons.'

'I thought you'd be at school. That was why you wasn't along yesterday.'

'Partly it was school,' agreed Santa. 'Mostly it was because we had to go with Mrs Schmidt to buy wellington-boots and jerseys. These are them I've got on, as a matter of fact. Then when we got back we did some lessons, because we are so backward, and we had to write to Bill, who is a man in London who was terribly kind to us. And then we had to go to bed.'

Ben moved his straw to the other side of his mouth.

'I was having a lay down most of yesterday. I was up most part of the night. One of my ponies took sick.'

'Was it Prissy?'

Ben nodded.

'That's right. She had a temperature.'

'Isn't it awful,' said Santa, 'when you think a person has told a lie and he hasn't? Alexis said Prissy looked ill when she came in the ring on Thursday, and I thought he'd just said it to show off.'

Ben spat out his straw.

'Not much showin' off about Alexsis. If he says one of the 'osses is sick, he's most like right.'

'If he knows such a lot about them why doesn't he want to work in the act?'

Ben stooped and found another straw.

'Knowin' about 'osses comes natural when you're brought up with 'em. I was ridin' a pony pannier time I was two. You'll not have seen them. Baskets they were, hung across the pony's back. Wonderful way to carry a baby. Time I was four I was ridin'. Time I was five there was nothin' I wouldn't go on. But that don't mean to say I want to go doing a high-school or a jockey act in the ring.'

'Doesn't Alexsis ride well?'

'The Petoff ain't born that doesn't ride. But you know how 'tis when the dad's a master at somethin'. If you can't do as well as he does, may as well go into somethin' different. That's what I say when we're trainin' a new high-school 'oss. On account a 'oss don't shape first-class at high-school, it's not to say we'll not make a good liberty of him.'

'So Alexsis wants to do what the Elgins do?' Ben nodded. 'It's not so exciting as riding, is it?'

Ben chewed his straw thoughtfully.

'To me a circus is 'osses. I don't never want to see no other turn. But there's some as likes it. 'Tain't for me to offer no advice. But if young Alexsis was my boy I'd give him 'is 'ead. No good draggin 'at 'is mouth; only sour 'im that way.'

Santa was just going to ask who was dragging at Alexsis's mouth when Gus tapped her on the shoulder. He was dressed for the parade. He had on his sailor suit. He was holding up yards and yards of trousers which were meant to go over his stilts. Ted Kenet had on a real clown's dress. Satin one-piece heavily embroidered with diamanté. A little pointed white felt hat, white socks, and patent leather shoes. His face was painted dead white and made up with squares and triangles in scarlet and black.

'Well?' said Gus. 'How's things? Is this true what

I hear, that you and the Petoff kids went sucking lemons round the band?'

Santa got very red.

'Yes.'

Gus turned to Ben.

'What're we going to do with her?'

Ben chuckled.

'First time I played that game the ring-master took a strap to me.'

Gus smiled reminiscently.

'Same here. Could that fellow lay it on!'

Ted felt in the pockets of his dress. He brought out his little bag of sulphur sweets. He presented them to Santa.

'Better have one. Sounds like your blood'll need keeping cool.'

Santa looked up at Gus. Was he really going to beat her? Perhaps they did beat you in circuses.

Gus laughed and pulled her hair.

'We've scared her.' He examined the strand of hair in his hand admiringly. He held it out to Ted.

'Fine hair, hasn't she?'

'That reminds me.' Santa caught hold of his sleeve. 'Might I have it cut short?'

'Cut short!' All the three men spoke at once. Gus stared at her.

'Fried kippers, girl! What d'you want to cut it off for?'

'Well, it's in the way. It's awful to comb. It takes simply hours.'

Gus looked at her in shocked surprise.

'Never heard of such a thing. You leave it long. You never know when you may want it.'

'Hair's a woman's glory,' said Ted.

Santa did not like to be rude, because her cheek was puffed out with his sulphur sweet, but she did think it was a bit mean of him to take sides against her.

'That's what my Aunt Rebecca always said. She said it because it was what a duchess had said to her. But I don't see why you need to say it.'

There was the sound of horses' feet. The grooms were leading them up for the parade.

'That's us,' said Gus. 'And no matter who said it you'll keep your glory, my girl, or I really will take a strap to you.'

Santa watched Ted and Gus walk away. Then she turned to Ben:

'I would have thought circuses were not fussy places.'

But Ben was busy with his horses and did not answer.

Although Peter and Santa had gone to bed early, they seemed hardly to have been asleep at all when Gus woke them. He was dressed. He had the kettle on to boil.

'Get your things on, and then we'll have a cup of tea before we start. I'll just go out and warm up the car.'

It is cold in April at six o'clock in the morning, especially on a cliff pitch with the wind blowing off the sea. Peter and Santa were glad of their new, thick jerseys. They drank their tea almost in a trance, still half asleep. While they drank it Gus walked round the caravan locking cupboards and making any movable object fast.

Peter sat in the front of the car.

'Better make it turn and turn about,' Gus said.

It did not much matter where they sat, for after a bit both Peter and Santa were asleep. They woke suddenly when Gus said:

'Skin your eyes, you two, for the green stars.'

They were in a town. There were narrow streets. On the lamp posts hung green stars on a white ground.

'Is this Carlisle?' asked Santa.

Gus nodded.

'Done it in nice time. We're nearly first. That's the Kenets ahead of us.'

They looked out. Turning the corner just in front of them was another caravan. Santa gazed out of the window behind her. She could not see much because of the caravan, then as they, too, turned the corner it swung out a little, and up the road behind them she could see a perfect stream of cars, each pulling its caravan.

Peter pointed to a lamp post.

'There's another star.'

Gus drove a moment or two in silence. Then he said: 'Here we are.'

They bumped over the rough grass. The king-poles stood out against the pale blue of the sky. The men's mess-tent was up; from it came a lovely smell of frying eggs and bacon. A man was standing on the steps of the advance wagon; he called out 'Good morning' to Gus. The Kenet's caravan was in place. The car was being detached and backed into position. A stream of caravans, each painted green and white, was towed in. There was much talking and laughing. People said Gus and the Kenets could not have been to bed or they would not have been there first. Gus gave Santa the kettle. She stood a moment looking round.

'It's just like last Thursday at Bridlington,' she whispered to Peter.

Peter forgot that he had a grievance. It was all so gay it was difficult to feel cross. He took a big sniff of circus smell.

'Only this time we belong.'

9

The Pull-Down

It was not very nice at Carlisle. It rained all the time. Peter was still in his bad mood and hated himself for being in it. Gus was worried because Peter seemed unhappy. Between being certain he was suffering from snobbishness because he did not like going to school, he had moments when he wondered if he were to blame. When he felt like that he tried to say something nice, which Peter answered in an off-hand manner, then Gus lost his temper and scolded him, and Peter sulked more than ever. Santa did not feel very cheerful; she never was when Peter was miserable.

It was a pity the three days turned out so badly, because Sunday had been nearly perfect. It was almost hot. Peter and Santa stood in the sun and watched every bit of the build-up. Then, when the horses arrived, Ben gave them bunches of carrots and they went round and fed them all.

Lunch was cheerful. The niceness of the day had got into them. The stew was especially good. Gus did not jump down Peter's throat and Peter did not argue.

In the afternoon they went and played with the other children, who were practising acrobatics on the cloth used for the water act, which had been laid out to dry in the sun. The others tried to teach them to turn cartwheels. Peter nearly did turn one. It was not a very good one, but they all clapped, and it made him feel better. Even to turn half a not very good cart-wheel was something. Santa heard him whistle as he walked across the ground for tea.

They had tea with the Schmidts. Gus had gone to look at a car the Kenets thought of buying, and he had arranged with Mrs Schmidt to give them something to eat. They had a lovely time. The Schmidts did not much care for tea, and drank coffee instead. Being Sunday, Mrs Schmidt had bought some cream, which she had whipped stiff and put in great spoonfuls on the top of each cup. There was some specially good bread, with caraway seed all over the crust. During tea they had a most interesting talk about sea-lions. Mr Schmidt explained the difficulties of bringing them up.

'When mine wife start she buy three sea-lion boys. Three year, eight year, twelve year. At first not one word of Germans do they speak.'

Mrs Schmidt nodded.

'That is so. Not one word of Germans do they understand.'

'So every day mine wife talk to them. And every day understand they a little better like a child who is in school.'

'How long did that take?' Peter asked.

Mrs Schmidt swallowed a mouthful of coffee, and wiped the cream off her lips.

'Three month. Four month.'

'Then when they speak she must learn them the little trick,' Mr Schmidt explained.

Santa leant on her elbows.

'Where did you teach them, Mrs Schmidt?'

The whole Schmidt family looked at each other. It was obvious that question was one which meant a lot to them all.

'But where?' Mr Schmidt leant forward. 'If you, Santa, or you, Peter, have four sea-lion and you have taught them English good, and you wish space for them a trick to teach, where would you take them?'

Neither Santa nor Peter had ever considered the problem before. But now they thought it over it was difficult. You could have four sea-lions in a wagon somewhere. But if you wanted a place as big as a ring, where would you go? You couldn't take them into a park; they would attract far too much attention.

'Where?' asked Peter.

Mr Schmidt held out his cup for some more coffee.

'Sometimes it is impossible. Sometimes there is in winter a swimming-bath that empty is. Always it is the great question where to teach them. Will we find a place?'

'Well, you must have.' Santa spread another bit of bread with butter. 'They're awfully clever now.'

Mrs Schmidt smiled.

'These are not the same ones. Those have we no longer.'

'I speak,' Mr Schmidt pointed out, 'of many year ago. Those were mine wife's first three. After she have teach them German three month, and then a room found to teach the trick, one he is stupid. He cannot learn. He must go. She buy another.'

'That new one I buy' – Mrs Schmidt smiled at the memory – 'he was the great artiste.'

Mr Schmidt sighed.

'Kolossal!'

'He stay,' Mrs Schmidt went on, 'for many year. I have him when the childrens is born. His name is Hans. I call Hans after him. He play the trumpet as I have never heard a sea-lion. It was as if he the music could feel. We was in Germany. I teach him a German song to play. It begin *Du, du liegst mir im Herzen*. In Germany all know it and all sing with him. Then it is that he begin to go blind.'

Her eyes filled with tears. She looked across

at Mr Schmidt to finish the story. He patted her hand.

'One day mine wife come to me. "Hans can no longer see," she said. "We must Willi put the trumpets to play." That night Willi play the trumpets. He is not so good, but all the audience sing. Always after that he play. Then one day mine wife say to me: 'Heinrich, you must come to the back. You must Hans watch while Willi the trumpets play." That afternoon I do not stand in the middle of the ring, I go back to the artistes' entrance. I see Hans.' He stirred his coffee in silence a moment. Then he looked up. 'That old sea-lion's head it go *Du, du liegst mir im Herzen*. The perfect time is keep. He raise and drop his head so he the right trumpet blow. When he have finish and all the audience clap he roll on his side laughing, and his flippers slap together. He is so glad he play so well.'

Santa laid down her knife.

'Do you mean he never knew that he wasn't playing? That Willi was doing it instead?'

Mr Schmidt nodded.

'He never knew. Till he go dead he never knew. He is blind, he cannot see. It is the kindness of the lieber Gott. I think if he knew Willi for him play, he break his heart.'

There was silence for a bit after that. It was obviously not the moment to break in with more questions. Each Schmidt was, by their silence, paying a tribute to the dead sea-lion. Then Mrs Schmidt looked up.

'It was as if Hans brought us the good luck. After he go dead things is not so good. We get an offer to England to go. That is good. We are pleased. But it is to us not lucky. Always plenty time sea-lions go dead.'

Peter leant back in his chair. The coffee had been awfully good, but three cups, with whipped cream on them all, gave a very full feeling.

'Do you mean they die easily?'

Mr Schmidt lit a cigarette.

'So. When we to England come it is for the tenting. That year was very hot. It goes to their hearts. One morning I go to the wagon. One was dead. Another two was dead. In the end we have no sea-lion. Always it is so. You train them. They are clever. They are like your childrens. Then it is hot. They go dead.'

'Do they like going into the ring?' Santa asked.

Mr Schmidt puffed at his cigarette.

'In the beginnings they must be teach. You must to them give noise and light. Then when they are to it used they are the perfect artiste. They can as an actor say "feel" their audience.'

Hans was still eating. He swallowed a mouthful.

'On Sundays they are bored. They do not eat their fish so good. There is no show.'

Mr Schmidt got up.

'In the ring they are all excitement. You watch

them and you will see they shake like a dog who is come out of the water. Each one say: "It is me next. To me that ball will come. I on my nose will balance it." Then perhaps something go wrong. One sea-lion miss the catch. I am a little slow. One lion he does not get the ball. He has been quiver with excitement. He wait to show what he to it can do. Then the ball does not come. The spirit is gone out of him. He has no heart to try more. He go to the side of the ring. He will not work in the act.'

'What, never again?' said Santa horrified.

'Oh, yes, tomorrow. All artiste are great children. A little thing go wrong it is an earthquake. One man give the extra clap and the sun shines.'

Peter got up to shake down his cream.

'Do they know if they have done anything wrong?'

All the Schmidts smiled. It seemed to them a very funny question. You might as well ask Gus if he knew when he made a mistake in a comedy routine. Fritzi spoke severely.

'That is foolish. Of course they know.'

Her tone made Peter argumentative.

'I bet it's only because they don't get any fish.'

Mr Schmidt patted his shoulder.

'No, Peter. It is true. They miss a ball. They do not balance so good, and they have no fish. But they themselves know when it is bad. They take a pride in their work. They with themselves angry are. It is so with an artiste. It may be that other people will then praise. They may say: "That is good." But with an artiste they know what is good and what is bad. It is so with mine lions. One may do bad. I may pretend I have not see, and give him his fish as if he had done good. But though he eat the fish he is not please. He has done bad, and he know it here.' Mr Schmidt tapped his heart. 'When you know a thing there to have a fish will not the comfort make.'

The Schmidts took them to church in the evening. Gus said they must go once each Sunday but they could choose their own time. It was a nice service and they sang *Fight the good fight* as a last hymn, so they were glad they had been.

When they came in Gus was back. He had supper ready for them. It was a good supper of welsh rarebit. Nobody could make a better welsh rarebit than Gus. He was famous for it in Cob's Circus.

Gus went out after that and Peter and Santa washed up and then went to bed. Just before they put out the light they had a last look out of the window. The caravans were like a well-lighted village street. In the men's mess-tent somebody was playing *Shenandoah*. One of the lions roared. A little wind blew and brought with it a faint smell of animals and sawdust.

Peter drew in his head.

'Well, good night.'

'Good night,' said Santa. She did not say any more, but she knew that, for this night anyway, he was glad they lived in a circus.

They woke up on Monday to find it pouring. It poured off and on for the three days they were there. The circus was very different then. The ground that had looked so nice on Sunday slowly churned up into a bog. The grooms and tent-men hurried along wrapped in oilskins, and wearing great boots. In spite of the big wooden clogs that the artistes always wore to go from the dressing-tents to the big top they had to pick their way with the utmost care to save their ring shoes from getting splashed.

To add to the general depression, business was bad. It was the week before Easter. The week before a bank holiday is never good for the entertainment world. People are saving their money for the Monday. Mr Cob counted on pulling an audience in mostly on the fact that he had a first-class entertainment to offer, and the news that it was good soon got round. He counted as well on stimulating interest by a fine street parade.

The day after the build-up there was always a call for all the animals and most of the artistes. They formed up, led by the band, outside the big top. The horses followed, ridden by Mr Petoff, the Kenets, and Paula. Then would come the clowns and augustes, some on stilts and some on comic bicycles, and Gus driving a fearful old crock of a car. Then came the ponies drawing their coach. Then the elephants holding each other's tails, with Kundra riding on the leader. Then Ben driving a four-in-hand with all the dancing-girls in crinolines sitting in the coach. That was followed by Lucille standing on a float with the poodles posed round her. Then the rest of the horses led by the grooms. Finally, another float, with the Martinis, Frasconis, and Elgins giving displays of balancing and acrobatics.

But that Monday in Carlisle there could be no thought of a parade. The rain came down in sheets. In a very discouraged mood the artistes hung about the big top, some gossiping and some working.

The children, of course, were at school at street parade time. They missed the general feeling of discouragement. But they had a disgusting walk to and fro. They felt it a distinct hardship that they had to go to school in such weather. They all came back to their respective caravans prepared to grumble.

The trouble was that everybody felt they had a right to complain. Living in tents and caravans is hateful when it rains. The only question was, who was going to complain to whom? Everybody thought it was nastiest for them.

By Wednesday night everything was sodden. Standing in the ring looking up at the canvas overhead, every bit of ribbing was visible, a sure sign the tent was soused. The tent-master stared at it gloomily. With all that weight of water in it they would have a fine time on the pull-down. He could see himself up to his knees in mud till two or three in the morning.

School was finished for that term. The children were starting their Easter holidays at Whitehaven. Santa reminded Gus of his promise they should watch the pull-down. Gus laughed bitterly.

'You've picked a good night for it. But I don't know why not. You may as well see tenting is not all beer and skittles.'

Peter and Santa saw the second house from the artistes' entrance. They slipped through the curtain at the side and crawled under the seats and watched from there. It was a lovely view, because they could see the artistes as well where they waited for their entrances. They had already learnt from Gus that every artiste had to be waiting to go into the ring two acts before their own; that they knew which act was on simply by listening to the music; that the music was the only means they had of knowing what was happening and it was considered quite sufficient. If an artiste did not hear it, and came late for his entrance, he was fined. But what they did not know was what went on in the artistes' entrance. Most of the time they found it more enthralling than what was happening in the ring.

It was the Frasconi sons who first caught their attention.

'Look!' Santa pulled at Peter's sleeve to make him take his eyes off the clowns. 'Fancy, in those clothes!'

The Frasconi brothers had come across from the men's dressing tent with mackintoshes over their fleshings. The bearer brother kicked off his clogs, but without taking off his mackintosh raised the other one over his head. The one raised still had his mackintosh on. He looked very odd lying in it across the palm of his brother's hand.

Peekaboo walked in with the two men who made him standing upright. He had clogs on all four feet, and a mackintosh over each half of him. In some ways he looked even sillier than he had in the ring. He was like a real horse folded up.

The show had begun with Satan's lions. The moment they had finished Satan superintended their removal into their travelling cages and saw them off to the station. He came back to the artistes' entrance to speak to Mr Cob just as the Arizonas were going on. The paint was dripping off his face.

'Hot work tonight, Satan,' said Ten Kenet.

Satan nodded.

'You've said it. Rain always upsets cats. But this rain we've had here has sent them crazy. I shan't be sorry to get out.'

'Why don't lions like rain?' Santa whispered to Peter.

Peter shook his head. It was one of those odd bits of information you seemed to be always picking up in a circus.

The Elgins, wrapped in mackintoshes, came hurrying along. They hung their mackintoshes on the stairs leading up to the orchestra. They kicked off their clogs and rubbed their feet in the tray of rosin. They then began limbering-up. Peter and Santa stared at them with amazement. Their idea of the way to get their muscles loose would have broken the bones of an ordinary person. The girls held out first their right legs and then their left for one of the men to hold straight over their heads. The men not only held them there but gave them two or three good jerks when they had got them in position. They picked each other up. They threw themselves over backwards standing on their hands and in that position leant against the tent side. Two of the men picked up one of the girls. One took her head, the other her legs. They bent her into a hoop and held her over their heads.

Peter dug Santa in the ribs.

'And that's what Alexsis wants to do. Sooner him than me.'

Santa, gazing in horror at the girl, expecting every moment to see her break in half, nodded.

'Or me. I'd much rather ride, even if I didn't do it as well as my father.'

The sea-lions arrived in the artistes' entrance with an incredible amount of fuss. They came barking out of their tank, almost falling over in their excitement. Each bark sounded as though they were saying: 'It's us! It's us! It's us!'

Peter and Santa had a good look at the Risley act while it was waiting to go on. Close to, it was quite clear, in spite of their rompers and socks, that the two Miss Martinis were not children. The younger one, though she was not much taller than Santa, looked about seventeen. Directly the family arrived for their entrance, they threw off the towelling dressing-gowns they had round them, took off their clogs, rubbed their feet in the rosin tray, and began their own kind of limbering-up. This meant Mr Martini took the elder of the girls and juggled with her, and the son took the younger one. The two girls were completely unmoved and went on with a conversation they were holding in Italian.

Peter and Santa were getting a bit cramped under the seats. They came out and went for a walk through the stables, which looked oddly depleted.

All the horses, except those the Kenets and Paula were using in the high-school act, had gone to the station. The bereiters were just riding the last of the liberties out of the stables as the children came in.

The sea-lions, poodles, and lions had gone. Only the elephants were still on their platform. They were dressed for their act, which came next. The elephant man had already unfastened their feet. The thought that it was almost their entrance had excited them. Each was desperately rehearsing. Trunks swinging from side to side, feet raised. As Peter and Santa came near them, Ben caught hold of each of them by a shoulder and drew them into one of the loose boxes which had not yet been pulled down. At that moment Kundra gave an order in Hindustani. The first elephant stepped off the platform. The second caught hold of his tail and followed. In a neat line they hurried to the artistes' entrance.

'You kids want to watch out,' said Ben. 'You'll get kicked or trodden on one day. None of the animals wouldn't mean to do it, but they get kind of excited like when it's their act.'

Peter and Santa were just going to step out again when there was the sound of horses' hooves. Round the bend in the tent came one of the Kenets. He was leaning out of the saddle to watch his horse's forelegs. It was pretty to see the way they were picked up. Left, right, left, right. At the end of the tent they turned. The horse went false. He was checked a moment, then off he went again in perfect rhythm.

'Would the horse do it wrong if he didn't practise before he went in the ring?' Peter whispered.

Ben chuckled.

'There was never a high-school rider yet who didn't have to show off. Be out at the front if they were allowed to.'

Peter sighed.

'I wish I could ride.'

'Do you, son?' Ben gave him a thoughtful glance. 'Your dad was a groom, so Gus was tellin' me. Maybe it's in the blood. You come along one mornin' when I'm exercisin' the 'osses in the ring. I'll put you up and see how you shape.'

'Would you?' Peter glowed. That was something like. If he were allowed to learn to exercise the horses he would feel much better.

Santa came out into the centre of the tent. A groom was pulling down the wall of the stall.

'Why don't you exercise them outside? It's dull for them in the big top. They'd have much more fun in a field.'

Ben chewed at a bit of straw. It was rather an old bent one, but there were not many clean bits lying around.

'They ain't shod right. A 'oss what's shod for this work won't never stand up to hackin' across country. We don't exercise 'em just for exercisin' in a manner of speakin'. It's on account of their gettin' a roll. Those Suffolk punches what the Arizonas ride, you watched them at work?' Peter and Santa nodded. 'Well, which way did they go round the ring? Clockwise or against the clock?'

182

They tried to remember.

'Clockwise,' said Santa.

Peter thought a moment longer.

'Against the clock.'

Ben chewed placidly.

'Peter's right. No matter where you see a bare-backed act it goes that way. Well, when the 'osses has done twelve rounds of the ring somebody' as got to ride them twelve times clockwise. If they didn't that 'oss would get a roll. Stands to reason. You try runnin' round in a circle always goin' the same way. You'd get lop-sided like, and then you'd roll.' Ben spat out his straw. 'Well, I must be movin'.' He gave Peter a nod. 'You come along. I'll see how you shape.'

Santa walked back up the tent kicking up the earth with the toes of her gum-boots. Peter looked at her.

'I expect he meant you too.'

Santa made a proud face.

'As a matter of fact I wasn't wanting to ride a horse.'

Peter shrugged his shoulders.

'You are a fool. Why don't you ask him?'

Santa skipped up against the wall of the tent.

'You want to watch out,' she said nastily. 'Anybody who was attending would hear six elephants coming.'

Peter jumped across to the other side of the tent. He would have liked to tell her not to be so cocky, but by the time the six elephants had hurried by it was too late.

They watched the elephants go to the station. They saw them splash their way out into the rain and mud. As usual they held on to each other by the tail. One of the keepers rode on the leader. Peter lifted the tent flap. They watched them disappear into the night, their greyness almost at once giving them the look of shadows.

'If anybody in Carlisle doesn't know there's been a circus and suddenly meets those I should think they'd get a shock,' he said.

They went back to the artistes' entrance. The Whirlwinds were just finishing, Gus and Ted Kenet swinging round faster and faster. Then the music stopped. They slid to the ground and stood bowing in the ring. The bandmaster held up his baton. The band burst into *God Save the Queen*.

Crash! Bang! 'Pass along outside quickly, please!' Everybody busy. Everybody working very quickly. For a minute or two Peter and Santa were too fussed they were in the way, and too confused, to see what was happening. Then they began to sort things out.

The audience were leaving. The 'Pass along outside quickly, please!' was for them. Of course they were not passing out quickly at all. Who would when such exciting things were going on? The uniformed men from the entrance had come inside and were driving them forward.

They looked rather like sheepdogs folding a stubborn flock.

Not that anybody belonging to the circus was paying any attention to the audience. As the last notes of *God Save the Queen* died away, artistes, ring-hands, tent-men, had swarmed in from the artistes' entrance. The band came hurrying down from their balcony. Mr Cob stood in the middle of the ring.

The crashing and banging was the seats. Starting on those farthest from the audience, they were being pulled down and stacked in heaps. The queer thing was the people who worked on them. Of course all the men were there, but with them, dressed in fearful old overalls, were some of the clowns and three of the Kenets.

Then the artistes were surprising. It had already upset all Peter's and Santa's ideas of what was what to find that the dancing butterflies were also the people who sold programmes. It did not seem to them at all suitable that such lovely ladies should do a job like that. Now they had a further shock. The butterflies had changed into cotton overalls, and were busy pulling covers off those seats which were expensive enough to have them. Two great baskets had been dragged to the ringside, and into them, neatly folded, the butterflies put the covers.

Gus and Ted Kenet had pulled disgraceful old dressing-gowns over their Whirlwind clothes.

They took down their trapeze quite unmoved by the pointing and nudging of the departing audience.

The two Frasconi sons and their father packed the trampo-line. The Frasconi sons had changed into dark suits. They did not look interesting. Santa gazed at them with disapproval.

'If I was a circus artiste and wore pink all over and a little bit of velvet fur, I wouldn't let the audience see me except while I had it on. They don't look a bit nice now. And they were so lovely when they were on the trampoline.'

Peter pointed up at the roof, where Gus was sitting nonchalantly on the trapeze doing something to a rope.

'And if I was Gus I wouldn't wear that awful dressing-gown. It isn't even clean.'

One of the butterflies staggered towards them with her arms full of chair-covers. She looked at Peter and made a gesture with her head at the basket.

'Heave the lid up, would you?'

Peter was delighted. Even opening a lid made you feel as though you had something to do. He watched the butterfly put her covers in a neat pile in the corner of the basket. He hated her cotton coat. It was the sort of thing Aunt Rebecca had worn when she did the housework: It worried him to see her and the other artistes working. He might not be a sort of relation of the duchess, but he had comforted himself with the thought that at least in the circus he moved in the best world there was. He quite understood that everybody might help now and again as a favour; but all these people who so short a time ago had been looking marvellous in the ring, were appearing in dirty old clothes in front of the audience. It must be wrong. He leant against the basket.

'Why do you all help pack?'

The girl went on folding covers.

'Why not?'

'I should have thought somebody else would. Some of these men.'

The girl went off to uncover a few more chairs. She looked over her shoulder.

'I shouldn't fuss, Little Lord Fauntleroy. Work never hurt anybody.'

Peter came back to Santa looking very red.

'Did you hear what she said?'

Santa kicked up a little pile of earth with her toe.

'Perhaps she didn't mean to be as rude as she sounded.'

'Well, then, why call me Little Lord Fauntleroy?'

Santa shrugged her shoulders.

'He's a boy in a book. Mrs Ford saw a film of it. She told me about it. She said he was a dear little boy.'

Peter gave her a look.

'You would say a thing like that. You've grown

hateful since you came here. You never used to be.'

Santa sat down on a box somebody had put near them. She thought of the way Peter had sulked lately, and of how Ben had said he would let him ride and had not said anything about her. She looked smug.

'If you want to know, I've been a Christian martyr of goodness. It's you that's always cross.'

'I like that—'

Santa put her fingers in her ears.

'It's no good talking. I'm not listening. I'm watching the pull-down.'

Peter could have hit her. Nothing is more annoying than a person not listening when you want to argue. He put his hands in his pockets and walked off to the other side of the ring.

In a few minutes they both forgot they had been quarrelling. The seats were still being taken down but fewer men were working on them, the rest were carrying away the tent-props. It was queer, as the seats vanished, and the props were carried out, and the ring fence was taken away, how gradually you could see the rough ground beginning to be just the empty ground again that it was last Sunday. Peter came across to Santa.

'There's masses and masses of straw just come. They're going to put it in here. I heard the men say so.'

'Why?'

Peter did not know.

'I didn't like to ask anybody. They all look so busy.'

They went outside to look at the straw. It was very interesting out there, though horribly wet. The wagons had drawn up in a circle round the big top. They were being loaded. It was a queer light. It was made by great arc-lamps fixed to lorries. It gave a greenish tinge to everything. The moving figures looked quite ghost-like in it. A continual stream of men came out of the big top carrying props. The props were long and heavy, and the ground slippery with mud. It was amazing that nobody skidded and dropped one.

There was added to the crash and bang of the seat-packing a sound of hammering on metal. The men were loosening the staples. Ben came stalking through the rain. He went up to one of the stable hands who was unlacing the side-flaps of the stable tent.

'Tell 'em I'm ready for my straw.'

He was turning away, but Santa caught him by the arm.

'What's the straw for, Ben?'

Ben smiled. His face was dripping with rain.

'You both here? It's a nasty night. Still, may as well see things all ways.'

'That's what Gus said, more or less,' Santa agreed.

Peter nodded at the straw now being carried in armloads into the stables.

'Why the straw now? All the animals have gone.'

Ben picked a straw off a bundle that was being carried by. He put it in his mouth.

'You take a look at your boots.' Peter and Santa looked at their legs. 'Look at all that mud 'n' water. What d'you think these tents would be like if we laid them down in this?'

Ben was moving away, so Peter caught up with him.

'But why should you lay them down.'

Ben shook his head.

'Where's your eyes, boy? You've seen the build-up. How did the big top come?'

'Folded in bundles,' said Santa.

Ben went into what was left of the stables.

'You must put it on the ground to fold it. Of a wet night we put down straw. Keeps it dry like. Most of this is for the big top. I only need a little on account of what I already 'ave for the 'osses. Very partic'lar Mr Cob is about straw. "Keep everythin' dry inside," he says, "and maybe God'll dry the outside."'

'But suppose it's raining in Whitehaven?' said Santa.

'Well, then it's lucky we're dry inside. I'ave known it rain off'n on for near a month tentin'. The canvas was always soused. The men lost heart on the pull-down. That big top weighs somethin' terrible when it's soused. But there's one thing a wet spell tentin' teaches you, and that's gratitude for small mercies. Bit of wind and a few hours' sun and you have all the place singin'.' He nodded to the children. 'See you in the mornin'.'

Peter and Santa went round to the front entrance. They had to keep well away from the big top, as the men were hammering at the staples and loosening the guy-ropes. It was not so easy to get along farther out. The wagons were everywhere. The caterpillar tractors were manoeuvring more lorries and wagons into position to be packed. Those lorries and wagons which were ready to go to the station were surrounded by men putting planks under their wheels, trying to lever them up out of the mud.

'Do you know,' Peter said, 'that Ben sleeps on the train and he won't get there till late, and then he's wet, and he'll be on the ground at Whitehaven about seven in the morning.'

Santa made a gesture covering all the drivers, tent-men, ring-hands, electricians, carpenters, and grooms.

'So will they all.'

'I know.' Peter hopped over a staple. 'But Ben's seventy-five.'

Santa thought about Ben.

'He never feels old. He's the nicest person we know, I think, except, of course, Gus.'

'Yes, excepting him, of course,' Peter agreed. 'And I don't know if we'd like him if he wasn't an uncle.'

Santa hurried on to get under the shelter of the big top.

'Well, he is an uncle, so we have to like him. Anyway I do.'

Peter followed her.

'So do I. But I think he simply hates me.'

Santa did not answer. She did not think Gus did like Peter much.

The seating was gone. The last of the props were being carried out. Gus and Ted Kenet had disappeared. The boxes with their trapeze gear lay in the ring, locked and roped. All the Frasconis had gone. Their stuff, in an iron-bound box and a kind of canvas hold-all, lay beside Gus's. The electricians were up in the roof disconnecting their lights.

'Bring in the straw, boys,' said the tent-master.

Everybody helped with the straw. A few odd hands collected Gus's and the Frasconis' stuff and carried it out. The rest scattered the straw in a fine carpet so that not one bit of wet ground showed. Mr Cob beckoned to the children.

'You kids come and stand along here beside me. They'll be dropping the tent now. Mustn't stand in the ring.'

It took a long time to spread the straw. The tent-master came up and spoke to Mr Cob.

'It'll be two before we're away.'

Mr Cob nodded.

'Maybe it'll be fine for the build-up. The glass is rising.'

The tent-master grunted.

'There's no wind. That's one thing.'

Peter was so interested he had to interrupt.

'Do you mind a wind? I thought it dried the tent.'

Mr Cob gave a short laugh.

'Not much good the wind trying to dry it while it's still raining.'

The tent-master looked at Peter.

'You'll be Gus's nephew. Well, you ask Gus whether we like a wind. He'll tell you.'

Peter and Santa had hardly ever been up so late before and they were getting cold and tired. The last part of pulling down the big top seemed slow. They could not see what everybody was doing. Ropes were loosened, and there were still some men in the roof. Then suddenly Mr Cob had hold of them.

'Come on.'

They were outside, standing beyond where the tent walls of the big top had been. They looked up to the top of the king-poles. Then suddenly, as if a giant pin had been dug in the tent, it collapsed and slid in a white heap on to the straw below.

Even that was nowhere near the end. Every bit of the great tent was laced. The lorries with their lamps drew nearer and threw their light on the lacing. The tent-men knelt round, nimbly unhitching the ropes.

Peter and Santa were chilled all through, and terribly sleepy, but they had stayed so long they had to see the end. They wanted to see the king-poles fall. But first the tent had to be packed. It was unlaced and the portions lay on the straw lead-like with water. There was not work for everybody now. Some of the men lit cigarettes. The others leant against the wagons talking. Then suddenly the tent-master gave an order. The effect was terrific. Many of the tent hands came from Wales and the North. They all seemed to be able to sing, as people from those parts usually do. They began now. Each piece of canvas had to be folded and refolded till it was a handlable bundle. The men lined up holding one side. Then they marched across dragging the weight behind them and put one side against the other, and so backwards and forwards till the folding was done. It was obviously a great strain to move that mass of sodden stuff. Each man leant forward, the rain shining on his face. They needed a swing to get themselves going and so they sang. Sea shanties and folk-songs, old stuff with simple melodies just right to pick up the rhythm of their united pulling.

The canvas was folded. It was put on things like wooden stretchers. The stretchers were carried to the waiting lorries. The ground was almost empty now. Just the king-poles, the lorries with the lights, and in the distance the line of caravans. Peter and Santa had almost to hold their eyelids up, they were so sleepy. Then Mr Cob took them each by an arm.

'Watch that,' he said. 'There it goes.'

It was the first of the king-poles. It swayed. It was lowered to the ground. A few minutes later and the other one was down. As if it were an omen, with the pull-down of the king-poles, the rain stopped.

'Go on, you two. Hop it,' said Mr Cob.

Peter and Santa fumbled their way across the dark ground to the caravan.

'It seems so odd,' said Santa sleepily, 'to think that in quite a little time it'll all begin again.'

Peter felt the caravan steps.

'Here we are,' he whispered. 'What seems to me so queer is that some of it's there already. You know the other pair of king-poles. Like we saw at Bridlington before the circus came.'

Gus stuck his head out of the window.

'Haven't you two had enough circus for one night? You've no need to stand around talking about it.'

'I am sorry, Gus,' said Santa. 'Did we wake you?'

Gus yawned.

'I was sleeping with one eye open. I knew you

two kids would come in half drowned without the sense to get yourselves a hot drink. Hop into bed, now, and I'll give you both a mug of something to keep out the cold.'

10

Santa's Violin

It was Good Friday. A holiday for all the circus people. The weather was nice. Blue skies, and a small breeze. Just the weather to dry the tents.

'Us for the station to fetch that box,' said Gus. 'The better the day the better the deed.'

Gus went outside to start up his car. Hans and Fritzi came bustling up.

'You go for a drive?' Hans inquired.

Gus shook his head.

'No, old son. Me and Ted are working on the trapeze later on. We're only off to the station to fetch Peter and Santa's box.'

Fritzi opened the car door.

'We will also to the station.'

Gus nodded and got into the driver's seat. Fifi joined them. She came over to Gus and made a bob curtsy.

'Good morning, Gus. Can I drive with you?'

Gus looked over into the back of the car.

'Squeeze up, kids. There'll be four of you in there.' He leant across and opened the other door and patted the seat beside him. 'Hop in, Fifi. You sit here.'

Peter and Santa were coming out of the caravan. They had just arranged that Santa should sit in front going, and Peter coming back. The first thing Santa saw was Fifi in her seat.

'Good morning, Santa and Peter,' said Fifi politely. 'It is a beautiful day.'

Fifi was wearing a smart little hat at a great angle over her left eye. There was something definitely annoying about her appearance. Santa did not like the way she wore her clothes, but all the same the effect was chic.

'Hallo! I say, that's my place. I'm sitting in front going and Peter coming back.'

Fifi threw up her hands and eyebrows and got up.

'I am so sorry.' She turned to Gus. 'That was you. You said to me: "Sit here."'

Gus caught at her skirts and pulled her back. 'Sit down.' He jerked his head at Peter and Santa. 'Hop into the back, you two. Hot cross buns, whose car is this, anyway?'

Peter and Santa got in. Santa was most hurt. Of course it was true the car was Gus's. But they were his nephew and niece. If anyone had a right to choose where they would sit it should be a nephew and niece. She looked hard out of the window. She knew her eyes had tears in them and she did not want the others to see.

Fritzi pulled at her arm.

'Mine mother says she would not me permit to wear such hats. She says for a child they not suitable are.'

Santa felt better. She did not altogether like Fritzi, who she thought much too cocksure about everything. But when it came to the right way to dress and behave they thought exactly alike. In fact, in her bad English Fritzi said lots of things the duchess had said, or at least things which meant the same. Santa had never cared for the things the duchess had said, but she had been brought up on them, and she felt on home ground when she heard other people saying them.

They all went into the station to look for the box. They all saw it at once because it was the only box there. They all pointed to it and made exclamations in their three different languages, all, that is, except Santa. She saw something else which made her tongue-tied with horror. Lying on the ground beside the box was her violin. They hung over the counter while Gus signed for the box.

'There's this come, too,' said the man.

'But, Santa, your violin has come,' said Hans.

Fritzi clasped her arm.

'But that is good. Yes? You will be able to us your music to play.'

Fifi made a magnificent gesture with both hands.

'For an artiste not to be able to work. That is terrible.'

Peter giggled.

'When you've heard Santa play you won't say anything about artistes.'

Santa flushed.

'She isn't going to hear me play, or anybody else. So sucks to you.'

Hans looked at Peter in shocked surprise.

'To tease one because they music love, that is not good.'

Fritzi gave Santa a comforting smile.

'Do not trouble, Santa. This very day we will all come to hear you play.'

'Goodness, I hope you won't!' said Santa. 'Because I can't. At least only one tune.'

Gus told a porter to bring out the box. He gave Santa her violin.

'Didn't know you played the fiddle.'

'I don't.' Santa caught at his arm. 'Honestly I don't. Don't let them think I do.'

'But,' Fifi said, 'you told us in the school that you played.'

She turned to Fritzi. ' "I play the violin." That was what she said. Olga was there too. She will remember.'

Fritzi did not like siding with Fifi against Santa. Fifi was a good artiste; in other things she considered she should be kept in her place. All the same, this time in honesty she had to admit she was right.

'That was how you say, Santa.'

Gus helped the porter to tie the box on the back of the car.

'Tomatoes and cheese! There's a lot of talk about this playing. We'll have the fiddle out tonight, Santa, and see how you shape.'

'Perhaps at five o'clock,' Fifi suggested. 'Then all can be there.'

'But I can't,' Santa said desperately. 'I can only play one tune, and that's *Art thou weary, art thou languid?*'

Gus got into the car and put his foot on the self-starter.

'And nothing nicer for a Good Friday.'

Peter and Santa left unpacking the box until the afternoon. Santa was feeling in no mood to bother with boxes, she was so upset about the violin.

'Do you really think they'll make me play?' she asked Peter.

Peter could not cheer her up. He was perfectly certain they would. There was no false modesty about circus people. If they could do a thing they did it. Santa, having said she played the violin, would have to play it.

'I wouldn't fuss,' he said. 'Even if they do come

to hear you, about two notes will be enough. Come in the big top and watch Gus and Ted Kenet working.'

Santa followed him, but she did not feel comforted. It was not a bit cheering to feel nobody would stand more than two notes. That would mean they would laugh, and she felt she could not face being laughed at. How she wished she played beautifully, so that all the people in the circus came round to hear her. And she and Peter, instead of being just Gus's nephew and niece, became important.

Gus and Ted Kenet were working on the trapeze. It was something new they were trying. Peter and Santa could not see what, as they did not know anything about trapeze work, but they could see that, instead of being free on the bar, their ankles were held to it by wires. Presently they slid down to earth. Gus went off to talk to Maxim Petoff. Ted Kenet came and sat beside the children. He had pulled an overcoat over the tights he had been working in. He felt in the pockets and produced a bag of his usual sweets. Peter took one.

'What was that you and Gus had holding you on to the trapeze?'

Ted chewed at his sweet.

'A lunge. That's a safety thing. You use'm for all aerial work, and training kids for jockey acts and such.'

Santa moved her sweet to the other side of her mouth.

'Did you learn on a lunge?'

'Me! There was no way I didn't learn. You see, I was born in my grandfather's circus. You'll have heard of Kenet's?'

'No.' Santa leant forward. Her voice was apologetic. 'I expect everybody else has but us. This is the only circus we know about.'

Ted did not seem to mind that they had not heard of Kenet's. He leant back in his seat, sucking noisily.

'Rare old chap was my grand-dad. He'd been ringmaster to old Pinker, who'd run a one-eyed circus, doing one-night stands in the small towns. Well, when old Pinker was dying he sends for my grand-dad. 'Charlie,' he says, 'I've no one to leave the turn-out to. I've a mind to leave it to you. I've well-nigh starved for it the last fifty years. It's time you had a bit of trouble.''

Peter was interested.

'Did he starve?'

Ted helped himself to another sweet.

'Him! No. Ambitious, he was. He looks round and he sees the turn-out wants improving. So he marries a lady lion tamer. She brought three fine beasts along with her. Then after a time there's children. My father was the eldest. My word, he was put through it! Time he could stand he was working in a Risley act and augusteing, and doing some jockey work.'

'Now that's a thing I've always wanted to know,' Santa broke in. 'What's the difference between being a clown and being an auguste?'

'Not much. Your contract's mostly for both. A clown, he wears clown's get-up and does clowning. An auguste wears funny clothes, but not a clown's dress. He does much the same work, but it's augusteing. A good clown or a good auguste can work in any act, aerial, horses, all the lot.'

Peter wanted to hear more about Kenet's circus. 'Then your father married and had all of you?'

'Not for a while he didn't. His dad, my grand-dad, kept him too busy. Time he was twenty he was seeing to the beast house. In it was a big monkey, two leopards, a wolf, two lionesses and one lion, four black Himalayan bears, and a llama. That's down one side. Down the other he had seven camels.'

'Goodness!' said Santa. 'What did he have to do with them?'

'What didn't he! Feed 'em. Clean 'em. Show some of 'em. Teach most of 'em. You may say, why did he do it? Why didn't he get an easier job somewhere else? It was on account of the riding. Crazy on horses, my dad was. My grandfather knew that, and he let him have the run of the horses if he looked after the beasts.'

Santa rested her elbows on her knees and put her chin in her hands.

'To ride them, do you mean?'

'Ride them! He had the rough stuff and had to try and make them for the ring. He used to tell us that sometimes he would ride as many as ten or twelve a day. And even that wasn't the end. He was a good tent-man. When he wasn't breaking horses, or acting teacher to his bears and that, he'd be sitting cross-legged on the tent putting in a patch, or splicing a lot of ropes.'

Peter wanted to get to the Kenets themselves.

'When you were born did you learn the same way?'

Ted passed round his bag of sweets.

'To start with. Then when we was still small kids my grand-dad dies. My father ran the circus a while, but there were bad seasons, and there never had been much money behind it. Then my father's interest was all in the horses. So was my mother's. She was from a riding family. My dad sold the whole outfit, only keeping the horses we needed, and we went off to America.'

'Doing what?' asked Santa.

'Jockey, and high-school. My three brothers and dad and mum were all working. I did a bit sometimes.'

Peter felt they were getting near what he wanted to know.

'Did your father teach you?'

'Did he! Wherever we went, and there wasn't a fair-sized country we hadn't tented in time I was fourteen. First thing he'd say after the build-up: 'Off and change, boys, while I put up the lunge.' Same when we were doing a season. We'd get to the place. Mother'd fix up our rooms. Dad wouldn't work the horses. Not if it had been a bad voyage. He'd settle them in gently. But for us it was always the same: "Get your things, boys, and come down to the ring."'

'But you couldn't work without the horses,' Peter objected.

'Couldn't we!' Ted gave a loud suck at his sweet. 'Jockey acts are most tumbling.'

Santa looked at Ted. He did not seem bruised.

'Tumbling! Do you mean falling off?'

Ted was not a man who was shocked at ignorance. He was quite placid.

'No. It's what you see the kids doing all the time. Those Petoffs are always at it. Fifi Moulin's good.'

'Do you mean somersaults and things?'

Ted nodded.

'Yes. You work a routine. The flip-flap that the kids are always practising is the connecting bit. Suppose you were wanting to do a set of tricks. That's a routine. Well, something's got to give you the impetus to get round, hasn't it? Well, the flip-flap does that. This is the usual routine. Flip-flap; round-all; flip-flap; back somersault. You watch.'

Ted stepped into the ring, throwing his coat and clogs on to the ring fence as he passed. He rubbed his hands on his tights. Then he began to turn over. It was quite easy to see which was the flip-flap. It came between the other tricks, just as he had said it would. It was what Olga was always doing. Throwing herself on to her hands, over, and finish standing upright. After it he did a sort of cartwheel with a half-turn to it. Then another flip-flap. Then the somersault. He came back to the children.

'You see? Of course, you can change the combination. You can put in some back pirouettes. Anything you fancy.' He pulled on his things and sat down again.

'Goodness!' said Santa enviously. 'I do wish I could do that.'

Ted looked at her appraisingly.

'How old are you?'

'Eleven.'

Ted took another sweet.

'That's late to start, but not too late. You're a good build for it. I'll come along and show you how some time, if Gus has no objection. It's good exercise.'

Peter gave Santa a glance out of the corner of his eye. Exercise! Ted had spun over so fast they hardly had been able to see him. It was not what he would call exercise. He turned to him.

'Go on about the horses. You said when they were tired after a voyage, you still had to work at tumbling.'

'That's right. We worked when we were travelling, too. I remember that first time we went to America. I was sick the whole way over. I was only a nipper, but dad said: "Have him up on deck. I'll just take him through a routine. Do him good."'

'Did it?' asked Santa.

Ted thought over the question.

'Not that trip it didn't. But maybe later. Fine teacher, my dad. Never believed in bringing kids up soft.'

Peter wriggled more comfortably into his seat.

'Then when did you learn to do things on a trapeze?'

Ted gazed at the ceiling as if trying to remember.

'We was over in Stockholm. We were working the jockey act. The horse went false. Dad was bearer. You know, like my brother does, holding the rest of us on his shoulders. Dad slipped. I was at the top of a pyramid. Down I came and broke my hip. They had to leave me in hospital. Well, while I was there they bring in another fellow from the circus. German he was. He'd been doing a flying trapeze act, and missed the catcher and broken his arm.'

Santa hated to interrupt, but she hated more not understanding.

'What's a catcher?'

'Someone who catches. If you look at an aerial act you'll see there's always one doing the catching.'

Peter frowned at Santa for muddling the story.

'Do go on.'

'Well, us lying in bed with nothing to do, we got talking. The act he was with had got someone in his place. Nor was he crazy to go back to them. He had a trapeze, and he'd worked out a nice routine for a double act. He suggested I came in with him.'

Santa was aghast.

'But you had a broken hip and he had a broken arm and you'd never been on a trapeze.'

Ted got up.

'Must be dinner-time. My hip mended and his arm got all right. I soon picked up the routine. We did very nicely.'

Santa caught at his coat.

'When did you go back to your father and brothers?'

'When dad died. The four of us took on the horses.' He held out his bag of sweets. 'Have another? You should, they're cooling to the blood. You need them in the spring.'

'Will you really teach me to tumble?' Santa called after him.

Ted did not exactly answer, but he gave a kind of nod as he went out.

Peter and Santa got up to go to lunch. They walked round the ring fence and out through the front entrance.

'Do you really want to learn to tumble?' said Peter. 'What for?'

Santa hopped over a guy-rope and opened the gate in the fence.

'To have something to do while you're riding.' She shut the gate in his face. 'Bet I get back to the caravan first.'

Gus had a stew nearly ready. Peter and Santa laid the table. Gus looked round from his stirring.

'We've all the kids coming to tea.'

A cold feeling gripped Santa's inside.

'Why?'

'Cabbages and cheese! Why not?' Gus tasted the stew and added a little more pepper. 'It's a good day for it; no performances.'

Peter knew what was worrying Santa.

'Fifi doesn't have tea, and I don't believe the Petoffs do. And the Schmidts drink coffee.'

Gus put three plates on the stove to warm.

'But they can eat hot cross buns, can't they?' He nodded at an enormous bag on the floor in the corner. 'Just been out and got two dozen of them.'

Santa put the cruet-stand on the table. She looked at Gus with suspicion.

'What made you ask them?'

Gus gave his stew a final stir.

'Seems you told the kids you could play the violin. They've gone home and told their dads and mums you can play the violin. Now the whole circus has heard you can play it. Well, if you can, what's the harm in your doing it?'

Santa held out a plate for him to fill with stew.

'But I can't.'

'Then why did you say you could?'

Santa's eyes filled with tears.

'Well, they were saying Aunt Rebecca had taught us nothing; that we were like new-born babies.'

'I see.' Gus turned to Peter. 'Is that why you said up at your school that you'd had a tutor to teach you Latin?'

Peter looked at Santa, with her flushed face and held-back tears. He saw red.

'All right, laugh. Perhaps everything we've been taught is wrong. But at least we aren't sneaks, coming home and telling all the circus what somebody said at school.'

Gus helped out the other two plates of stew. He sat down. He looked apologetic.

'Look here. I don't want to be hard on you kids. But you don't seem to have any horse sense. You come up here dressed for Buckingham Palace—'

'That's mean!' said Santa.

Gus sighed.

'This tutor business.' He took a mouthful of stew. 'Can't you see you go about things all wrong? I never have known what's the good of Latin, but as sure as eggs, if there's any good in it, then it'll turn up handy. One day somebody'll say: "Anybody know Latin?" Then you just say "Yes," and there you are.'

'I had to say something,' Peter burst out angrily. 'The boys were saying I didn't know anything.'

'What if they did?' Gus finished chewing his mouthful. 'Maybe they're not far out. But, boy, why do you want to go telling the dancing-girls that they shouldn't help with the pull-down? You had them all laughing fit to split their sides. They've christened you Little Lord Fauntleroy.'

Peter scowled at his plate.

'I don't see why.'

Gus ate a moment in silence. Then he looked up.

'There's none of us can see ourselves. But there are people going around just asking to have their legs pulled. You're like that and you want to watch your step. Don't go talking silliness. It's all right to speak nicely and be clean and all that. But you want to look as if you could give someone a sock on the jaw if you had to.'

'Well, perhaps I could. You don't know that I couldn't.'

Gus nodded.

'That's right. Perhaps you could. All I know is when I was your age if I'd found myself in a circus I'd be around with the men or the other boys. I wouldn't be walking around with my sister looking as if I'd come to sing in the choir.'

Santa got up to get some more stew.

'It's no good trying to separate me and Peter. We're used to each other. And you like us to be clean, otherwise why are you always sending us to the public baths?'

Gus looked at the stewpot.

'Give me a bit more of that while you're up, Santa.' He passed her his plate. 'I'm no good at putting what I mean into words. I don't want you to get me wrong, Peter.'

Peter looked at him bitterly.

'I shouldn't think I could.'

Gus took his plate back from Santa.

'Can't you really play that fiddle?'

'Only one tune, and that terribly badly.'

Gus laughed.

'Puts me in mind of a clown was once with us. He wasn't much of a clown. Never knew how he got round Mr Cob to take him on. But could he talk! To hear him, there was nothing that man couldn't do. One day old Ben hears him criticizing the jockey act. "You ride?" Ben asks. "Ride!" The clown, Fred his name was, laughed. "Ridden since I could stand." Well, Ben he says nothing more at the time, but he goes to Mr Cob and together they fixes a joke. All the circus is in on it. "Fred," says Mr Cob, "I hear you ride. There's a horse we want breaking. Would you come in the ring in the morning and see what you can do with it?" Well, Fred tries to find an excuse. But it's no good. Mr Cob keeps saying: "Just as a favour, Fred." In the end he has to say he'd be there.'

'Goodness! Could he ride?' asked Santa.

'Him! No. Didn't know the back end of a horse from the front.'

Peter laid down his fork and knife.

'Why wasn't he killed, then?'

Gus chuckled.

'That next morning we was all there. All the men and everybody. There was Ben holding the horse. It was kicking and rearing all over the place. Fred took one look at him and turned the colour of a lettuce. But it was no good. Ben was there, and he and Cob shoved him on. He was in such a state he looked like a sack of coals. Ben gave the horse a slap on the flank. Away they went into the ring. Laugh! I never saw such a sight. I thought I'd split.'

'But didn't he fall off?' asked Santa.

Gus chuckled at his memories.

'He couldn't. While Mr Cob and Ben were fussing around getting him up they slipped a lunge round him. Specially made, it was. A light thing he never noticed, being in the state he was. Well, first buck and he's sent flying, but not on the ground, for the boys pulled on the lunge rope and there he is dangling in the air. Then they caught the horse and back he's put again. Must have gone on putting him on best part of half an hour. Then in comes one of the Kenets. They can hang on to anything. Gets up on the horse, and rides him round as if he'd got him out in a park. We never heard much talk from Fred after that.'

Peter and Santa washed up the lunch things. They looked round the circus. A holiday peace was over it. The children's voices could be heard playing round the big top. There was some barking from the poodles. One of the horses neighed. Otherwise everybody was resting or asleep. They washed up without talking for a bit. Their minds were on the argument at lunch.

'It's funny,' Santa whispered at last. 'Being here is the nicest thing that ever happened to us, but it keeps getting spoilt somehow.'

'Anything would with Gus,' Peter said bitterly. 'He isn't even fair. It's not my fault we've been brought up differently to the way Gus was. I say things wrong, but they weren't wrong when we lived with Aunt Rebecca. How'm I to know?'

Santa washed out a teacup. They always had tea after lunch. Gus liked it.

'Gus doesn't mean it. He means to be nice.'

'Funny way to show it. It's all right for you. It's me he minds.' He leant over the basin to Santa, and whispered: 'I'm going to ask Ben not to tell him he's letting me ride. If he knew he'd bring people to laugh.'

Santa nodded.

'That's a good idea. But Gus is often in the big top. Won't he see?'

'No. Some of the horses are exercised early. I'll get Ben to let me learn then.'

Santa said nothing. She thought it a good idea. It was just what Gus wanted. Peter going off alone. Queer how lately people kept trying to separate them. Not that they could, but she wished they would not try.

Olga, Sasha, Fritzi, Hans, and Fifi came tearing along to tea at half past four. They could not comfortably all have tea in the caravan, so the boys sat on the steps and Gus passed out buns as they wanted them.

'Has your violin come safely, Santa?' asked Olga.

'Good deal too safely to please Santa,' said Gus. 'She says she can't play it.'

Fifi laid down her bun. She shrugged both shoulders and lifted both hands.

'Impossible! Why should one travel with a violin which one cannot play?'

'But I didn't travel with it,' Santa protested. 'I left it behind.'

'You said that you could play,' Fritzi broke in. 'How is it then you cannot?'

Sasha stuck his head in at the door.

'Have you got a mood, Santa?'

Peter pulled him back.

'Shut up, you fool. She can't play. She makes a beast of a row.'

Hans shook his head.

'Always it so is. There is one artiste in the family the rest they cannot understand.'

Peter took a large bite of bun.

'Rot.'

As soon as the tea was eaten Gus pointed at the violin case.

'Come on, Santa, tune up.'

'But no.' Fifi jumped up. 'I must fetch papa and maman. They too wish to hear her play.'

'That is so.' Hans climbed down the caravan steps. 'Mine father and mother they too her will hear.'

Fritzi nodded comfortingly to Santa.

'They the music understand.'

Santa went miserably to the corner and took out the violin. The E string had broken. She looked in the box part of the end of the case and found a new one. Most unwillingly she fastened it in. How awful this was going to be. How she wished the caravan would fall over or something, anything so that she need not play.

The Moulins and the Schmidts arrived. Gus, with a twinkle in his eye, put chairs for them outside. He put down a rug so the children could sit on the ground. He made Santa stand on the caravan step where they could all see her.

Santa rosined and tightened her bow. She had tuned the violin as well as she could, but she had not much ear and was lost without a piano to give her an A. She put the velvet pad into her neck. Then she looked beseechingly at Gus.

'Please. I can't. You know I can't.'

Gus grinned.

'Come on. You told the other kids you could. Now let's hear you.'

'I can only play *Art thou weary, art thou languid?*'

Gus turned to the Schmidts and Moulins.

'That's a hymn.'

Mrs Schmidt nodded in contentment.

'That will beautiful be. It is nice on a Good Friday.'

The Moulins made approving noises. They sat like people at a concert. Holding their breath for the first note.

Santa, seeing that she had got to go through with it, put her bow across the strings.

There had never been a moment since Santa started the violin when she had not made a disgusting noise on it. The noise she made that afternoon was worse than she had ever made before. The violin was out of tune. Her fingers, damp with fright, slipped on the notes. The bow scooped. *Art thou weary, art thou languid?* is rather a doleful tune. As played by Santa that afternoon it sounded like the moan of somebody in the most excruciating pain.

The Moulins were polite people. Mr Moulin and Lucille sat with fixed smiles as if they were pleased. Fifi, less controlled, put her fingers in her ears. Lucille at once gave her a slap, so she took them out again and also sat with a fixed smile.

The Schmidts were musical. They came of families who all played some instrument or other. When together they made up quite a good little orchestra, playing purely for pleasure. It was to them sacrilege for anyone who could make such a noise as Santa was making to touch an instrument. They shut their eyes and tried to think of other things.

Olga and Sasha had been brought up without hearing much music. But they had a little music in their blood. They thought at first that Santa was being funny. They looked round at the serious pained expressions of all the others. They bore it for three lines of the hymn, then they could stand it no more. They rolled on the ground screaming with laughter.

It was very rude, but from Santa's point of view much the best thing that could have happened. In a moment she had stopped playing and they were all laughing. Mr Schmidt was the first to recover.

'Never,' he said, wiping his eyes, 'have I such sounds heard.'

Mrs Schmidt tapped him on the knee.

'That is not kind, Heinrich. The poor little Santa. It is not the wish of the lieber Gott that all gifts should have.'

Fritzi got up.

'But how is it, Santa, that you tell us you do play?'

Mr Schmidt shook his head at his daughter.

'It is finish. We will some music make to take the noise away. Stand up, Hans, and you, liebchen. We will sing.'

People who can sing always collect other people round them. The Schmidts sang German folk-songs. They sounded lovely. Some of the ring-hands and tent-men came across to listen. Then they sang in Welsh. Then someone started a tune that was familiar to them all even if the words they put to it were in various tongues. One song led to another. Half the circus people were standing outside Gus's caravan. It began to get dark. Lights popped up here and there.

'What shall we finish with?' said one of the men.

Gus looked round. He caught Santa's eye. She could see his lips forming the word 'Art'. She gave him a desperate look. He couldn't, he wouldn't be so mean. Gus grinned at her.

'How about *The long, long trail*?' he said. 'I was always partial to that.'

11

The Riding Lesson

Two things happened in Blackpool. The first was on Easter morning. Gus had a puncture on the way down and his was the last caravan to arrive. As he turned the car into the ground Olga and Sasha jumped up on the running-board. Olga stuck her head through the window.

'Peter and Santa, will you come to our caravan? We have eggs and paska.'

Sasha pushed his head through beside hers.

'We have asked Fifi and Fritzi and Hans. But Fifi has gone to Mass, and Fritzi and Hans have eaten something bad. They have both been sick. They had to stop the car on the way over so they could be. So it will only be you. Will you come?'

Gus stopped the car.

'Hop out, you two, and go and get your Easter eggs. I'm not driving any farther with these two hung on like that.' He leant out and gave Sasha a slight slap. 'One jolt, and you'll be under the wheels. And what's the good of Easter eggs then?'

Olga did a flip-flap and turned a cartwheel.

'I'm so glad it's Easter,' she said, when she was the right way up again. 'We have a feast.' She held out her hand to Santa. 'Come on.'

There were eggs dyed all colours. There were some kind of herrings soaked in oil with mushrooms round them. There were salted cucumbers. There was a meat dish. Most exciting of all was the cake, the paska. Peter and Santa had been given small chocolate eggs on Easter Day but there had been no kind of party. They stared at the table in amazement. Especially at the paska; they had never seen a cake like it before. Mrs Petoff was making a pot of tea. She turned beaming to Peter and Santa.

'A happy Easter. We had thought maybe you was lost on the road.'

Peter explained about the tyre. Maxim patted the place next to him.

'Come, Santa, you will sit beside me. We are the good friends. Peter will sit by my wife. Sit down, all of you.'

It was extraordinary how they all fitted in, but somehow they managed. And what a meal they all ate! Something from every dish. Then, to finish up with, a great slice of paska. You would not think a rich cake was the sort of food to have for breakfast as well as meat and herrings and cucumber, but it all went down very well. When they had finished Mrs Petoff handed round the eggs. They were in a basket. Santa took a red one and Peter a green. They were ordinary hens' eggs, boiled hard and dyed. They stared at them curiously, because they had never seen Easter eggs like that before. Maxim had a blue one. He turned it over in his fingers. He smiled at Santa.

'You have never seen such an egg? No? When I was a little boy in Russia I have seen these being coloured. I would think then time is so slow. Easter will never come.'

'Did you always have a party for Easter?' asked Peter.

Mrs Petoff nodded.

'I do not remember, but I have heard it was the great feast. Before there was a long fast.'

Maxim made a face.

'For that there was sunflower-seed oil instead of butter, and not much to eat. Three days it lasted. And imagine what was going on. The kitchen was in excitement. Dish after dish is cooked. The herrings as we have today, only better, you cannot get them good in England. The cucumbers. The great roasts. Then the paska! We children would stand round, our mouths watering. Such a mound of curds and sugar and raisins and almonds. It was hard to see it made when we were fasting.'

Santa could not bear to think of the children being hungry.

'Never mind. On Easter Day you ate it all for breakfast.

The Petoffs laughed. Maxim shook his head.

'Not for breakfast. No. In England, yes. There is the pull-down and we travel early. But when I was a little child it was at night.' He dropped his voice and his eyes had a far-away look. 'All the evening the table is set out. All the food and the vodka. Then at perhaps half past eleven my mother bring in the paska. Then we go to church. The church will be so full it is hard to get in. We kneel on the floor. On the floor is laid twigs of fir-tree. There is an image of the dead Christ. Then suddenly all the bells sound. The priests and choir come to the door. They have many banners, and lanterns. Then we follow. We have candles. They blow in the wind. There are many stars. The lanterns are on high poles. We march round the church, and sing the great hymn. Then quick like that' – Maxim clicked his fingers to show the passing of a second – 'all that is solemn is over. It is as if all had gone mad. The bells clash. All kiss each other. All cry "Christ is risen, Christos woss krese." '

Maxim's voice tailed away. He sat holding his egg with the tears running down his cheeks. Peter and Santa looked round. All the Petoffs were crying. Very quietly they got up and left the caravan. Outside they looked at each other.

'My goodness!' said Santa. 'How awful. Poor Mr

Petoff. Fancy having to live in England when it makes him cry to think of Russia.'

Peter had been thoroughly embarrassed by the tears.

'Must be pretty bad to make him cry. I wonder he doesn't try and go back. I expect he could. There must still be circuses in Russia.'

Olga came bounding down the caravan steps, followed by Sasha. She stood on her hands.

'Wasn't that a lovely Easter?'

Peter stared at her.

'It was. But it seemed to make you all pretty miserable.'

'Miserable!' Sasha did a flip-flap and finished facing Peter. 'We wasn't miserable. It was beautiful.'

Santa looked at him severely.

'That's not true, Sasha. Two minutes ago you were crying. We saw you.'

Sasha turned to Olga. They were obviously puzzled.

'Every Easter we cry,' Olga explained. 'So it should be. My father is an exile from Russia.'

'I know,' Peter agreed. 'And it's awful for him. That's why, though everything was very nice to eat, you can't say it was a lovely Easter when it made you all remember you were unhappy.'

Olga walked a few steps on her hands.

'But we was not unhappy.'

'You may not be,' Peter argued, 'but your father is. He wants to go back to Russia.'

This statement stopped both Olga and Sasha from practising tumbling. They stood upright, looking very earnest.

'Never,' said Olga, 'would my father wish to return to Russia. He is naturalized English.'

Sasha thumped his chest.

'We was British.'

Peter gave a despairing shrug. He would never understand.

'Then why did you all cry?'

Olga stamped her foot.

'You can be stupid, Peter. It's beautiful to cry. It's a mood. If you never cry how can you enjoy it when you laugh?'

Peter put his egg in his pocket.

'Gus laughs a lot and he never cries.'

Olga did a cartwheel.

'For the English it's wrong to cry. My father says they cannot feel.'

'Then why's he got naturalized?' said Peter. 'He oughtn't to if he doesn't like the English.'

Olga skipped away.

'You are stupid. He loves England. It isn't not loving a country if you say the people don't feel.'

Peter did not like to say any more as they had just been to a party. He gave a nod to Olga and Sasha and went towards their own caravan. Santa hurried after him.

'I think Russians are very odd, don't you?'

Peter kicked up the grass.

'I don't know what they're talking about. But perhaps we shall later on.'

The other thing that happened in Blackpool was Peter's first riding lesson. He went by himself and found Ben. He hung about beside him while he looked at the horses. He knew exactly what he wanted to say, but he didn't know how to start. Ben stopped suddenly and looked at him.

'What's the trouble, Peter?'

'Well, I was wondering – I mean to say – well, you said—'

Ben put up a hand to stop him. He picked up two straws and gave him one.

'Either you got something to say, or you haven't. If you have, speak out. I never could abide talk that had to go a mile round where it was gettin' to.'

Peter leant against the post between Halfpenny's and Robin's stalls. Ben leant against a tent prop.

'You remember,' said Peter, 'that you said some time you'd see how I shaped at riding.'

'That's right. Come tomorrow, if you like.'

'Well, it isn't only that.' Peter looked straight at Ben. 'People here think I'm a fool.'

Ben chewed at his straw thoughtfully.

'Lot a people don't see no more'n the outside. I say about people what I always say about 'osses. No good fixing everything on looks. What about the heart? That's what I want to know.'

Peter felt a bit discouraged. He would have liked Ben to have said: 'Nobody thinks you're a fool. How could you have imagined it?' He kicked at the straw under his feet.

'Why do they think I'm a fool?'

Ben spat out his straw.

'It's not so much a fool as maybe soft. The day you come, and I sees you and Santa in the stable here, you remember, I sees you look soft. It was your way of walking careful in case you should tread in something, and the way you have of brushin' bits of dust and that off your things. It's more like a girl.'

'Gus can't bear me,' Peter blurted out. 'So I thought if I could come and ride early when he didn't know, it would be a good idea. If he knew he'd come and laugh.'

Ben carefully chose another straw. He put it in his mouth.

'I always say to the lads in the stable here: "Don't come grumblin' to me. You knew what you 'ad to do when you signed on. If you don't like it, sign off." '

'But I can't sign off.'

Ben gave him a shrewd look.

'Wasn't there talk of an orphanage?'

'Oh, that!' Peter thought the argument silly. Obviously nobody would want to go to an orphanage who could live in a circus. 'I don't mind being here as much as that.'

'Then there ain't no point in grumblin'. Gus has took you both in. A caravan ain't all that big. Must 'a' done away with most of 'is comfort havin' you.'

Peter stared at Ben. Aunt Rebecca had run her house for them, and they had always taken it for granted she liked doing it. They had come to Gus. They had thought that perhaps to please Mr Stibbings they would be sent to the orphanages, but they had never thought that it would have suited Gus. It was a new idea. Peter could not accept it right away. He felt he had a proper grievance, that he was being picked on unfairly. It was not easy to switch his mind to what Gus was putting up with on his account. He went back to the question of his riding.

'Could I come early? I'd much rather.'

Ben nodded.

'Be along at seven. I'll be exercisin' Mustard. He's just built to start you on.'

Peter went to Mustard's stall. He looked very like the other chestnuts, he thought.

'Why's he specially good?'

Ben came slowly down the stables. He gave Mustard an affectionate pat.

'Well, he's slight. Must start you on something slight on account of the length of your legs.' He went into the stall feeling in his pocket. He brought out some sugar and gave it to Mustard. He fondled him. 'He's a grand 'oss. Ain't you, old fellow? He was a hunter when Mr Cob bought him. Intelligent! This 'oss is almost 'uman. Eighteen months after his last hunt he was workin' in the ring. Bit of a change for 'im, but he took to it like he'd been born in a circus.'

'Do you think he misses his hunting?'

Ben came out of the stall.

'Sometimes I think he does. 'Course, all 'osses has their moods, same as 'umans. Mustard here, he does get a bit down at times. There's mornin's, especially at the end of tentin', when it's sharp, and you get a smell of dropped leaves like. Then Mustard, 'e'll go off 'is feed. And I'll see a look in 'is eye as if he were rememberin'.'

'Poor Mustard.' Peter went into the stall and gave him a pat. 'Poor old boy.' He turned to Ben. 'Couldn't you take him out when he feels like that?'

Ben shook his head.

'Once a 'oss is trained to the ring, he's got to stop there.'

Ben and Peter walked slowly up the stables.

'Must be pretty dull for all the horses,' said Peter. 'Just standing here all day. It isn't as if they could talk.'

'Can't talk!' Ben stood still. He tapped Peter with his straw.

''Osses talk just as good as you and me. They've all got their pals that they chats to. Mustard don't make the close friends some do. He's on his own, like. But if he didn't find himself alongside Vinegar and Tapioca there'd be trouble. They was here when he came. They was trainin' too. They gave Mustard a helpin' 'and, and he hasn't forgotten.'

Peter was not sure Ben was not pulling his leg.

'Do you really think they mind which horse they stand next to? And they can't really talk?'

'Can't they! You come along here.' Ben led the way across to the four creams. 'These are a funny mix-up. Two years back Mr Cob wanted four creams special on account of a tableau he was puttin' on for a season at Christmas. He did it with four of the girls. Pretty it was, but too fancified for me. Well, near a year beforehand we was looking for these cream-coloured 'osses. They 'ad to match nice, and they weren't easy to get on account of another circus having matched up ten recent. In the end he gets two from Scandinavia, and one from a greengrocer's cart, and one from a titled lady. Well, the one from the greengrocer hadn't a name. The two Scandinavians 'ad names, but no one could get their tongues round 'em. So, seeing the one from the titled lady was called "President", we called the others the same way. The greengrocer's 'oss we called King, and the other two Rajah and Emperor. Naturally we puts the two foreigners together and King and President alongside each other. Then the fun began.'

'Why?'

'All on account of President bein' above hisself. He thought, comin' from where he did, he was too good to stand alongside a 'oss what come out of a greengrocer's cart. He started the mischief. Straight away he was savaging King. We didn't give in at once, but we 'ad to in the end. President 'ad us beat. You see now we 'ave 'em separated. King's up this end, where he can say a word now and then to Wisher and Pie-crust. The two Scandinavians only speak to each other, that's on account of their never 'avin' learnt English.'

'Then who does President talk to?'

'No one. Not unless it's Satan's lions. They say they're the king of beasts so maybe they're good enough for 'im. Mind you, you got to understand a 'oss. Every one 'as 'is little ways, and all different. But 'osses is like 'umans. Now and then you comes across one you can't do nothin' with. President's like that. I tried all ways, all the boys 'as tried, but he thinks hisself too good for us, and that's a fact.'

Peter looked carefully at President. When you knew about him he had got rather a proud face.

Ben took out his watch.

'Dinner-time, I reckon. See you tomorrow at seven.'

Peter told Santa he was to ride the next morning. They always had done things together, so he was quite fair and asked her if she would like to come and watch. She would have liked to, but she thought Peter would like to go alone, it was less annoying to fall off if nobody was watching, and besides it would please Gus if he did something by himself. But all she said was:

'Thank you for nothing. I wasn't thinking of getting up early just to watch you kicked off.'

Ben did not think either the shorts Gus had bought Peter, or his own suits, the right clothes to ride in, so Alexsis was confided in. He lent an old pair of jodhpurs. Peter had been worried about how he would wake up, but Alexsis solved that too. He had to go to early exercise anyway. he was called by an alarum clock. he offered to give Santa a shake as he went by, and she said she would wake Peter.

'But you said you didn't want to be woken up,' Peter objected, quite fussed by her generosity.

'I don't mind waking. It's going over to that cold big top I don't want. As a matter of fact, as I'll be awake I'll cook the breakfast. It'll be a surprise for Gus.'

Peter was leaning against the caravan door. he ran his finger up and down the woodwork.

'D' you suppose he likes having us?'

'I suppose so,' said Santa. 'It must have been lonely for him living all alone.'

'Ben said today that a caravan wasn't very big, and that Gus must have done away with a lot of comfort to have us.'

'Did he?' Santa was undressing. She put on her dressing-gown and joined Peter in the doorway.

'You mean he's only having us because he's got to?'

'He hasn't. He could have sent us to Saint Winifred's and Saint Bernard's.'

Santa began combing her hair.

'Not very well, he couldn't. It would look a bit mean for an uncle to put his nephew and niece into an orphanage.'

'Ben didn't think so. He seemed to think it was awfully nice of him to look after us.'

Santa struggled with a knot.

'But people always look after children. I mean, if you've only an uncle then he has to.'

'Ben didn't think that. And Ben's the most sensible person we know.'

Santa groaned as her comb fought its way through a tangle.

'Well, what are you going to do about it? We can't say we'll go to orphanages, because we wouldn't, and there's nowhere else.'

Peter shut the door and went into the other room. He did not know exactly what he did want to say. Only things like one of them cooking the breakfast seemed fair.

'I just thought I'd tell you. Good night.'

Santa thought about Gus for a minute. It was quite a new idea that he might not want them. Suddenly she had a plan. She banged on Peter's door.

'I say.'

Peter opened the door and looked in.

'What's up?'

'We might make him want us. I mean, want us so much we always stayed with him. He only said we could stay for the tenting tour. I thought that meant always, but perhaps it doesn't. Perhaps he means to send us to Saint Winifred's and Saint Bernard's after that.'

'How could we make him want us?'

Santa dragged at another knot and considered.

'Well, one of us could always cook the breakfast. And then I could do his mending. I suppose there's lots of things we could think of.'

'Whatever we do I expect he'll say we do it wrong.' Peter grumbled. 'I did try and help with that tyre on Sunday, and all he said was: "Get back in the car. I'll be quicker alone." '

'Well, you did drop those screw things from the wheel.'

'It's not my fault I don't know about cars.'

Santa divided her hair in half and began plaiting it.

'Well, I wouldn't learn on Gus's. Perhaps Ted Kenet would tell you things. He's awfully nice.'

Peter watched Santa fasten the end of a plait with wool.

'Why don't you always wear it like that? It gets in a terrible mess loose.'

Santa examined her head in the glass.

'Wouldn't Gus mind?'

'Why should he? It's still there, even if it's plaited. It's only cutting it off he doesn't like.'

'I haven't any ribbon or anything to tie it up with.'

'That wool looks all right.'

'Does it?' Santa once more stared in the glass. It did look neat. The part round her face curled, so it would keep tidy. The back part had been very straight ever since she came to the circus. Nobody who was not mad was going to curl their hair in rags every night unless they had an Aunt Rebecca who made them. 'It doesn't look bad. And if wool would do I've heaps.'

'Good,' said Peter, and shut the door.

Santa got into bed. She thought about the comfort of not having a lot of hair to get in her eyes and mouth. Really Peter did have good ideas. Why hadn't she thought of wearing it plaited?

The big top was cold at seven in the morning. Peter had not put on his jodhpurs in the caravan in case Gus woke up and saw them. He went under the seating and changed. He felt terribly self-conscious when he came out. He had never worn jodhpurs before, but he had heard so much about Lord Bronedin wearing them that it was rather like putting on Puss's boots or Red Riding Hood's cloak. Something you had heard of always, but known you would never wear.

He need not have worried. There were only four people about: Ben, a groom holding Mustard,

Alexsis just getting on to Vinegar, and a bereiter already exercising Salt. Ben beckoned to Peter and they sat down in two of the ringside seats.

'There's a right way and a wrong way of doin' everythin',' said Ben. 'You could sit on old Mustard same as if you was sittin' in a arm-chair. He'd carry you round and round the ring takin' no more notice of you than if you wasn't there. But that ain't ridin'. The first thing you've got to think of is how you're goin' to sit. And the answer is, just as natural as you know how. There's some no sooner see a 'oss than they stiffen up. That's all wrong. You want to keep yourself easy, your head up, but all your neck muscles loose so you can see what's comin'. Can't expect the 'oss to do everything. Ridin' 's a job for two. You want your neck muscles loose and your eyes easy, so you can tell old Mustard if there's anything unusual about so he can watch his step. Then you want your shoulders down. Funny what a lot of people hunch them up ridin'. Looks terrible. Then your arms have got to hang natural just as far as your elbows. Then you've got something to do. You've got to keep them close to your sides. If you turn them out you'll never have good hands. We ain't comin' to hands today, but they're what make the good rider.'

Peter tried to attend properly. But being told how you sit was not his idea of riding. He tried to hurry Ben up by coming to the end of riding.

He tried to hurry Ben up by coming to the end of the parts of him.

'How about my legs?'

'We're coming to them. They want well stretchin' down. Your thighs want keepin' flat. Then there's your knees. You want to take particular account of them. You're ridin' with a saddle to start with. If you keep your knees close to the flaps as you can, you'll be right. You want to turn your toes a bit out. That's particular important in high-school ridin', 'cause that means the 'oss'll feel the touch from your leg before he feels the spur, and same time your foot's right for usin' a spur.' Ben stopped and smiled. 'You won't remember one 'alf of that. So come on. Up you go.'

Out of all the things Ben had said the only one which had stuck was the first thing: 'You must sit just as natural as you know how.' Peter was not a bit nervous. He did not look upon horses as things to be nervous of. The groom gave him a leg into the saddle. There was some rearrangement of the stirrups. He held the reins in a bunch in his hands. Then he sat down.

'Keep hold of Mustard,' said Ben to the groom. 'Lead him into the ring so I can have a look.' The groom made a clicking sound. Mustard obediently stepped forward.

Peter was thrilled. He did not worry at all how he was sitting. There was something about being on a horse which satisfied some bit of him that had never been satisfied before. He turned and grinned at Ben.

Ben came into the ring. From one of his pockets he picked a bent, scraggy piece of straw. He put it in his mouth. He walked thoughtfully round Peter and Mustard, sucking as he went.

'Not so far out,' he said at last. 'Straighten that back. You don't want no hollows. Keep your head up, your hands down, and your heels down. Keep those toes turned out a bit. Remember 'oss ridin' is balance. You don't want to hold on nowhere. When you do 'ave to your knees are there to do it. If you 'ave to get a grip it's from your knees to your ankles it's got to come. If you tell me tomorrow you ache above the knees I'll be wantin' to know why. You'll be grippin' wrong. Now off you go. Walk him round.'

'What about these? How do I hold them?' Peter held up the reins.

'You be here tomorrow same time and I'll tell you. Just 'old them loose. Mustard knows what 'e's got to do.'

It was lovely riding round the ring. It felt like being a real circus performer. Of course the seats were empty, but it was not very difficult to fill them with applauding people. Peter looked up at the band balcony. Of course the band was not there, but it's easy to hum a tune in your head, and see a band playing it. Alexsis and the bereiter were going round too. It was simple to turn the three of them into a daring act. Ben sat peacefully

239

chewing. Now and then he said: 'Remember that back,' or: 'What's happened to your head? Is your neck weak?' The groom smoked. From the stables came champings and neighings and the hoarse barks of the sea-lions. Through the tent flap a smell of bacon and eggs blew in from the men's mess. The circus smell of animals, rosin, sawdust, and earth came to the nose in a rich jumble.

'Breakfast,' said Ben. 'Come on, Mustard.'

Peter slid to the ground. He looked up at Ben. 'I say, thanks awfully.'

Ben signalled to the groom to lead Mustard to his stall.

'There ain't nothin' to thank for, son. Mustard needed exercisin'. Must keep him from gettin' a roll.' He looked at Peter with a queer smile. It was as if he was not only seeing him, but somebody in his memory. 'You was happy ridin', wasn't you?' Peter nodded. Ben turned away. 'I thought you was. See you seven tomorrow.'

Peter went under the seats and changed back into his shorts. He rolled the jodhpurs up in a bundle and hid them until he could find a minute when Gus was not about. He went outside.

The sun was shining. It was a gorgeous day. The air smelt of sea. High up above a lark was singing. Peter was so happy he had to let some of it out. He made a wild whooping sound. Then he dashed through the gate in the fence and went bounding back to breakfast.

12

Parade

It was not as easy doing things for Gus as it seemed as if it would be. He was the most independent man. The first day when Santa cooked his breakfast he seemed surprised to find it ready for him, but not a bit pleased or grateful. He did eat his bacon and eggs, but he turned every mouthful over suspiciously with his tongue.

'Bacon crisp, eggs soft, that was my old mother's, your grandmother's, rule. Apple sauce, girl, you've got 'em the other way round!'

After breakfast he went outside and looked at his frying-pan. Santa had noticed he never washed it, but cleaned it out with paper. There was a bit of paper waiting in it, so he could see she was going to do it the way he liked. But all the same he did not look pleased. He just made a grunting noise and lit a cigarette and went off to the big top.

Santa was discouraged. She thought there were

times when Gus was difficult to like as much as people ought to like an uncle. She did not say this to Peter because he was finding it difficult to be fond of Gus anyway, and certainly did not need any encouragement not to like him.

She did not try cooking the breakfast again for a bit. Her next effort to please was on Sunday afternoon. They were in Southport. Peter was away feeding the horses. Gus was talking to Ted Kenet. Santa decided to do the mending. She got all Gus's socks and took them and her work-basket outside and sat on the caravan steps looking for holes. She hoped Gus would bring Ted Kenet back with him. Even if Gus could not see things for himself, Ted Kenet probably would. He would be almost sure to say Gus was lucky to have a niece to do his mending for him. But Gus came back alone and was not a bit pleased.

'What are you up to?'

'Mending your socks,' said Santa, trying not to sound as smug as she felt.

Gus looked at his socks with a surprised air, as if he were wondering how they came to be out of doors.

'They got holes in 'em?'

'No.' Santa gave a regretful sigh. That she had not found any holes so far was rather spoiling her gesture. 'There aren't, but I expect I'll soon find some.'

Gus picked up the socks. He took the one off her hand which she was examining.

'You'll soon make some, poking your finger through the wool that way.' He looked down at her. 'I should have thought a kid like you could have found something to do round the ground. What do you want sitting around on the steps for? If my socks wanted mending I'd have mended them.'

Santa was hurt. Besides, he must be talking rubbish. The duchess had often said, and Aunt Rebecca repeated: 'The home is made by the woman.'

'I've plenty to do,' she said crossly. 'But I didn't know you could sew. Most men can't.'

Gus laughed.

'How d'you think I've managed all these years?'

Santa had not thought. She was just determined to be useful. She still wanted to be.

'I should have thought,' she said with dignity, 'you would be glad of a woman about the –' She stopped there because a caravan is not a house. 'Well, homes are made by women, you know.'

'I don't.' Gus pulled one of her plaits. 'My home's always been made by me. Now you run along and play with the other kids. You don't see Fifi and Olga sitting around with work-baskets.'

Santa got up.

'Fritzi does.'

Gus yawned.

'Well, you go and sew dolls' clothes with Fritzi. I'm going to have a lay down.'

Santa glared at the shut caravan door. Sew dolls' clothes, indeed! and she getting on for twelve. Gus really was a most annoying man. Then she heard Olga and Sasha laughing. It was a nice afternoon. Perhaps it was quite a good thing Gus did not want his socks mended.

Peter had no better luck with his effort. It was worse for him because the reason he tried to be useful was different. Santa wanted to be so useful that Gus could not bear to part with them. Peter could not forget what Ben had said. He found himself looking at Gus when Gus was not looking at him. Didn't he want them? Had he been much more comfortable before they came?

Peter cleaned the car. He spent all the time that the first evening performance was on doing it. He borrowed the right things from Alexsis, who showed him what cloths and polish to use. When Gus came back between the shows Peter was looking very hot and dirty, and the car very nice indeed. Gus blinked at his car in surprise.

'Kedgeree and rum! look at the car! Mr Ford himself wouldn't know her.'

Peter grinned.

'She does look better, doesn't she?'

Peter only said that because he had to say something. He had never driven in a car until he met Gus, and had no thought of suggesting it was not clean enough for him. But unfortunately Gus was touchy about his car. He never had kept it very well. Ted Kenet and Maxim Petoff were always making jokes about it. When they made jokes Gus did not exactly mind, but it made him make resolutions to clean it up, which he never kept. He gave it a lick and a polish now and again, and that had to do. But that Peter should hint the car was dirty was quite a different thing. He lost his temper before he had time to think.

'Sorry it wasn't good enough for you as it was.'

Peter was indignant. It had been nice of him to clean the car.

'I never said it wasn't good enough for me. I just thought you'd be pleased, that's all.'

Gus walked round his car, examining it as if to see if Peter had hurt the paint. He felt ashamed of himself and did not know how to say something nice to make up.

'If I'd wanted you to clean it I could have asked you.'

'But you never do,' Peter flared at him. 'You always look as if you thought I couldn't do anything.'

This was so exactly what Gus did think that he did not say any more. He was afraid if he did he would make things worse. Instead he went into the caravan and shut the door.

Peter stood staring a moment at the door. He

would have liked to burst it open and shout something rude. But he did not. Angrily he stooped and collected all the cleaning things. He moved to take them back to Alexsis. Then suddenly he had an idea. He put the cleaning things on the ground and picked up a handful of dirt. The jug of water was standing outside the caravan. He poured some of it on the dirt and made some mud. Then he looked at the car. He had taken a lot of trouble with the wings, which were clean enough to eat a meal off. Savagely he rubbed his mud on them. It spoilt the look of the car but he felt a lot better.

It was at Southport Santa had her first lesson in tumbling. She was playing on the cloth used for the water act with Olga, Sasha, Fifi, and Fritzi. Peter and Hans were sitting nearby making catapults. Fifi and Fritzi had been practising quite seriously. Olga and Sasha had been throwing themselves about in the way they always did. Fifi was the first to stop working. She looked at her watch and put on her jersey.

'I have completed my half an hour. Papa says that is all that I should do without him, or it may be that I will do wrong and make a bad habit.'

Olga turned three cartwheels.

'Me and Sasha work all day and we never make bad habits.'

Fifi looked under her eyelashes at Fritzi. She

said nothing, but the look expressed a lot. The rough and ready way in which the Petoff children were allowed to work was a constant topic of conversation between the Schmidt and Moulin mothers. In fact, without it they would not have had much to talk about, for they did not like each other very much although they were always polite. But Mrs Moulin considered that the Schmidt children were well brought up, and Mrs Schmidt, though she could not go as far as that about Fifi, at least thought she was being well trained for her profession. Neither of them thought the Petoffs either well brought up or trained, and they liked to put their heads together and click their tongues and say so. Of course things like that are catching, and Fritzi and Fifi put their heads together and clicked their tongues about the Petoffs too. Not because they did not like them, on the whole they did, but because their training really was very casual. Besides, seeing their mothers clicking and gossiping made them think it was a smart thing to do.

Fritzi was not so easily satisfied as Fifi with a look or gesture to express her feelings. She liked to put things into words. She looked at Olga severely.

'But you and Sasha many bad habits have.'

Sasha was trying to walk on his hands. He fell over at Fritzi's feet.

'We have not. My father says we can do a floor act this Christmas.'

Fifi and Fritzi looked shocked.

'Such a child to tell such lies,' said Fritzi.

Fifi did not use words, but the way her eyebrows and shoulders and hands flew up expressed a lot.

Santa did not know what it was all about.

'Are you, Sasha? Is it a lie?'

'But of course it is a lie,' Fritzi explained. 'In England such children may not work. Sasha is only eight.'

Sasha took some strutting bragging steps.

'I didn't say we was going to work in England. Maybe we go to Russia.'

Olga was holding her right leg over her head. She took her eyes off her foot to glare at Sasha.

'That's stupid. We can't go to Russia. We shouldn't be permitted.'

Fifi patted the foot Olga had on the ground.

'We know. It's that naughty Sasha. Always he is telling lies.' She turned to Sasha. 'If you are British you must not be in the circus as a child. For me, I can if I wish.'

'Are you going to at Christmas, Fifi?' Santa asked.

Fifi shrugged her shoulders.

'I do not know. Perhaps. It may be in a theatre.'

Fritzi pursed up her mouth.

'Mine father would not let us work. He says it will be time when we fifteen are.'

'But what are you going to work at?' said Santa. 'You haven't any sea-lions.'

Fritzi moved back a little to get out of the way of Olga, who was doing a series of flip-flaps round the canvas.

'Mine mother has a sister. She was good on the flying trapeze. She marries an American. He is a great artiste. They have with them a man to work. They are "The Flying Mistrals".' She looked at Fifi, who nodded to say she had heard of them. 'When we was in Germany mine aunt she teach me. It may be I work with mine aunt's husband. It is that she get fat.'

'Goodness!' Santa was enormously impressed. 'You mean you'll be like Ted Kenet and Gus?'

Fifi tapped Santa's hand with her finger.

'But no. That is not flying. To fly there are two trapeze. They are wide apart. You swing from one to the other.'

Santa had never seen a flying trapeze. That Fritzi was even training for something so difficult she found very impressive. She looked at Fifi. It was funny now she came to think of it that she was always watching them practise but she had never thought what they were going to do. Somehow she had thought vaguely that the Petoffs would ride, the Schmidts train sea-lions, and Fifi would help with the poodles.

'What are you going to do, Fifi?'

'Next year I shall not go tenting with papa and

maman. I am to stay in France. I am to be the pupil of Mink.'

She said 'Mink' in the sort of voice that people use when they expect other people to say: 'Really! Mink! Just fancy!' But Santa, of course, looked blank.

Olga dropped panting on the canvas beside them.

'It's no good hoping Santa'll know, she never knows anything.'

Sasha crouched down on to his ankles.

'She's better than Peter. He knows nothing and then looks grand, like as if it was good to know nothing.'

'He doesn't!' said Santa indignantly. 'It isn't our fault we don't know things.'

'That is right,' Fifi agreed. 'It is the fault of their dead aunt.' She turned to Santa. 'Mink is the greatest clown there has ever been.'

'But you don't want to be a clown,' Santa objected.

Fifi spoke slowly, as if she was speaking to a rather small and stupid baby.

'You mustn't say "clown" like that. Mink is a great artiste.'

'Kolossal,' Fritzi agreed.

Olga lay on her back and raised her legs over her head.

'When he was seven he could do a routine and play the violin.'

Fritzi breathed heavily at the thought of such artistry.

'And never one time breaks he the tune.'

'When he was ten,' Olga went on, 'he could play all the wind instruments, and while he plays he juggles.'

'He is a great musician,' Fritzi explained. 'And while that is so he is also the great tumbler. There was never a clown like him. Never.'

Santa turned to Fifi.

'Isn't he being a clown any more?'

Fifi looked dramatic.

'All the world over he was the greatest artiste. People ran in the streets in London and New York and Berlin, it didn't matter where. Always they said: "Look, there is Mink." Then when he was one time in France war came.'

Sasha wriggled towards Fifi.

'It was in your country they put him in prison.'

'But certainly,' Fifi agreed with dignity. 'When there is a war there is no place for artistes.'

Fritzi picked a daisy.

'He was not long in prison. Soon they know who he is and he is free. But he is detained. When the war over is all say:

"Where is Mink?" '

Fifi took up the story.

'And Mink said: "Here I am, but I cannot be a clown any more." '

'Why not?' asked Santa.

Fifi shrugged her shoulders.

'He wrote in the paper: "Monsieur, Madame, I was in the world to make laughter. I have seen war, so I have no laughter to give. I retire!" '

'Goodness!' said Santa. 'What a grand way to write.'

Olga, Fifi, Fritzi, and Sasha looked at her with varying expressions of pity.

Fritzi explained her to the others.

'She is English.'

Santa saw that in some way she had said the wrong thing about Mink. She got the subject back to his work.

'And now he just teaches?'

'Yes.' Olga, still lying on her back, held her toes. 'He is the greatest teacher. He only takes those who have talent.'

'Oh!' Santa gave an admiring glance at Fifi. No wonder she always looked so self-assured. She would look self-assured if someone like Mink, who only took people of talent, had said he would teach her.

'Are you going to do a routine while you play the violin, Fifi?'

Fifi giggled. 'If I could play a beautiful hymn like you, I would.' Then she patted Santa's hand to show she was only teasing. 'No, I will work two years to be an acrobat. Already I have worked with him a little. He doesn't work like everybody here.

See.' She got up. 'Here is how Paula does when she is working with the Arizonas.' Very neatly she went through the routine that Ted Kenet had shown Peter and Santa.

Sasha and Olga got up and did it too, though not so well. Fritzi made disparaging noises through her teeth when they started.

'It is well as Fifi does it,' she said to Santa loudly. 'You see how it is. She backwards turn and the same way as a clock go.'

Fifi finished neatly. She held out her two hands palms uppermost just as if an audience were there. She came back to Fritzi and Santa. 'With Mink he turns the other way. As an Arab. He goes forward and not the way of a clock.'

Olga stood on her head.

'Is that all the difference?'

'If it is,' said Sasha, once more trying to walk on his hands, 'us could do that without going to Mink.'

Fritzi and Fifi exchanged another glance.

'It's not all,' Fifi said with dignity. 'The impulse is different. With Mink there is no flip-flap. There is a forespring.' She got up again, threw herself over, and came back neatly the right way up. 'Do you see, Santa?'

Santa saw that one way Fifi went forwards and the other backwards, but it was all one to her. Either was impossible to do.

'I suppose so. But I can't do any of it anyway.'

Fifi caught her hand.

'Come on, I'll teach you.'

Santa had on the same green frock she had travelled in. It was getting very shabby. She wished it would get hotter so that she could wear one of her cotton frocks. Fritzi, Olga, and Fifi had on practice clothes. Rather like bathing-dresses, with a jersey to match to put on when they finished working. Santa would have liked to learn how to tumble, but she felt self- conscious. To be the only one with skirts made her feel embarrassed.

'I can't. I haven't the right clothes.'

Fifi dismissed the need for special clothes with one gesture of her hands. But Fritzi was more understanding.

'Come! I another practice clothes have. I will lend them. Then mine mother can clean your frock. Each day she say: "The frocks of the little Santa dirty are. I would wish to have them to clean." '

Fifi nodded. 'That is the same with maman. But I said: "Impossible! Santa has no more clothes. What she wears is all there is." '

Santa was very glad to think she might borrow a practice dress. Of course she had never worn anything like that, and she felt she would look really circus in it. All the same, she did wish Fifi and Fritzi would not make her sound so poor. She knew she could not do the things they did, or have the clothes they had, but she did not need to have them saying so.

Peter got on well with Hans. Hans was serious, and liked to talk of serious things. To him the most serious thing in the world was training wild animals. To Peter, horses and riding. They sat side by side shaping the branches which Hans had chosen for catapults.

'Shall you have sea-lions when you are big enough to work?' Peter asked.

Hans chipped a small piece of wood from the fork of his branch.

'Maybe some. But mine father wish I should go to mine uncle. He has the animals that were mine grandfather's.'

'What sort of animals?'

Hans stopped cutting and considered.

'Now there was five lion. One go dead just two month ago. Three panther, four bear, and two tiger.'

'Will you have to go in the cage with them?'

'But yes. It is a fine show. They work together.'

'But aren't you afraid?'

Hans thought.

'Maybe a little sometimes.'

Peter peeled the last bit of his forked twig.

'I'd be all the time. I mean, they could kill you.'

Hans nodded.

'That is so.'

'Ben says he doesn't like wild-animal acts. He says he doesn't like any act behind bars.'

'That was right. I too wish they was not have to perform. I could not take an animal from a forest. I could not shut him up all the time; I know how unhappy he is.'

'Well, what about your uncle's beasts? They're shut up. Aren't they unhappy?'

'No. They was come as cubs. I see them train. They was like babies. They know nothing.' Hans took hold of Peter's arm to make him attend. 'First they must know each other. It is not natural that lions, tigers, panthers, and polar bears friends could be.'

'I should think it wasn't. How do you make them like each other?'

'First they was all in cages that was touching. So they all speak to each other. Then each mine uncle visit. Each one he bring a small present. So it is they to each other say: "See, our friend who bring the little things in his pocket is come!" Then one day after many weeks they are all together put to play.'

'My goodness!' said Peter. 'I wouldn't like to be there that day.'

'No,' Hans agreed. 'It is a time of great anxiety. The cubs was very valuable. It was bad if they should fight. You see, they was like little children who goes to a kindergarten. One boy maybe will another boy kick. He does not mean to be bad, it is he feels strange. So is it with mine uncle's animals. They play the great games, they get hot, and they are excited. Then maybe a little bad one pull a lion's mane. The lion think that not much fun. He hit whoever near is. Then mine uncle come. He is like the teacher in the school. He keeps order.'

'Sooner him than me.'

'If you was like us you would not be afraid. Always we have the wild animal. Always we have love them. It is with them as with the horses. Never mind they their own way have. Always must each know who the master is. So it is we the tricks teach. Some trainers make a great show with the whip. That is bad. It is leather pocket in which the little pieces of meat are that should make each little one wish to please.'

Peter put down his penknife.

'But Ben said lions and things like that don't like working in the ring.'

Hans frowned.

'I don't know. Sometimes I think "This is not kind. The animals was not happy." Then I think: "These was born in captivity. Each one, if he was not in the ring, he must to a zoo go. That is bad. Animals was like us. Each one he like to have something to do. If he is free that is best. But if he cannot be free then it is kinder he should work. Just to sit in a cage with all day nothing to do, that is terrible." '

Peter looked across in the direction of the stables.

'Well, I'd much rather have something to do with the horses.'

'So,' Hans agreed placidly. 'For me it must be the wild animal. I was afraid if I was not there another trainer not so kind would be.'

'Mr Cob wouldn't have a trainer who wasn't.'

'No; but there was others.' Hans looked suddenly angry. 'If I the peoples was who paid the circus to see and there was some beasts who do not happy look, of which you could say: "That is not kind", I would get up, and I would walk out, and as I go would cry to everyone: "You must not stay. You must not the money pay to see an animal perform who was not love his trainer!" '

Peter thought rather regretfully of Satan and his lions. There was no question that they did not love him. He had seen him sit with one who had toothache, ad he knew that the lion had let him pull the bad tooth out. It was a pity, in a way; it would have been exciting to see Hans making a row in the big top.

Santa came along. She was wearing an emerald green practice suit. She had green wool on the ends of her plaits. She looked nice like that. Peter felt proud of her. Santa was very conscious of her clothes. She stood on one leg.

'I borrowed it from Fritzi.'

Hans looked up.

'You was practising?'

Santa sat down beside him.

'I'd meant to. Fifi said she would show me how to tumble, but while I was changing she and Olga went off somewhere.' She looked anxiously at Peter. 'Do I look all right?'

'Um. Not bad.'

Ted Kenet came by. He had been working and had a coat over his practice things. He was, as usual, eating a sweet. He nodded to the three children.

'Hallo, kid. How's things?'

'I was going to practise tumbling with Fifi,' said Santa, 'but she's gone.'

'Oh! Well, if you'll come along past my caravan first, I'll show you how to work.'

'Will you?' Santa jumped up. 'Are you sure you don't mind?'

Ted walked off. Santa had to run to catch up with him.

'If I minded I wouldn't have offered. You ever drink sarsaparilla?'

'No.'

'Well, you should. That's what I'm going to get now. Nothing like it in the spring for keeping the blood cool. I'll give you a glass.'

'Thank you.' Santa tried to sound pleased, but she felt nervous it would be nasty. 'Of course you need cool blood on a trapeze.'

'You've said it.' Ted stooped and picked a dandelion and put it in his button-hole. 'Though it's all right up there. Get a fine view.'

Santa thought of the way he and Gus spun round.

'I wouldn't have thought you'd have time to see much.'

'You'd be surprised. Why, only last night at the second house I saw a lady faint. I'd a lovely view of her.'

They reached the caravan. Santa leaned against it. Ted went inside to mix the sarsaparilla. He cam out with two glasses. He handed one to Santa.

'Drink up. May you never break any bones!' Seeing this was obviously a sort of toast, Santa took a sip. She did not care for the taste at all. But Ted swallowed his in three gulps, so she made a valiant effort and got hers down. Ted took her glass. He smacked his lips. 'A glass of that three times a day and you'll live to be a hundred.'

Santa did not say so, but she thought she would rather not be as old if it meant drinking all that sarsaparilla.

Ted was a first-class teacher of tumbling. He took Santa into the ring.

'It's all being supple and balancing right.' He took hold of one of her legs and tried to lift it over her head. It was something all the other children did quite easily, but Santa's legs would not do it.

'I think I'm made wrong,' she gasped.

'No.' Ted dropped her leg. 'Stiff. That's your trouble. You want exercises. Nothing like it.

They'll make you so you can jump over the moon. Come on.'

The next half hour was the most hard-working that Santa had ever spent. Ted did not believe in amateurs. He told Santa that he was teaching her just for fun, but he worked her as if she had to earn her living doing acrobatics. Some of it was fun. He played leap-frog with her. Not just leap-frog as anybody might do it, but with a special way of taking-off and landing. A lot of the time was spent on just dull exercises like those she did at school. He made her stoop and touch her toes after everything she did. At the end, he picked up first one leg and then the other and again tried to hold them over her head. He still could not make her do it, but he said they were a good inch higher than they were before the lesson started.

'You work at those exercises two or three days.' He felt in his pocket and found his bag of sulphur sweets. 'I'll give you another lesson at Preston.'

Preston, which they moved to for the last three days of the week, was not very popular with Peter and Santa. It rained a great deal, and Gus said that it being too wet to be out much was a good opportunity for writing letters. They could each write to Mr Stibbings, Mrs Ford, Madame Tranchot, and Miss Fane. Rain and four letters to write was very depressing. If it had not been that they were both try-ing to please Gus, they would probably have grumbled. As it was, they only grumbled to each other.

'It's sickening, with the holidays nearly over,' said Peter.

Santa sucked her pen.
'And I can't find anything to say. I don't believe any of them ever saw a circus. And they're not travelled like us.'

There was one nice thing at Preston. They rode in the street parade.

It was Mr Cob's idea. He saw Peter and Santa hanging about outside the big top.

'Hallo,' he said. 'What are you two up to?'

They explained they were waiting to see the parade start.

Mr Cob looked at the sky. 'I'm not betting on there being one. Looks more like rain.'

'Goodness, I hope not,' said Santa. 'Of course it's always nice with a circus, but it's not as nice when it's raining.'

Mr Cob laughed.
'Glad you always find it nice. Some of these wet days I wish the whole contraption under the sea.' Then he looked at the children. 'How would you two like to ride on the coach?'

Peter and Santa got quite red with excitement. 'Might we?'

'Yes.' He nodded at Santa. 'You go along to the girls' dressing-tent. Tell the leader one of them can stay at home, and to fix you up with clothes.' He scratched his head and stared at Peter. 'What are we going to do with you? I have it. You find the coach boy. He'll have a spare coat and topper. If you're sitting, your breeks won't show.'

Half an hour later Santa and Peter climbed on to the coach. Santa had on a crinoline and bonnet, Peter a green coat and a top-hat. They were given the seat in the front beside Ben. Ben was looking very smart in a coat with a lot of collars, a top-hat, and yellow gloves. He nodded at them.

'Proper circus folk you're gettin'.'

'Which of the horses are you driving, Ben?' Santa asked.

Ben jerked his head towards Peter.

'You ask him. He's gettin' to know my' osses most as well as I do myself.'

Peter looked at the four. They were fairly well-matched bays.

'That's' – Peter pointed to the leader – 'Wisher; the one with him is Pie-crust; the one behind Wisher is Rainbow, and the other one is Whisky.'

Ben's lips tightened in a sort of smile. He looked pleased. Santa was startled at Peter being so clever. She knew Mustard by sight because she went with Peter to feed him every morning, but she was not positive she could have picked him out. As for these bays, she just knew they existed, that was all.

'My goodness! how did you know?' she whispered.

Peter kicked her ankle. Not hard, but just enough to make her shut up. He did not want Ben or the girls behind to hear Santa asking how he knew the horses' names. In the circus people did know things, and nobody thought it clever of them.

The girl Peter had opened the basket for at the pull-down was sitting behind them. She tapped Peter on the shoulder.

'Good morning, Little Lord Fauntleroy. Nice of you to honour the coach.'

Peter turned scarlet, but to Santa's surprise he did not lose his temper.

'Good morning,' he said. Then, after a pause, he added: 'I didn't know it was your coach, or I'd have thanked you for letting me ride on it.'

The other girls sitting round laughed, and so did Ben. Ben said:

'He's learnin', Rosa.'

Rosa seemed to like Peter for having had an answer ready. She was only about sixteen, and though as a dancer and acrobat she pretended to be grown-up, she was quite glad to talk to people near her own age. She had a bag of chocolates. She offered them to Peter and Santa.

'Have one. How are you liking living with us?'

Peter and Santa told her they were liking it very much. They went on to discuss the different towns they had been in, but Santa's mind was not on the conversation. Peter was changing. Only that short time ago when they ran away, people like the tomato man and Bill had found him odd. He had looked rather as if he did not want to know people. He still looked rather out of place in a circus, but much less than he had. Of course, knowing things made you feel much less queer. Fancy Peter knowing all the horses by sight. The people here would not think anything of that, but she knew, and so, she was sure, did Ben, that it was clever of a boy who a little less than a month before had never known a horse to speak to. She had a feeling like she always used to have before they came to live with Gus, that Peter was clever. She was proud of him. Lately she had not felt like that. She had begun to look upon herself as his equal. After all, neither of them knew anything, and on the whole, people found her less stupid than him. But now she did not feel his equal a bit. She did not know the names of the horses, and she would never have had an answer for Rosa, and she knew it.

Ben had been sitting with the ribbons loosely in his hands, but now he gathered them up. The float with the band on it was turning out into the road, playing a gay tune. Behind them, looking lovely and glossy, came Mustard, Tapioca, Coffee, Cocoa, Pepper, and Clove, with Mr Petoff, the Kenets, and Paula riding them, wearing smartly cut coats and breeches and bowler hats. Behind them came Gus in an awful old crock of a car. He wore a green coat with enormous white spots, a huge scarlet bow-tie, and a bowler hat with no top to it, through which his wig was sticking. He had a funny make-up, with a white face, scarlet nose, an immense mouth, and very long, curling eyelashes. Behind him came all the other clowns and augustes. Some were on stilts, one clown was riding an old penny-farthing bicycle, another was driving Peekaboo, who was cavorting about as if he were a new lamb. The rest were riding on a float, where they shot at each other with water pistols, and knocked each other down and were very funny. Behind them the ponies came spanking along drawing their little coach. Alexsis in a scarlet livery with a white-top-hat was leading them. Behind them trunk to tail came the elephants, with Kundra, in a gold suit, covered with what looked like precious stones, riding on the leader.

'Here's us,' said Ben. He made clicking sounds. The horses moved. The coach was in the procession.

It felt queer riding on a coach. Santa was frightened at first. She was afraid Peter would fall off. She was glad he was on the outside because she was quite certain she would not have held on for a minute. She was afraid the horses would bolt. Four horses seemed a lot for one man to be driving, especially a man as old as Ben. But presently she got used to the feeling, and then she began to enjoy it.

They came into the main streets. Everybody stopped what they were doing, to look. Everybody, no matter what they looked like before, began to smile. The children, in the streets and hanging out of the windows, roared with laughter. The police had to hold up the traffic. The people in their motor cars did not seem to mind; they hung out of the windows and laughed with everybody else. You could hear what was passing in front of people by the noises they made. There was conversation about the horses because everybody wanted to point out their good points to somebody else. There were roars of laughter for the clowns and augustes. There were cooing sounds of people saying: 'Aren't they sweet!' for the ponies, and again for the poodles, who were on the float behind the coach. There was a long 'Ooh!' for the elephants.

The excitement in the street was catching. Before long Peter and Santa were excited too. You could not help it. It was grand to be part of something which pleased such a lot of people. To be even a little bit of such a gay procession. To Peter and Santa it was lovely to see other children wishing they were them. To know they lived in the world where this sort of thing was always happening. That ahead of them, in Bolton and Oldham, children were reading the advertisements for next week. That in all the towns they were visiting between now and October, children were saying: 'The circus is coming! The circus is coming!'

13

'Mis'

It was in Sheffield in the third week in May that Mis got ill. The children heard of it when, with Fritzi and Hans, they went to fetch Fifi for school. Usually Fifi was dressed and ready, waiting to shake hands and say good morning in her polite way. Today there was not a sign of her, in spite of their knocking. Then suddenly she came running from the direction of the stables. Her face was white and her eyes red with crying.

'Something wrong was?' said Fritzi nervously. She gripped Peter's arm.

Usually Peter hated his arm held, but this time he was so worried he did not notice it.

It was quite a time before they could find out what had happened. The moment Fifi began to tell them she cried, and all they could hear was 'Mis'.

At last Fritzi asked a direct question:

'Mis was gone dead?'

Fifi raised her head.

'No, but she was very sick.'

Santa was sorry about Mis, but she could not think it would help if they were all late for school. She took Fifi's arm.

'I expect she'll get all right. Come on. Perhaps when we get back she'll be better.'

They were a very drooping procession going to school. Even Sasha and Olga, who joined them, had not the heart to do more than walk quietly. The illness of a dog of Mis's ability took the spirit out of them all.

'How did it start?' asked Olga. 'Santa and me and Peter was in front last night. Mr Cob passed us in. She wasn't ill then.'

'It must have started in the night. It was early in the morning that maman sat up. she woke papa. "Quick!" she said. "Mis is ill. I feel it here." ' Fifi clasped the place where her heart was, to show what her mother had done.

'How did she know?' Peter asked. 'Did she hear her whining?'

Olga, Sasha, Fritzi, Hans, and Fifi looked at him. Their faces showed they thought that he had said something very silly.

'With us,' Olga explained severely, 'our animals are the same as children. If a baby is put to bed its mother may go to sleep and not worry. But suddenly in the night she'll wake up, and some little thing that was different will come to her.

"My baby is ill," she'll say. Then she'll run. So it is with us.'

'Well, but Mis wasn't different last night,' Peter objected. 'We saw her. She was just the same as usual.'

'To you, yes,' Fifi agreed. 'But not to maman. And she was right.' She lowered her voice dramatically. 'Papa ran to the stables. He went to Mis's kennel. She lay still. At first he thought she was sleeping. Then he laid his hand on her. She was stiff and cold. She was unconscious.'

'Goodness!' Santa was appalled at the thought of energetic, lively Mis lying unconscious. 'What did your father do?'

'Maman had followed him. They picked Mis up. They wrapped her in blankets. They pour water on her head. Presently she opened her eyes. Then maman fed her with the white of an egg beaten with brandy. They feel her to see if she has any pain. They think that perhaps she has been poisoned.'

'Poisoned!' all the children exclaimed.

Fifi made a gesture to show that anything was possible.

'Where there is so great an artiste there is always jealousy.'

'Well, had she been?' asked Peter.

'No. That very day there had been new kennels. ~etter in front. It is impossible for anyone to pass ~ything through. Besides, Mis has no trouble inside. She has no fever. It is just that she's unhappy. She cries and cries. My papa fetches a vet. A very good vet. He can find nothing. But today she's no better. Her lovely coat doesn't shine. She won't eat. She won't drink.'

Sasha pulled her sleeve.

'Will she be in the show today?'

Fifi shrugged her shoulders and raised her hands.

'Who knows? She cannot go on the parade this morning. She won't leave her kennel.'

'Perhaps the air of Sheffield disagrees with her,' Santa suggested.

Fifi shook her head.

'It's worse than that. Sometimes it may be the place doesn't suit. But then a little powder and all is well. Maman says she remembers now that since Sunday when we arrived she has been quiet. Last night she thinks she was still more quiet.'

'Nobody has brought a dog near her, have they?' Olga asked. 'Could she have caught anything? You know, she might have.'

'Perfectly,' Fifi agreed. 'But if that was so she would have fever. Nor has she a chill. On Sunday, when the stables are built, there was a dip in the ground where the dogs are put to play when the menagerie is shown. So papa went to Monsieur Schmidt and asked if for this one week he will change places. So he puts his sea-lions at the end next to the elephants.'

Fritzi and Hans had heard of this change. Mr and Mrs Schmidt had agreed to it, but at home they had sniffed and said the fuss the Moulins made about their dogs was ridiculous. There had been no rain for days to make the dip damp. However, this was no moment to say anything about being fussy. Fritzi and Hans just looked at each other and said nothing.

After school they all hurried home. They followed Fifi to the stables. Both Mr Moulin and Lucille were sitting by Mis's kennel. The other dogs were playing about in an enclosure in the sun outside, but Mis lay in her basket with lack-lustre eyes. The children looked expectantly at Mr Moulin and Lucille. Lucille got up and came to them. Even in a moment of extremis like this she could not forget her manners.

'Good morning, Fritzi and Hans. Good morning, Peter and Santa.'

They all spoke at once.

'Good morning. How is Mis?'

Lucille shrugged her shoulders and raised her hands. Her eyes filled with tears.

'Ill.'

'What's the matter with her?' asked Santa.

Lucille sighed. 'Who can say? The vet can find nothing.'

'Perhaps it's a mood,' Olga suggested.

'That may be,' Lucille agreed. 'I have said I elieve she is suffering here.' She held her heart.

'But why should she?' Peter argued. 'Nothing's happened.'

Lucille sighed again.

'Who can say? With a great artiste it may be a little thing. They are such children. Once we have a dog; she was a dog from Holland. A very clever dog, but to us she was quiet. "She has no temperament, that one," I said. My husband said: "She has temperament, but she is a Hollander. Hollanders do not show how they feel." He was right. One day that dog is ill. She cannot eat. We try her with everything. Still she will not eat. The next day it is the same. She takes nothing, but nothing at all. That night I wake up. I wake my husband. I say: "I know how it is that Gretchen will not eat. Come, I will show you." We get up and go to the stables. The watchman brings us a light. Gretchen is asleep in her basket in her kennels. I have with me some bread in hot milk. I call "Vooruit Gretchen, vooruit!" Gretchen jumps up. She comes to me. She eats. You see how it was. We had that week finished teaching her to speak French. We taught her so well that we spoke it to her altogether. In the ring she would not mind, but now we were speaking it for her food. That made her homesick. She will not eat. After that we speak Hollander and she is not ill again.'

Peter looked puzzled.

'But you haven't talked anything but French to Mis, have you?'

'But no. But it may be some little thing has hurt her feelings. She is so sensitive, that one.'

Fifi took her mother's hand. 'Will she work today, maman?'

Lucille stooped and kissed Fifi's anxious face. 'Yes. She will work. She is the artiste born. It will be in the ring as if there was nothing wrong. Now you must smile, my little one. Come, I have a nice déjeuner waiting for you.'

Mis was able to work at both shows. She gave her usual witty performance. Whatever her trouble, she never let the audience know anything was wrong.

Early the next morning, when Peter went for his riding-lesson, he went to the kennels to inquire for her. Violette, Simone, and Marie were playing about in their enclosure outside. Mr Moulin was hanging their blankets up to air. There was no sign of Mis. Peter felt a sinking inside as if he was going down in a lift. No Mis. Had she died in the night? Mr Moulin saw what he was wondering.

'It's all right, Peter. We took her to sleep in the caravan.'

'Is she better this morning?'

Mr Moulin fastened leads on to Violette, Simone, and Marie. His face was sad.

'No.'

Nothing could take away Peter's pleasure in his 'ing lesson, but inside he had that dull ache you get when something is wrong, even if you are not actually thinking about it.

He was getting on well with his riding. He needed no help to mount Mustard now. Ben had taken away his stirrups. He did not believe you could make a rider unless you could trot without them.

'Movin' by slow ways, that's my method,' he said. 'No stirrups now, not till August. Before then I'll put you up on a lot of diff'rent 'osses. You got to ride 'em when they're lively, and difficult to handle. When I can put you on any 'oss in the stables and you can make him know from the beginnin' you're not one he can take liberties with, then we're getting somewhere.'

'What'll I do in August?' Peter asked.

Ben chewed his straw thoughtfully.

'Maybe I'll see how you shape at high-school.'

Peter was so surprised he felt as if somebody had hit him in the wind. Haute école, of which Alexsis had said: 'This is the most best work in riding.'

'Do you mean what the Kenets and Paula do?'

Ben nodded.

'By the time I was second head of the stables I was teachin' it. It's pretty work for the 'osses, and fine control for the riders.'

'But it's proper circus riding. Could I?'

Ben moved his straw across to the other side of his mouth.

'From all I hear, it wasn't always used in

circus. There was a gentleman come round once. Artist he was. Always paintin' the 'osses. Tented with us one or two summers. He telled me that time of Oliver Cromwell, you know him in the history books, his special bodyguard like was all trained in it. The artist he tells me it was a right good idea. He says the passes left and right was just the thing for fightin' with a sword.'

Peter tried to picture himself fighting with a sword on horse-back. He saw a mental figure of himself dressed as a Roundhead, his sword thrusting left and right. And as he moved, he saw the horse moving with him.

'It would be a good thing to do. It would be much better than an ordinary horse that only goes backwards and forwards.'

'That's right.' Ben sucked his straw meditatively. 'Mind you, it's true. I heard tell there was a statue to King Charles what had a 'oss doin' high-school work. So last time I was at the winter stables I takes a day off and goes up to see. I had the name of the place where it was wrote on a bit of paper.'

'Did you find it all right?'

Ben nodded.

'Very nice it was, too. Nicely trained the 'oss seemed. Must 'ave come hard on him posin' that long. It's 'ard enough to get a 'oss to hold his position while his photo's took. Shouldn't care for the job of keepin' 'im quiet while they made a statue of 'im.'

'Can I start at the beginning of August? When my holidays begin?'

'Maybe. We'll see how you shape. You keep your legs down better. Sittin' the way I often sees you, with your toes turned in, you couldn't use a spur. I'd 'ave me 'osses ripped raw.'

'You wouldn't!' Peter said indignantly.

Ben never noticed when people were cross; his voice was as slow and mild as usual.

'Couldn't 'elp it, son. If your toes is turned in, then you forces the calves of your legs out. Sittin' that way your 'oss won't feel your leg before the spur like he should. And when you 'ave to use the spur, it won't be a gentle touch like is proper, you'll 'ave to jab. Sittin' that way, you can't do nothin' else.'

Peter longed to argue. He was certain Ben was wrong. If he only had some spurs on he would show him. But it was a waste of time arguing with Ben. He never seemed to notice you were arguing. He never supposed anyone would want to argue with him about horses or riding.

After the lesson Peter went with Mustard to his stall. He gave him a pat and some carrots, and walked down the stables. He liked it in there. He knew most of the stable lads by name now. At this hour of the morning they were all about. Doing the stables. Cleaning the harness. Grooming the horses. The bereiters leading the different horses into the ring for exercise. There was a nice cheerful noise of hissing during the grooming. The horses stamped. There was a good smell of stables. Usually most of the men had a word to say, but this morning they were all gossiping among themselves. Peter stopped by the stable lad he knew best.

'Has something happened, Nobby?'

Nobby pretended to be intent on Magician's hind-legs, which he was brushing. He spoke quietly.

'There's trouble with one of the elephants. Kundra's in a rare takin'.'

'Which elephant?'

'Ranee. The little one on the end of the line.'

'What's the matter with her?'

'Turned nasty-tempered. Got at one of the men this morning and threw him down. If Mr Cob hears he won't let her won't let her work. He'd never 'ave one you couldn't trust in the ring.'

'But all the elephants are good-tempered. I always feed them.'

'Well, you better not get too near Ranee today, or you may get something you don't expect.'

'Funny her getting suddenly angry.'

Nobby gave Magician a slap.

'Get over, can't you!' He gave a glance in the direction of the elephants. 'It all comes of keepin' wild beasts. You give me 'orses. You knows where you are with them.'

Peter walked towards the elephants. Kundra

was there talking to the head keeper. From a cautious distance Peter had a look at Ranee. As far as he could see she was exactly as usual. She swayed from side to side. Her trunk was held out hopefully on the chance that some passer-by might have a fragment to give away.

'Well,' Kundra was saying, 'give her that with her food. Maybe the weather has upset her. These spring days are apt to get them a bit down.'

'Right,' the keeper agreed. He and Kundra went out of the tent. They were talking so hard they never noticed Peter.

From his safe position Peter went on looking at Ranee. He felt sorry for her. Perhaps she was feeling as Ben said Mustard felt in the early autumn. Ben said Mustard missed the smell of falling leaves and would go off his food. Was Ranee missing the smell of new plants coming up? Peter had very vague ideas about what sort of country elephants were used to. Jungles, he supposed. He did not know what grew in jungles, but whatever it was probably got new leaves in the spring. Perhaps Ranee was missing the smell of them. He felt in his pocket. He had a few carrots. There were always carrots in the caravan and he took some to give Mustard. These were spare ones. It would be nice to give them to Ranee to cheer her up. But he did not at all want to be thrown on the ground. He took a few steps forward. Ranee did not look cross. He took another few steps. He got the carrots out. Perhaps if she saw he was bringing carrots she would know he meant to be nice. Three more steps and he could reach her. He looked round. Nobody was about. If he went back to the caravan now nobody would know he had meant to give Ranee carrots and had not because he was afraid. He stood irresolute for a second. Should he go home? Then he looked at Ranee. She must have seen the carrots. It would be mean to take them away now. He took the steps forward. He held out his hand.

Ranee took the carrots. She put them in her mouth. She crunched them up. But although she ate them and seemed to enjoy them, Peter got the impression that titbits were not what she was asking for. He forgot to be frightened. He put his hand on her trunk. He had often done it to elephants before. Sometimes one of them would hold him so he had to pull to get free. Ranee did that now. She put her trunk round his arm. After a moment he gave a little pull to get free. She held him tighter. He gave his arm a tug. Ranee not only gripped him more firmly but pulled him towards her.

'Let go, Ranee.'

Ranee had no intention of doing anything of the sort. She drew Peter forward. His feet touched the wooden platform on which the elephants stood. He was cold with fright. Any moment he expected o be picked up and thrown on the ground.

He pulled. He struggled. But it's not much use struggling with an elephant.

'Let go, Ranee!' he gasped. 'Let go!'

He looked up. He was staring into her eyes. Elephants' eyes are not the sort most people admire. That small, pig-like shape is not handsome. Standing as close to them as Peter was he thought they looked awful. Then suddenly he saw something in them which surprised him. He had thought they looked fierce and cruel. Now, seeing them more closely, he saw they were miserable. He was so sorry for her he forgot the way she was treating him.

'Poor Ranee,' he said. 'Poor old girl.'

It looked as if a little sympathy was just what Ranee was wanting. As suddenly as she had gripped his arm, she let it go. Peter, instead of moving out of her range, stood where he was. He fondled her trunk. He looked round. What could she be miserable about? The stable was as usual. On the left the ponies munched their breakfast. On the right came pleased hoarse barks from the sealions' wagon. Then suddenly he had an idea.

Kundra and the keeper came back. They stood staring at Peter. Kundra came forward gently.

'Don't be frightened, Peter. Move slowly backwards away from Ranee. She's in a bad mood this morning.'

Peter stayed where he was. He went on fondling Ranee's trunk.

'I know, but I don't believe she has a bad mood. I think she's unhappy.'

'Maybe.' Kundra still talked in a quiet voice. 'But do what I say. Come towards me slowly.'

Peter still did not move. He looked round again at the sealions' wagon. He was shy of saying what he thought because, of course, everybody in the circus knew about animals and he did not.

'Could an elephant be fond of a dog?'

Kundra and the keeper knew at once what he meant. They looked at the sea-lion wagon standing in the position where the poodles always played.

'I wonder,' said Kundra. 'Something's upset Mis.'

The keeper nodded.

'D'you remember that lion we had out with us? The Rajah of Bong? Remember that little fox-terrier he had along of him? Had to live in his cage?'

'It can happen,' Kundra agreed. 'There's been some funny friends. My father had one elephant which palled up with a pony.'

'Shall I fetch Mr Moulin?' the keeper suggested.

'Yes.' Kundra beckoned to Peter. 'Come on, son. You may be right, but she's bashed one of the men's arms this morning and we don't want to take you to hospital too.'

Peter gave Ranee a final pat. He moved away from her. She made no effort to hold him. He had a feeling she had been listening to the conversation and was pleased with him.

A smell of bacon blew in through the tent door. It woke Peter up to the time.

'Do you know what the time is?'

Kundra looked at his watch.

'Ten minutes past eight.'

'Goodness!' Peter started to run. 'I shall be late for breakfast.'

'Aren't you going to wait and see if you're right about Mis?'

'I can't,' Peter called over his shoulder. 'I have to go to school.'

Peter scuttled out of his jodhpurs and into his shorts. He raced across to the caravan. Gus and Santa were having breakfast.

'What's happened to you?' said Gus. 'Breakfast is eight when there's school, and you know it.'

'Sorry.' Peter helped himself to bacon and eggs. 'I was talking to the elephants.'

Santa gave his back a shocked look. Peter was getting into very bad habits, she thought. He need not have told Gus he had been riding, but he could have said feeding the horses. He always gave Mustard carrots, so it would be true.

Never had Peter so hated going to school. To make it worse Fifi stayed away, at least when they went to fetch her she was not in the caravan.

Nobody was there. Fritzi and Hans, who were with Peter and Santa, looked disgusted.

'Such a fuss about that dog to make. Mine father say she not ill was,' Fritzi muttered.

'It was true,' Hans agreed. 'She was spoilt.'

'I don't believe it,' Santa argued. 'You don't faint just because you're spoilt.'

'But yes,' Hans explained. 'When there is temperament it might be.'

Peter said nothing. He looked towards the stables. He wished he was there. He could not tell the others what he thought was wrong. Somehow, now that he was out of doors, doing a prosaic thing like walking to school, the idea seemed ridiculous. They would probably laugh.

Fifi came to school late. Peter did not, of course, see her until they were going home.

'Imagine,' she called out, as Peter, Sasha, and Hans joined herself, Santa, Olga, and Fritzi. 'Mis is well. It was an affair of the heart. She has such affection, that little one. And she had given it to Ranee. Nobody knew. Always they have been placed side by side. Now she is back by her friend and all is well.'

'What, Ranee the elephant?' asked Hans.

'Yes,' Fifi agreed, prancing up the road. 'It was at breakfast. There comes a knock on our door. Maman hold her heart. She has a migraine since Mis is ill. She cannot bear any noise.'

Olga turned a cartwheel.

'Was it Ranee come to say she was missing Mis'

Sasha giggled. He did a flip-flap.

'Did Ranee and Mis kiss each other?'

'Imbecile!' Fifi retorted. 'No, it was the keeper. He come to say that Kundra and he have a thought.'

Peter gasped.

'He came to say what?'

Fifi sighed at his stupidity.

'He came to tell us of he idea that Ranee and Mis might be friends.'

Peter could not believe it.

'He said that he and Kundra had thought of it?'

Fifi nodded.

'But yes. Who else?'

Directly they got to the ground Peter hurried to the stables. The sea-lions had been moved. The poodles were back in their old playground by the elephants. A lot of people who had paid to see the menagerie were passing through. It took a minute before Peter could get close to the poodles' enclosure. When he got there he found Kundra talking to Lucille and Mr Moulin.

'But it was wonderful,' said Lucille. 'How was it we did not think? You have a pretty great understanding of animals, monsieur.'

Kundra smiled in a pleased way.

'Oh, well, I've been in the business a long time. One senses things, you know.' He stopped, catching Peter's eye. He turned red.

The Moulins, after saying a few more polite words, moved off to have their déjeuner. Kundra looked at Peter. He grinned.

'I know, son. But it's no good my saying you thought of it. It's no good to you. You aren't going to train elephants,'

'What good is it to you?'

'Mr Cob is thinking of renewing our contract for another three years.'

'Oh!' Peter stopped feeling angry. It was not fair of course, but at least Kundra was not pretending with him.

Kundra felt in his pocket. He brought out a pound note. He handed it to Peter.

'Spend that. You've done me a good turn.'

Kundra went out of the stables. Peter stared at the note. He did not really want it, though, of course, it was grand to have money to spend. But he hated having been given it in exchange for what was a sort of lie. He liked Kundra and wished he had not pretended. Then he looked at Mis and Ranee. Mis had her paws on the fence dividing the poodles from the elephants. Her tongue was hanging out. She looked her amusing gay self. Ranee had her head turned towards her. It was obvious the friends were having a good gossip.

Peter put the note in his pocket. What did it

matter who had thought that separating them might be the trouble? All that really mattered was that Mis and Ranee were their old selves again. He walked off whistling.

14

Making Plans

Cob's Circus was moving south. It was a slow sort of moving because often they went backwards. The last week in May they were at Lincoln and Leicester. Then they went a little north again and spent a week in Nottingham. From there they went to Stoke and Burton-on-Trent. Then north again to Chester and Crewe. Then in the last week in June they went over the border into Wales. The first stops there were Rhyl and Colwyn Bay.

Peter and Santa got so used to their wandering life that they hardly knew in which town they were. They liked the week stands best. It was fun moving on to a new town with the caravan trailing behind the car, but once a week was enough. There was something extra nice about the Sundays at Blackpool, Sheffield, and Nottingham. The build-up finished, a kind of settled feeling came over everybody. It was done for the week. Tenting made you feel a week was an enormous time to spend in any place.

When they got to Wales a new feeling came over the circus. It was lovely weather. They were going to do the seaside towns. This would be tenting at its nicest, with bathing parties and long afternoons lying in the sun.

Gus was a surprising man. Neither Peter nor Santa felt they were making any headway as to his needing them. He was exactly as he was the first time they met him. Practical, taking them as a matter of course, but showing not a sign as to whether he liked having them or not. He got on a shade better with Peter, but then Peter argued less. What with school and his riding lessons and the way he was getting to know the grooms and tent-men, he had less time. Besides, though he had no idea of it, he had changed. He never now thought anything not good enough for him. To everybody in the circus he was just 'Gus's nephew'. Feeling just Gus's nephew was as catching as Aunt Rebecca's idea that they were too grand to know anybody. Of course being just Gus's nephew was rather humbling. All the other children had a future in the circus world. They might not be anybody yet, but they would be. But Peter and Santa did not really belong. What they liked best was when people treated them as if they did. There was no sign from Gus what he meant to do with them later on, so it was comforting when other people behaved as if they would be with him always. The first really hopeful sign that he was fond of them came when they crossed the Welsh border. That was why he was so surprising, you never knew what he was thinking. It was on the Sunday at Rhyl. They were eating their stew.

'Time you kids had a summer rig-out,' said Gus, 'and bathing things.'

Santa helped herself to some butter.

'I've got two more cotton frocks like this, and Peter's got a grey flannel suit. You don't do much about it being summer in London, except not wearing a coat.'

Gus ate a moment in silence. Then he looked up.

'The other kids wear a practice dress playing around here. Might as well have one of them too.'

'Might I?' Santa beamed at him. 'I borrow one of Fritzi's sometimes. It's green. What I would like is a blue one.'

Peter felt Santa was accepting everything too easily.

'Well, but if Gus is going to buy us bathing things, he won't want to get you one of those as well.'

'Cabbages and cheese!' said Gus. 'Why not? I'm coming to you in a minute, Peter. No need to be jealous if I buy Santa a few things.'

Santa put her hand on Gus's.

'My dear Gus, Peter and I are never jealous of each other. He just meant I mustn't let you spend too much money.'

'If I couldn't afford it I wouldn't have offered, would I?' Gus grumbled.

After that small disagreement they had a cheerful lunch. It seemed as though Gus had been thinking about clothes most seriously. He liked Santa's cotton frocks for school, although by Aunt Rebecca's standards they were on the short side. But he did not like to see her in socks and shoes. The other girls had bare legs and sandals and he thought she should too. Then he thought the blue one-piece play-suit a good idea for wearing about the ground.

'You kids are always standing on your heads,' he said. 'May as well look neat to do it.'

He had strong views, too, on bathing dresses. He had, it seemed, had a talk about them with Mrs Moulin.

'You may as well get good stuff for bathing in and make it last. Lucille Moulin tells me the cheap bathing things stretch. She says she'll take you both out shopping and get something made of decent wool and a couple of those bath wraps so you don't mess up all the towels. And something strong in the way of a bathing-cap for you, Santa. Your hair's neat now you plait it. Don't want it full of sea-water.'

Santa stared at him.

'I never knew you knew I had plaited it, Gus. You never said anything about it.'

'Why should I? If I don't say nothing it don't mean I haven't seen nothing. My old dad, your grandfather, used to say: "Seeing's better than speaking." '

'Not always it isn't,' Peter objected. 'If you saw somebody being burnt in a fire it's no good just seeing, you'd have to speak too or they wouldn't be saved.'

'That's seeing and speaking. You see, my old dad, your grandfather, was a gardener. He'd just go round his plants looking. He never needed to say much. He could see if his plants wasn't doing well.'

Peter got up and helped himself to more stew.

'That's like Ben and the horses. He can see in a minute if anything's wrong with any of them.'

Gus passed his plate.

'Fill mine up while you're there.' He looked at Peter as he took his refilled plate. 'You'll want some more grey shorts and some of these short-sleeved shirts Hans wears. When we're in Tenby next week you can slip along after school and buy them.'

Peter said: 'Thank you.' Inside he felt that swollen feeling you get when people are extra kind. It was so nice of Gus to say he could go alone. He was quite capable of buying those sort of things by himself, but he was not sure if Gus knew it.

After lunch Peter and Santa washed up outside. Gus went to sleep. Santa stood with her hands in the basin looking at Peter. It was an inquiring face she made. Peter made a Fifi shrug in answer. Santa went on, as if they had spoken:

'He must like us a little.'

'They're only summer things,' Peter pointed out. 'It doesn't say what he's doing with us after tenting.'

Santa washed a plate and handed it to him.

'I believe he's beginning to like us.'

Peter dried the plate.

'He might be,' he agreed. 'At least he notices what we wear. I never knew he did that.'

Santa leant over the basin.

'He's got a birthday in August. It's when we're at Torquay. On the Wednesday.'

'It's all one-week stands then. We shan't have to move.'

'No.' Santa passed over another plate. 'I thought perhaps we could do something. We've a little money left, haven't we?'

'No. Gus took it. It's to help get our things out of pawn when we go back to London.'

'Oh!' Santa washed the third plate gloomily. 'You can't do much without money.'

'I've got a pound.'

'A pound!' Santa nearly dropped the plate

she was passing to him. 'How ever did you get that?'

Peter fixed her with his eyes.

'Will you swear to keep a secret?'

Santa took her hand from the basin. She held up her first finger. 'See this wet.' She dried it on her frock. 'See this dry.' She drew it across her throat. 'Cut my throat if I lie.'

Peter was satisfied. Nobody would tell a secret after a vow like that. And as a matter of fact he trusted Santa anyway. He told her about Mis and Ranee. Santa was furious.

'How dreadfully mean of Kundra. And I always thought he was nice.'

Peter dried a knife.

'I didn't mind. With a pound we could get Gus a lovely birthday present.'

'But don't you want it?'

Peter put the knife down and took up another.

'I was going to get some jodhpurs, but it doesn't matter because Alexsis goes on lending me his. I don't think he wants them really. They are too small for him and too big for Sasha.'

Santa swished the soap-flakes into a better foam.

'I think we'd better ask all the others what's the best thing to do for a birthday. Perhaps we could give Gus a party.'

'Not if people don't usually have parties for their

birthdays in a circus,' Peter objected. 'We've been living with Gus nearly three months and never had a birthday party yet.'

'Children do.' Santa plunged the teapot into the water. 'Hans and Fritzi had one just before we came.'

'I don't believe grown-ups do,' said Peter, 'but we'll ask.'

But what with school, and all the other things there were to do, the days slipped by. It was not until they got to Carmarthen that they caught all the children doing nothing, and had a chance to hold a meeting about birthdays.

It was a wet Saturday. They were playing in the big top. Peter beckoned mysteriously. Hans and Fritzi came at once. Fifi grumbled a little because she had on a new frock and thought it a pity to sit in a corner where no one could see it. Olga and Sasha had to be fetched. Sasha only came because he could walk on his hands to the seats where they were sitting.

'What is it, Peter?' said Fifi. 'Why should we sit here?'

Peter looked at Santa. She made a face at him to say he should do the telling. He explained about Gus's birthday and said he had got a pound. He did not make any suggestion how it should be spent because he wanted to know what they thought would be suitable.

'A pound!' said Fifi. 'But that is magnificent. Gus can have a beautiful fête.'

'Yes, but what shall we do?' Santa asked.

Hans counted on his fingers.

'Next week is Cardiff. That is one week. Then Bath. That is two weeks. Then it is Taunton. That is three weeks. Then Exeter. That is four weeks. Which day is the birthday?'

'Wednesday,' said Peter.

'One month and three days before the birthday we have,' Fritzi announced.

Santa gave her a look. Of course they had asked everybody's advice as to the best way of keeping a birthday, but that did not mean that they wanted Fritzi to take it on as if it was the birthday of *her* uncle. The way she said 'we' sounded very much as if she would.

'We must sing,' Hans suggested. 'A song for his birthday we must write. Very early outside the caravan will we it sing.'

Peter looked doubtful.

'Gus doesn't like to be woken early.'

Fritzi dismissed the suggestion.

'On his birthday he will not mind.'

Olga stood on her head. She leant against the nearest chair.

'Your mother will make a beautiful cake, Fritzi.'

'Maman will make some little ones,' Fifi broke in, 'the same as she made for your birthdays.' She nodded at the twins.

'Then,' said Olga, 'we will have a lovely picnic. We will make a fire. My mother has a samovar. Perhaps she'll lend it.'

Sasha hopped about with excitement.

'And after we've eaten we will give Gus a concert. Each of us will perform.'

'Except Peter and Santa,' Fritzi reminded them. 'They can nothing do.'

'But naturally not,' Fifi agreed. 'That is understood.'

'Could we—' Sasha was so pleased with his idea he lost his voice. 'Could we spend the pound on fireworks?'

'Certainly,' said Fritzi approvingly. 'That was a very good idea, Sasha. We will fireworks have.'

'Feu d'artifice!' Fifi gasped, carried away by the glory of the idea.

'But—' said Peter.

'What will you do at the concert, Fifi?' Sasha asked.

Fifi got up.

'I will practise. I will work out some little thing.'

Fritzi turned to Hans.

'We will together work.'

'So,' Hans agreed. 'And our father shall write the song.'

Olga, who had been walking on her hands, suddenly sprang the right way up.

'Come, Sasha. You remember that floor show

we did at Christmas for the charity for children? We'll do that.'

Sasha was enchanted. He dashed down to the ring.

'Come on then. Let's practise.'

Peter and Santa, left alone, stared at each other.

'I think a pound is an awful lot to spend on fireworks, don't you?' Santa suggested.

Peter nodded. Then he sat down and took out a piece of paper from his pocket.

'Let them get on with the singing and the picnic and the concert. Here's a list of things I thought of.'

Santa looked over his shoulder. She read:

Mascot for car. To fix over the radiator cap.

A pipe.

New driving gloves.

Ties.

Thermos flask.

'I think the new driving gloves.'

Peter put the list back in his pocket.

'So do I.'

'We'll have to spend some money on things to eat at the picnic.'

Peter looked worried.

'I know. I wish we hadn't asked them. I believe Gus will hate that sort of fuss.'

15

Gus's Birthday

The weather grew nicer and nicer. Of course there were wet days, but they sank into the background, and the sunny ones stood out. Gus bought a tent and Santa slept in it. Just at the beginning she was a little nervous. She thought: 'Suppose the lions should escape,' or: 'Suppose a burglar should come. Would Gus hear?' But after a day or two she got to love it. It was like having a house of her own. She got fussy about how it looked. She tied a picture up, and put flowers in a vase. The hot days they had all their meals outside. So did everybody else. The tables were set between the caravans, and the most enchanting smells of other people's dinners floated up the line, as did cheerful conversations in various languages. When the children came back from afternoon school they would find everybody resting in the sun. Of course the shows came first, and nobody forgot that was what they were there for. All the same, tenting began to feel more and more like a never-ending picnic.

Peter and Santa were busy. Peter, of course, had his riding lessons before school. He was getting on well, and there was not a horse trained to a saddle that he had not been on. Nor one of the more difficult ones he had not fallen off. Ben liked people to fall off now and again.

'It's like life,' he said. 'You goes along all confident thinkin' all's going nice. Then one day somethin' happens and you fall on your nose. When you gets up you're careful for a time. Watch where you're goin' so you don't trip. It's the same with 'osses. You get so easy you gets careless. Then the 'oss stumbles or rears a bit at something and off you come. I never could abide a rider what treated a 'oss like he was a bed. Somethin' just to go to sleep on.'

Santa had her exercises to do for Ted Kenet. She meant to do those before breakfast. She did for a bit, and then slacked off. People were always passing when she was going to work. It was more fun gossiping with the milkman or the postman, or helping somebody clean a car, than limbering up. Besides, she had got far more supple since she had occasional lessons from Ted Kenet, so she did not really think there was need for her to work.

Both Peter and Santa had less and less free time. Even the bit from after school to bed was partly filled up. Now they were at seaside towns Gus was having them taught to swim. He employed one of the ring-hands called Syd to teach them. Syd took Gus's commission very seriously. For three days at Carmarthen, a week each at Cardiff, Bristol, and Bath, he had them for half an hour, lying balanced on upturned wooden boxes, practising their strokes.

'Half an hour has to do for now,' he said. 'What with your school, and me bein' wanted in the top, we 'aven't more time. But I reckon on the first two weeks in August at Exeter and Taunton when you 'ave holidays to get you into fine trim. So when we gets to Torquay it won't take more'n a couple of lessons to have you like fishes.'

Peter and Santa did not say anything to Syd, but away from him they groaned. Learning to swim in the sea is all very well. Swimming week after week on a wooden box is a terrible bore. The thought that they were to do more of it when the holidays began was unbearable.

Both Peter and Santa hoped that if they said no more about it the plans for Gus's birthday would die. But they were reckoning without Fritzi. Fritzi was not the sort of person who believed in plans dying. Almost every day, either going or coming from school, she mentioned them.

'How was your practice, Fifi?'

'Such children as you, Olga and Sasha, must

hard work. It most unsuitable is that work that is careless should before Gus be done.'

'Mine mother will buy the icing sugar for the cake of Gus to make.'

She never mentioned the fireworks again, but Peter and Santa expected every day that she would.

'I wish we could just buy the driving gloves, and then if they ask for money for the fireworks, say it's gone,' said Santa.

Peter did not bother to answer. Although after nearly four months of living in a circus they were getting more confidence, they still had not enough to risk annoying all the other children. There had been some short-lived quarrels that they had seen, and they knew how quickly other people who had nothing to do with the original row took sides. If the Petoffs and the Schmidts and Fifi Moulin managed to persuade their families they had been badly treated over the fireworks, it was possible a whole lot of other people would side with them, and that would mean that they would be ostracized for quite a time, and perhaps Gus too, a situation too awful to be contemplated.

The school holidays began while they were at Bath. Santa met Ted Kenet as she was coming back from the last day of school.

'Holidays start tomorrow, don't they?' he asked.

Santa skipped along beside him. She was so

pleased it was holidays her feet simply would not walk.

'Yes.'

'What are you kids going to do with yourselves?'

'Well, Syd's teaching Peter and me to swim; he's going to give us extra swimming on a box so when we get to Torquay we'll be able to go straight in and swim.'

Ted laughed. He took his bag of sweets out of his pocket. He handed them to Santa.

'Bet you don't.'

Santa took a sweet.

'So do I. But that's what he says. We hope we'll be able to soon, because until we can we mayn't go on the beach except for a swimming lesson.'

Ted sucked thoughtfully.

'How's my exercises going?'

Santa stooped and pretended to do up her sandal while she thought of a good answer to that. After all, she reasoned, even if she could not say she had worked hard, she could say they were going well. If they were not, how was she so much more supple than she had been?

'Very nicely, thank you.'

'Practising every day?'

Santa took a deep breath.

'Well, of course, I can't always. You see, there's school, and then we wash up for Gus, and there's my tent to tidy, and—'

'You haven't been working?' Ted interrupted.

'Oh, I have sometimes, but not every day.'

'I see. How long since your last lesson?'

Santa considered.

'The Sunday at Tenby.'

Ted thought a moment.

'Tenby and Carmarthen, Cardiff, Bristol. That's a month next Sunday. Come in the big top tomorrow round about half past eleven. We'll see how you've been getting on.'

Santa practised twice before her lesson. Before she went to bed that night, and before breakfast. She could catch hold of her heels now and raise her legs above her head like all the others did. It was true her knees still had a bit of bend in them, but she did not think it showed much. She could sit on the ground and hold her ankles and almost knock her forehead on her knees. She could bend down and without bending her knees put first her palms and then the backs of her hands on the ground. She could lie on the ground and raise herself on her arms while she raised her legs, and almost touch the back of her head with the soles of her feet, but not quite. She could stand in a hoop with the palms of her hands and the soles of her feet on the ground, but only for a second; she could not hold the position. In fact, she was beginning to do a lot of things she had not been able to do when she came to the circus. She was beginning to think herself something of an acrobat.

Ted was waiting for her in the morning when she got to the big top. He and Gus were working every morning now for something new they were planning for Christmas. He was in his practice things and dressing-gown. He was drinking sarsaparilla. He tapped his glass.

'You ought to see Gus has some of this. Do him good.'

Santa stepped over the ring fence. She made a mark in the sawdust with her toe.

'Does his blood need cooling?'

Ted took a gulp of drink.

'Must do. 'Tisn't natural it shouldn't this hot weather.' He put down his glass and came and sat on the ring fence. 'Now then, off you go. We haven't much time, the Elgins are coming to work at twelve. Do your exercise routine. Then the back-bends.'

Usually Santa had to work somewhere outside. Only the artistes had the right to work in the ring, though nobody minded the children using it if it were not wanted. Santa loved practising in the ring. It made her feel like a real acrobat. She liked the circus smell of animals and sawdust. As she bent backwards she could see the tiers and tiers of seats. Anybody in a proper practice dress lying in the ring trying to make the soles of her feet touch the back of her head would have been able to imagine crowds of people watching.

Santa imagined it so hard that when she got up she took a slight skip forward and held her palms upward. Almost as she did it she could hear the roars of applause.

'What's that for?' asked Ted.

Santa came down to earth with a bump. She turned red.

'I don't know. It's how the others end their practice.'

Ted got up. He wrapped his dressing-gown round him.

'Well, so long.'

Santa stared at him.

'Aren't you going to teach me a new exercise?'

Ted walked towards the artistes' entrance.

'No. I'm not bothering no more.'

Santa jumped over the ring fence. She ran after him and caught him by the arm.

'But why, Ted?'

Ted stopped.

'When I said I'd show you how to tumble I thought you really wanted to know. I didn't know you only wanted to fool around.'

'But I don't. I want to learn frightfully.'

Ted moved off again.

'Funny way of showing it.'

Santa gripped hold of his dressing-gown.

'Do stand still. You might tell me what you mean.'

Ted hesitated. Then he came back. He climbed

under the barrier and sat down. He patted the chair next to him.

'All right.' He handed Santa his sweets and took one himself. 'I'm a pro., see. I told you how I was born in my grand-dad's circus. I learnt to walk pushing one of those big balls, we use clowning, round the ring. There was never a time when I fooled around learning to do anything, and I don't figure to start doing it now.'

'If you mean I'm fooling around,' said Santa indignantly, 'you're wrong.'

'Maybe, from the way you look at it,' Ted agreed mildly. 'But me, I don't understand bothering with anything unless you mean to work at it.'

'I have worked.'

'Worked!' Ted's voice was full of scorn. 'You don't know what work is. From what Gus tells me it isn't your fault. You were brought up all wrong. He says you two came here supposing you'd just be fed and looked after until you were older and then jobs found for you.'

'Well, what else can children do?'

'Work. Time I was your age I had it all clear what I was going to do.'

'But you were born in a circus. You were trained by the time you were little.'

'That's right; but if I hadn't been I'd have known what I was about. You take Peter. He'll be old enough to be on his own soon. What's he going to do?'

Santa wriggled on her chair.

'I don't know. I suppose Gus'll find him something.'

'Well, what? You're neither of you any good at your schooling from what I hear.'

Santa sighed.

'No, we're not. We're very bad, both of us.'

Ted sucked his sweet a moment without speaking.

'You know, I don't understand you kids. If I wasn't any good at my books, I'd start practising up for something I could do. I wouldn't want to be pushed into some job just because I hadn't worked at anything special.'

'Everybody can't be good at something.'

'Yes, they could. Now supposing you thought you'd like to be a cook. Your grandmother was, wasn't she?' Santa nodded. 'Is there any reason why you shouldn't be a good one?'

'Gus does the cooking. He doesn't like me doing it much.'

'I bet if you said to him you wanted to do it on account you hoped to be a cook some day he'd let you fast enough. But he won't want you fooling at it. That's what I mean about this tumbling. You say you'd like to learn now. I say: "Right, I'll show you." Well, there's a chance for you. I know what I'm doing. You got a good chance to learn to do it first class. I don't say it'll be any good to you. But they have people to teach exercises in these schools. Might come in handy. Anyway, no good wasting my time fooling at it.'

'I'm not,' said Santa.

Ted handed her his bag of sweets.

'Take another, and don't talk so foolish. If you'd practised even half an hour every other day you'd show it. You haven't.' He looked at her. 'Have you?'

Santa looked at her sandals.

'No.'

'All right. No need to look ashamed about it. It's just a game to you. No need why you should work. But if it's a game no point in me troubling to show you how. The other kids can do that.'

Santa looked at him out of the corner of her eye.

'I don't want it to be a game. I want to learn to do it properly.'

'Enough to practise half an hour?'

'Yes.'

Ted got up.

'Right. Come outside and let's see you touch your feet a dozen times.'

After her lesson Santa went to look for Peter. She knew she would find him in the stables. He spent all his spare time there. He was leaning against one of the tent props watching Nobby clean some harness. Santa came and stood beside him.

'What d'you want?' said Peter.

'I just thought you might walk round with me a bit.'

Peter gave her a look. If she said a thing like that she must want to talk about something. He followed her outside.

They skipped over the guy-ropes. They went between the forage tent and the men's kitchen. They sat down on the ground at the back of the staff wagons.

'Have you thought what you're going to do when you leave school?' Santa asked. To her surprise he did not say at once 'No' and 'Why should I?' and then change the subject. Instead he said:

'Why?'

She told him about her talk with Ted. She found it a relief telling Peter because, of course, with him she did not have to pretend she had worked. He knew quite well she had not. Peter did not answer at once. Then he put his arms round one of his knees. His voice was embarrassed, as though she were dragging a secret from him.

'I'm going to be a groom.'

'A groom! What, like one of the men in the stables?'

Peter nodded.

'There's no need to sound grand about it. Our father was. Anyway, it's a jolly good job. You can ride the horses when you like.'

Santa just stared at him. In the old days she had known what he was thinking about things, even though they never talked about them. But now Peter seemed changed and she never knew. Fancy him thinking he would be a groom. It was only a little time ago that he had been angry to find their father had been one. She was changing too, she knew. But all the same not enough to make her think being a cook like her grandmother would be a good thing to do; when Ted had spoken of it she had taken it for granted he was joking.

'Would you try to be one in the circus?'

He shook his head.

'No. Not to begin with. They don't have boys of fifteen. I've talked to some of them. Nobby and some of the others. They say the best chance for a boy would be in private work, where somebody keeps hunters.'

'Could you get that?'

Peter picked a grass. He put it in his mouth.

'I think it's the thing I'd get easiest. All those people, the duchess and that Lady Vansittart, are just the sort of people who keep grooms.'

Santa stared in front of her. She saw the sitting-room in London, just after Aunt Rebecca died, when they were so miserable.

'Do you remember our lessons?'

'It was lucky we came away. We were awful fools.'

Santa thought of school.

'Are you getting cocky? We aren't all that bright now.'

Peter threw himself on her. He rolled her over and tickled her.

'Pax!' she screamed. 'Pax!'

'Not till you say you're sorry for calling me cocky.'

'I am,' she wheezed. Peter let her go. She sat up. 'Fancy me calling any one cocky who only wanted to be a groom.' Peter made a move to roll her over once more. She stopped him. 'No. I won't say it again. How are you going to get to them as a groom? Will you write to that Lord Bronedin?'

'When I get a chance I'm going to ask Gus to write. That Mr Stibbings asked if the annuity could go on is all they know about us. But they might remember Gus. At least the old ones would.'

'Is it because you want to be a groom you're always in the stables?'

Peter got up.

'Partly.'

'What else?'

'It's the horses. They're much more interesting than people, and much easier. They aren't different every day.'

They began strolling back towards the caravan. Santa stopped to pick a daisy.

'Nor are people.'

'Yes, they are. When they have a mood they feel angry inside and then they're angry with somebody else to work it off. When a horse has a mood he's just miserable. He doesn't get angry with other people.'

Santa stuck the daisy through the wool of her practice dress.

'Well, you can have them. I like horses all right, but I can't tell them apart. Their faces are so alike,'

Peter snorted with disgust at such a silly statement. Then he stopped and sniffed.

'What's for dinner?'

'It's chicken. I'd forgotten. Goodness, I'm hungry. Let's run.' On the Sunday at Taunton directly the build-up was finished Peter went to find Ben. He found him in the stables. He was leaning against a post staring at Canada. He was chewing his usual straw. He did not look up, but Peter knew that he realized he was there.

'Mr Cob's gettin' rid of old Canada here.'

Peter was horrified. He had come to feel getting rid of a horse was like getting rid of a child.

'Why?'

'He's going to America. We had six other greys we sold there.'

'But why? He's very good in the liberty act. He does a decapo.'

Ben moved his straw over to the other side of his mouth.

'One of the other 'osses can do that, son. We're breaking in a whole lot more greys before next tenting. Maxim and Mr Cob, they want sixteen of them.'

'Well, then, they'll need Canada.'

'No. He's not as good a match as the others. Matchin' up well is a lot to do with smartness in the ring.'

'When's he going?'

'Couple of weeks. I'll be sending one of my boys with him.'

Peter looked at Canada with pity.

'I do hope he won't hate it.'

Ben nodded.

'So do I. Never could bear to sell a 'oss I'd had any time.'

'But what's Lorenzo going to do without him?'

'Or 'im without Lorenzo. That's what I've been tellin' Mr Cob. He says they'll settle, but I says I doubts it. I broke both of them. Never been parted, they haven't.'

'Poor Canada!'

'It's more Lorenzo what's troublin' me. Seems like the one that's left always feels it most. Canada, he'll 'ave strange people and all that. Lorenzo will jus' stand and look at Canada's stall. I don't like it.'

'Couldn't they both go?'

Ben nodded.

'They could. They was wantin' a pair for America, but Mr Cob, 'e says "No." 'E's a wonderful waltzer, is Lorenzo, and he won't part with 'im.'

Peter gave Lorenzo a pat. He felt in his pockets for some sugar for him and Canada. He went into Canada's stall and fondled him while he fed him. He looked at Ben over his shoulder.

'Do you know it's August this week?'

'I'aven't forgotten.' He smiled. 'I don't think I said beginnin' of August, did I?'

'No. You said you'd see how I shaped. Am I shaping better?'

Ben spat out his straw.

'Yes. We'll start tomorrow. I'm going to have a doss down now. Didn't get much sleep. Seemed to be shuntin' us all last night.'

Peter looked after him. He felt swollen with happiness. Tomorrow he would start haute école. He would be allowed to try if he could make a horse obey every little movement that he made. To take a horse through that difficult routine must be the grandest feeling in the world.

He looked at President. He went across and gave him a friendly pat.

'It must be awful to be him,' he thought. 'Too proud to have a friend in the world.' Careful to keep well away from his heels, he sidled up the stall and gave him a lump of sugar. President ate the lump. Peter thought he looked surprised. As a matter of fact he was. It was a long time since anybody had singled him out for special attention. Not knowing Peter was starting to learn high-school riding in the morning, he wondered what he was celebrating.

What with Peter not having wanted her at his early riding lessons, and afterwards because she had other things to do Santa had never watched one. But at Exeter she was there by accident. Since Ted Kenet's talk on work she got up at half past seven and did her exercises before breakfast. There was an alarm clock which woke her. It was in a drawer in the caravan doing nothing and Gus said she could borrow it for her tent. This morning it went off as usual. She yawned and stretched and got out of bed. She poured some water into her basin. Washing was one of the few things about tenting she did not like. Even in the middle of August she hated cold water. She shivered as it ran down her. Having washed, she brushed and plaited her hair. She put on her practice dress. It was then she heard the pit-a-pat on the canvas. She went to the tent flap and looked out. It was raining, Not just a few drops but a hard, steady downpour. Much too wet to practise outside. She pulled her mackintosh off its hook and put on her wellingtons. She went out and across to the big top. At this hour she would find somewhere where nobody was working. As she splashed along she had become sufficiently fond of the circus to feel sorry it was a pull-down day. If this went on the men would have a bad time getting out.

The weather had kept most people away from

early work. There was nobody in sight except Ben, who was leaning against one of the king-poles chewing his usual straw, and Peter, who was riding. Santa chose a place in the main entrance to work. She took off her mackintosh and boots. She went into the big top to put them on a seat. Then she stood staring at Peter.

'Make him change now, Peter.' Ben spoke clearly in spite of the straw. "'E's cantered enough on that fore . . . Stop 'im . . . That's right. Now start 'im on the near fore . . . Circle to the right . . . That's it. Now start again . . . Keep doin' it over and over till you've got 'im nice and light to 'andle . . . Stop . . . Make 'im start clean at the first pressure of your leg. Remember 'osses is like children. They don't want more orderin' about than they must 'ave, but if you do give one see it's obeyed instant . . . That's nice an' clean . . . Don't let 'im 'urry . . . 'Urrying, 'e gets 'is aunches out of line.'

In the shadow in the entrance Santa was not seen. In any case both Ben and Peter were too absorbed to notice any one. To say Santa was startled was to put it mildly. If she had thought about Peter's riding lessons at all she had pictured him just sitting quietly on a horse which walked slowly round the ring. But all this cantering was startling. Besides, even to her ignorant eye Peter had a good seat. He looked part of the horse. Besides, he was so calm and confident carrying out Ben's orders. She made a face at herself. Look at him! Why hadn't he told her how good he was getting? No wonder he thought he had better be a groom.

She went back to the entrance and began her exercises. She worked especially hard. If Peter could ride like that it was time she did something well. She sat down and held her toes. She straightened her knees. She bent forward. She would get her forehead right down to her knees today. Peter wasn't going to be the only one who could do things.

It was while she was working that something made her remember what day it was. Saturday! Goodness, they'd be at Torquay tomorrow! Then it would only be three days to Gus's birthday. She must catch Peter after his lesson. Nobody had said anything more about fireworks. Perhaps they could risk buying the driving gloves that morning. Exeter was a big town. Just the sort of place to buy them.

She found Peter in the stables. He was feeding Mustard and talking to Ben.

'Hallo,' he said. 'What are you doing here?'

'It's raining. I couldn't practise outside.' She came up to Peter. She whispered although she knew it was rude, but really there was nothing else to do. 'Do you think we could get the gloves today? It's next Wednesday.'

Peter hated her whispering. It looked, he

thought, as if they were saying something about Ben.

'Don't whisper in my ear,' he grumbled. 'It tickles. Why can't you speak up? There's nothing Ben can't hear.'

Santa was indignant. They had kept all their plans for Gus's birthday secret. Peter was a fool. He might have thought what she was whispering. Very well, she would teach him. She raised her voice to a positive roar.

'I was saying it's Gus's birthday next Wednesday and shall we get the gloves today?'

Ben spat out his straw.

'Gus got a birthday next week?'

'Yes.' Peter suddenly thought what a good idea it would be to ask Ben's advice. He always knew things. 'We asked all the others what we'd do about it. We thought of asking some people to tea and a cake. Then we want to give him some new driving gloves.'

Ben picked up another straw.

'If you asked the kids what to do I reckon they'll 'ave fixed a fancy dress party or some such.'

Santa looked at Peter.

'I wish we'd asked him before.'

Peter gave Mustard another carrot.

'They want a picnic, and then to give him a concert afterwards. Not Santa and me, of course, because we can't do anything, but they will. And then they did say fireworks. But if we

321

buy the fireworks we shan't have enough for the gloves.'

Ben chewed thoughtfully.

'You don't want to go payin' much attention to what the kids say,' he said after a bit. 'Full of plans, they are. Most of' em won't come off. This one won't. For why? Gus, 'e wouldn't turn out for no picnic, not if you dragged 'im. You can't 'ave fireworks. One, on account the law don't allow it. Can't have a lot of folks sending off fireworks in the middle of the town. Second, Mr Cob wouldn't 'ave it. Not on account of upsetting the animals he wouldn't. They ought to 'ave thought of that.'

'As a matter of fact,' said Santa, 'they haven't said anything more about them.'

'Nor will.' Ben gave Tapioca a friendly smack. 'Like as not they spoke of them at home. They'd soon be told it was foolishness.'

Santa looked worried.

'But if we don't have a picnic what'll we do about the cakes? Mrs Schmidt has made a proper birthday one, or at least she's bought the things for it, and Mrs Moulin is making little ones.'

'Well, eat 'em.'

'Where?'

'Out or in. All accordin' to how the weather is.'

'Will Gus like that?' asked Peter.

'Well' – Ben sucked his straw – ''course as you're gettin' on you don't care for birthdays like you did.

More especial a man in Gus's profession. Don't want to be too old, doing the work he does. Mind you, when you get as old as me you don't mind. I have my birthday round Christmas. They 'ave a bit of supper for me now. Mr Cob, 'e proposes my health. 'Here's to Mr Willis," 'e says. 'May 'e live to be a hundred and still with us.' Then all the artistes and my boys they drinks to me. 'Mr Willis,' they says. Just as if they always called me that. I reckon Gus'll like a cake and that. He's not had much fussin' over, Gus hasn't. A little won't do him no harm.'

It was fine on the Wednesday at Torquay. Peter told Santa as he went off to his riding lesson.

'It's fine, Santa.'

Santa came outside to do her practice. The Schmidt twins came flying up to her.

'It's fine, Santa. It was a beautiful day.'

Fifi looked out of her caravan window at the Schmidt twins walking by.

'Good morning, Hans. Good morning, Fritzi. It's fine.'

They gave Gus his gloves at breakfast. They put the parcel by his plate. Gus picked it up.

'What's this?'

At that moment Hans and Fritzi came and stood outside and sang.

'It's for you, Gus,' Santa said anxiously. 'It's for your birthday. You must listen.'

Gus did listen. He stood on the steps of the caravan and heard the song right through to the end. Hans and Fritzi sang it nicely. When they had finished Gus grinned at them.

'Fancy you making a song for me. Very nice, thank you. Well, my breakfast will be getting cold. So long.' He came in and sat down and opened his parcel. 'Funny, these foreigners,' he said as he cut the string. 'Singing for my birthday!' But he seemed rather pleased.

He was quite stunned by the gloves.

'Cabbages and cheese, look at them! We shan't know ourselves on Sunday mornings.' He grinned at Peter. 'I'll have to clean up the car to live up to them.' Then he turned them over. 'Where did you kids get money? Thought you hadn't any.'

Peter expected that question.

'I earned it. I can't tell you how. But it's all right.'

Gus nodded.

'That's fine.' He looked at the gloves. 'Very handsome. Well, how about these bacon and eggs?'

The party was a great success. Directly Gus heard about the cake he asked the parent Moulins, Schmidts, and Petoffs, as well as the children. The grown-ups sat on chairs and had plates on their knees. The children sat on the ground. Gus even liked the concert. He grumbled about the way the Petoffs slurred their movements, and he told Hans he looked too solemn while he was working. Peter and Santa were worried that Olga, Sasha, and Hans would not like being criticized, seeing they were doing it specially for Gus's party. But nobody minded. In fact, it started a very good discussion on hand-stands. The party finished by Gus, Maxim Petoff, Mr Schmidt, Mr Moulin, Hans, Fritzi, Fifi, Olga, and Sasha all doing hand-stands at once. They were quite startled when Lucille looked at her watch and said she must go and make up.

'That's the worst of a good time,' said Gus. 'It goes so quick.'

Santa dug her elbow into Peter. He dug her back. Nobody could want a nicer compliment than that about a party.

16

Gus Speaks

It was not easy to swim, even after weeks of doing it on a box, as Syd had hoped. Every day at Torquay and Bourne-mouth they struggled, Syd, up to his waist in water, walking beside first one and then the other with a hand under their chins, saying: 'One, two. One, two.' Then at Portsmouth Peter did six strokes alone, and was too worried to be pleased about it.

On the Thursday night at Bournemouth Canada was boxed and sent with one of the bereiters over to Southampton to sail to America. Early on Friday Peter went to call Lorenzo to see how he was feeling and to bring him some carrots. He seemed quite cheerful. The same thing happened on Saturday morning. On Sunday he was waiting in the stables when Lorenzo was ridden up from the station. He was still all right. On the Monday morning Peter had only time to give him a pat and a lump of sugar after his riding lesson, as school had begun again. He had meant to run down and see him after afternoon school, but Syd was waiting to take them swimming.

'Have to make it snappy,' he said. 'We're not so near the sea, and I must be here by half past five sharp.'

Directly they came back from the bathing Peter got some lumps of sugar and hurried to the stables. Mr Cob, Ben, and two of the stable hands were standing round Lorenzo's stall. Lorenzo was looking wretched. He dropped all over. All the brushing he had received had not made his coat shine.

'I gave him a bran mash 'stead of his oats ration,' Ben was saying. 'He didn't finish it. There's nothing really wrong with him, except 'e's pinin'.'

Mr Cob shook his head.

'Looks like you were right, Ben. I shouldn't have separated him and Canada. Seems queer, though. He was all right at first after he went.'

'Not quite right, he wasn't,' Ben objected. 'Not quite hisself to me.'

Mr Cob shook his head.

'That's because you were looking for trouble. Nobody else saw any. Maxim was watching him in the ring. He said he seemed all right.'

'He wouldn't 'ave if he' had to follow Canada instead of Canada's place bein' behind 'im. Besides, he's always waltzed with Masterman these last two years. Far as 'is ring work' concernd there wasn't no change.'

'But if he was missing Canada all that much why didn't he start the hullabaloo on the Friday? That's what I can't understand.'

Ben chewed his straw thoughtfully.

'The way I looks at it, Mr Cob, is this. You bought Canada and Lorenzo when they were just off two. You gave 'em to me to break. On account of them coming same time they was stabled side by side. When they was broken to liberty work we takes them tenting. Again they're stabled side by side. Well, you know how 'tis, a 'oss don't think ahead like, same as you an' me. What 'e has is memory. All last week at Bournemouth he's fussed because Canada ain't there, but there's nothin' to mak 'im think he won't be by tomorrer. But yesterday when we builds up the stable we don't put up no stall for Canada. Lorenzo finds hisself alongside Pepper, and he don't like it.'

'Well, he'll have to learn.' Mr Cob turned away. 'He'll get used to it in time. And he's got Masterman one side of him. He's used to him.'

Ben spat out his straw. He watched Mr Cob disappear round the bend in the stables. He turned to the grooms.

'Put on his harness.' He shook his head at Peter. ''E's pinin'. 'Osses has eyes same as you an' me. Lorenzo's been fussed since Canada went. Now he's downright upset. 'E can see Canada' stall ain't been built. There'll be trouble. You'll see.'

'He's still got you,' Peter suggested.

Ben gave Lorenzo an affectionate pat.

'That won't do 'im no good. Tell you a funny thing, Peter, which most folks who loves 'osses tries to deny. But it's the truth. 'Ossess don't care for men. Maybe they'll come at the call of one voice, or neigh when someone comes into the stable. But that's 'abit. Sell the 'oss. Get another man to teach him the same tricks. Two or three days, and he'll be comin' to the call from the new voice, and neighing fit to bust hisself when the new owner comes in the stable.'

Peter hated this. He stammered with indignation.

'Mustard would miss me now if I went. I know he would.'

Ben turned away.

'That's the way I like to think, son, about all the 'osses. But 'tain't so, and facin' facts never hurt anybody.'

Lorenzo was a clever horse. He was the best waltzer of all the liberties. He had always been impetuous and excitable. A very different type from his quiet friend Canada. Habit made him conform to the circus routine. He knew just at what hours he would be fed and watered, just at what hours he would be dressed for the shows, just what was expected of him when he got in the ring, and what long, quiet hours he would have to gossip with his friend. A change in his routine not only upset him, but brought all his natural excitability and impetuosity to the top. He did not plan what he would do, he just let his feeling run away with him. If one bit of his routine was upset, then it was all upset. His friend of years had been taken away. Then he did not want to eat. He did not want to gossip. And when he got into the ring on Monday night he suddenly found he did not want to work.

Maxim was not expecting trouble. Of course he knew that Lorenzo was off his food, and missing his friend, but he had not known him in the early days when he was being broken. He did not know what a lot of temperament lay under that placid exterior.

The trouble started at once. The greys came cantering into the ring. Maxim cracked his whip and whispered to them. That should have been the signal for each of them to stop and put their forelegs on the ring fence. So all the horses did except Lorenzo. He did not move. He stood in his place in the ring with Masterman on one side of him and the leader Allah on the other. But Allah should not have been there according to custom. When they formed a circle it should have been Canada who stood between him and Allah. For days he had been uneasy at this change. Now he knew he could not stand it.

Maxim cracked his whip again. Gently he came over and fondled Lorenzo's head. 'Up,' he whispered. But Lorenzo would not move.

Maxim cracked his whip beside him so that the end just flicked him. He stood like a rock. It was bad policy to allow disobedience. There would be a rehearsal. For this performance Maxim let it pass. He could not go on keeping the audience waiting. The orchestra broke into the *Blue Danube* waltz. The horses stood in their pairs. Juniper led off with Ferdinand, Biscuit followed with Halfpenny, Robin with Pennybun. Then should have come Canada and Allah, but since Canada was gone Allah was sent out of the ring before the waltzing started, so that it was now the turn of the star waltzers, Masterman and Lorenzo. Masterman got into his position. Maxim cracked his whip. Masterman took his first steps. Lorenzo felt a surge of rebellion. He would not waltz. He would not do anything. His world was turned upside down and he could not bear it. He kicked up his heels, jumped over the ring fence, galloped through the artistes' entrance to his own stall, and there stood with hanging head, all the spirit gone out of him. It had done him good to rebel. But now the rebellion was over and he was just a lonely horse missing his friend.

No horse could be allowed to get away with that sort of behaviour. Directly the first performance audience were out of the big top, the greys were brought back. They were put through their whole performance, only this time Lorenzo had Alexsis on his back. It was weary work. It took ten minutes to get his forelegs up on the ring fence, twenty minutes to get him to waltz properly, and another quarter of an hour to force him to bow at the end of his performance. Long before they had finished the rehearsal the audience were coming in for the next house. As Lorenzo made his last bow, Maxim patted him and gave him two lumps of sugar. He followed him out of the ring. In the artistes' entrance he stood mopping his forehead. He had been able to get neither food nor rest between the shows, but he was satisfied. By nothing but patience he had once more taught the horses that he would have unswerving obedience.

Peter had, of course, heard how badly Lorenzo had behaved. He stood under the seats by the artistes' entrance to watch the second house. He watched the first half without seeing it properly. His mind was fixed on Lorenzo. Had he learnt his lesson? Would he do it right this time?

The liberty act came after the interval. Peter gave a silent prayer: 'Please God let him do it properly, they'll only make him do it afterwards if he doesn't, and he's so unhappy already.'

But Lorenzo did not do it properly. His will had been over-come at rehearsal. The combined cajoling of Maxim and Alexsis had worn him down. But now he had no one on his back. Things were wrong. Why should some parts of his life go on as usual while other old habits were changed? He had always stood by Canada. Why wasn't he now? He did not even wait in his place in the ring, much less put his forelegs on the fence. He kicked up his heels, pushed his way between Half-penny and Robin, jumped over the fence gate, and, disregarding everybody, galloped back to his stall.

Peter hardly dared go down the stables after the show. What would they do to a horse who behaved like that at two shows running? He peered out from under the seats to see if Gus were about. They were not allowed to watch the second house in term-time. But tonight he had risked it. He simply had to know how Lorenzo was getting on.

Gus was not in sight. Peter ran down the stables. A few of the audience were passing through. The voices of the grooms saying 'No smoking in the stables, please' came with monotonous regularity. To Peter's surprise the greys were in their stalls. He had thought they would be going back for rehearsal. Lorenzo was in his stall too. His head dropped. Nobody was looking at him. Peter knew it was not the thing to do to a disobedient horse, but Lorenzo looked so depressed he simply had to. he went into his stall and gave him all the food he had in his pocket. It was three carrots and five lumps of sugar. Lorenzo ate the lot. Peter was glad; he knew he had not eaten much all day. He might be a sinner, but he would feel better with something inside. He turned to go out. Ben was looking at him.

'When a 'oss has disobeyed,' he said quietly, 'it's actin' stupid to pet him.'

Peter was so sorry for Lorenzo he lost his temper.

'I should think somebody better. You know he's going to be beaten until he does it right.'

Ben found himself a nice straw. He got one for Peter.

'None of the 'osses is ever beaten. Mr Cob goes mad if a groom so much as speaks rough to 'em. I've 'eard 'im threaten to flog one of my boys because he saw him give old President a smack when he was playin' up. And if ever a 'oss needed smackin', President does.'

'Well, what'll they do to Lorenzo? I bet they don't let him off. And it's very unfair, because he only wouldn't work because he's miserable.'

Ben smiled.

'You're gettin' 'ot before you need, son.' He felt in his pocket and brought out an old envelope. 'Take a read of that. It's a copy of a cable what went tonight.'

Peter took the envelope. On it was written:

JENSON. JENCIR. NEYWORK.

If you still want that other grey you can have him stop Cable immediately as will ship Friday Cob.

Peter looked up.

'Is it Mr Jenson that bought Canada?'

'Yes.'

Peter looked up.

Peter handed back the envelope.

'Will he have him, do you think?'

Ben put the envelope in his pocket.

'Yes. Wanted him from the beginnin'.'

'Well, will you send a letter with him to say he must be stabled next to Canada?'

Ben put his straw on the other side of his mouth.

'The groom that goes with 'im will tell 'im.'

'But don't you think you ought to write as well? Just to make sure?'

Ben spat out his straw.

'Not to Mr Jenson. He knows more about 'osses than any man in this business. You don't need to tell Mr Jenson nothin'. He feels 'ow a 'oss feels. He was over here once. Wanted me to go back with 'im.'

'What, to America?' Ben nodded. 'Why didn't you?'

'Well, I reckoned as there wasn't no need for me an' Mr Jenson in one circus. You see, here I'm wanted. Mr Cob, the Kenets, and Maxim, they're all fine riders and know a lot about 'osses. But now and then there's somebody what does a bit more than know about them. Well, Mr Jenson's one of them and I'm another. I reckoned it were better we was split up like.'

'Would you have earned a lot of money in America?'

'Yes. Powerful lot. But what for? I got a place to sleep, enough to eat, and a bit put by for when I'm too old to work. No man don't want more. My work's with the 'osses and where I reckons it's best for them I should be, it's best for me.' He looked along the rows of sleek backs. 'Bless 'em. That's what I say. Good night.'

He moved slowly away, walking as quietly as he talked. Peter had a feeling the 'Good night' had been to the horses and not to him.

The lights were dimming, the grooms yawning their way to bed. Peter left the stables. It was a glorious night. Talk and laughter drifted across from the men's mess-tent. Here and there a cigarette glowed. One of the lions gave a sleepy roar. Peter hurried as fast as he could across the ground. Gus would be angry, but it was worth it to know that Lorenzo was going to join Canada.

Peter was lucky. Gus was not at home. He was still at supper with the Kenets. He scuttled into bed. When Gus came in he was asleep.

Peter swam at Bognor, Santa a week later at Brighton. Gus came down to Brighton beach to watch them both. He never bathed himself as he considered it put his eye out for his work. So he stood on the promenade where he could see.

Peter plunged straight into the water and swam with good, bold strokes. Santa floundered a bit. She took quick, nervous strokes. But there was no question but that she was swimming.

Gus was pleased.

'You've done well.' He felt in his pocket and brought out two new half-crowns. 'There you are. Buy something you want. You can go on the beach when you like, but keep in your depth till you're more used to it. Well, I must go back and put some paint on my face.'

Peter and Santa did not go back with Gus. They said they would like to walk.

'I say,' said Peter, 'that was awfully nice of him.'

Santa looked admiringly at her half-crown.

'I've been thinking lately he was liking us more. Quite often now he lets me cook the breakfast.'

Peter wrung out his bathing trunks.

'And he asks me to clean the car. I think he's finding us useful. I wish he'd say something. There's not an awful lot of time left. There's Eastbourne, that's one week. Then there's Hastings, three days, and Folkestone three days. That's two weeks. Then there's Canterbury and Maidstone. That's three weeks. Then Dover and Deal. That's a month. Then there's only one week after that. Whitstable and Margate. Just think, in five weeks this'll be finished.'

Even the pleasure of having learnt to swim and having got a reward of half a crown faded. They walked gloomily up on to the front and turned homeward.

'I can't believe he means to send us to Saint

Bernard's or Saint Winifred's,' Santa said hopefully. 'He must know we'd hate them worse than ever after this.'

'I hope not.' Peter did not sound very hopeful. 'But you remember he told us we didn't know they'd be awful as we'd never seen them.'

'Shall we ask him?'

Peter stopped to take a pebble out of his shoe.

'I'd rather we didn't. If he said we were going to Saint Winifred's and Saint Bernard's it would spoil the five weeks that's left.'

'I know,' Santa agreed. 'But if he said we were stopping with him near the winter quarters it would make the rest of the time more heavenly than it is.'

Peter stopped. He held out his half-crown.

'How about us tossing for it? Heads we ask him; tails we don't.'

He tossed. It was tails. Santa sighed.

'In a way I'm sorry. I've got a sort of pressing feeling just in the middle of me. It comes whenever I think about what's going to happen to us.'

Peter put his half-crown in his pocket.

'Let's go and have an ice. It'll make us feel better.'

'Yes, let's.' Santa skipped at the idea. 'But don't let's go into any shop that says "Vanilla", because I want strawberry.'

The weather went on being lovely. Every day

at Eastbourne, Hastings, and Folkestone Peter and Santa swam. When they got to Canterbury there was, of course, no bathing, so they had more time for games on the ground and violent practice on the water-act cloth. It was at Canterbury they first heard there was trouble in the Petoff family. Fifi mentioned it as they came back from afternoon school.

'There was a terrible noise in your caravan last night, Olga. It woke us up. Maman has a migraine today. She says it is because you make such a noise she cannot sleep.'

Olga turned a cartwheel.

'It's terrible. Father cried. Mother screamed. We all had a dreadful mood. It was already light before we felt better and had some tea.'

'To drink tea foolish was when one a mood has,' said Fritzi severely.

Sasha hopped along on one leg.

'Not to us. Tea makes us feel good.'

'What was all the row about?' asked Peter.

Olga took his arm. He tried to wriggle free but she held on. She lowered her voice dramatically.

'Alexsis said he would run away!'

'Why?' asked Santa.

Olga looked at her impressively.

'The Elgins have an engagement in Paris for Christmas. They wish Alexsis to go with them. Alexsis had to tell my father. There was a terrible row.'

'Me and Olga' – Sasha hopped to the other side of Peter – 'felt as if our beds was shook. Never we had a bigger row.'

Peter pulled his arm free of Olga's.

'Won't your father let him go?'

'Certainly not. He is needed for the horses.' Olga turned another cartwheel. 'This very Christmas he is to work in the act.'

'Has Mr Cob given him a contract?' asked Fifi.

Olga shook her head.

'Not yet. But he will.'

Fifi made an immense gesture with both hands. It expressed her complete disbelief in such a contract. Hans accepted it as if she had spoken.

'Fifi right was. Unless the contract signed is, nothing is known. It may be the Elgins will go to Paris, and Alexsis remain, and he no work will have.'

Olga finished a flip-flap. She caught up with the rest of them.

'And still my father won't let him go. He says he has to work with the horses. When Sasha is older it will be different. Even if Alexsis may not work this Christmas my father will train him all next year.'

'You see,' Sasha explained to Peter and Santa, 'the Kenets have no contract with Mr Cob after one more year. It may be they will stay. But it may be they will get more money if they go. If they go there's only my father and Paula for the high school. That's not enough.'

Hans, Fritzi, and Fifi nodded. It was not enough. Hans spoke for them all.

'Alexsis will not be able to go.'

'Well, I think it's shame,' said Peter. 'I hope he runs away.'

Fritzi looked shocked at such stupidity.

'That all talk is. Where would he run?'

'I don't know.' Peter's voice was stubborn. 'But I think it's a shame if he has an offer he can't take it. He could come back to his father if the Kenets go.'

Fritzi tapped his arm.

'When one has nothing of sense to say it is better to silent be. How will he practise when he has no horses?'

It was an unarguable point, but Peter felt (not for the first time since he had known her) that he would like to hit Fritzi. He could see Santa felt the same.

They told Gus all about Alexsis's troubles, driving to Maidstone on Thursday morning. It was not a very good day to talk about troubles, because the country was looking so nice. There were nuts in the hedges. Trails of traveller's joy looked like snow. The first berries were forming on the bushes. The leaves were turning colour. Peter sniffed at the air. This was one of those October mornings when Ben said Mustard missed the hunting. 'When it's sharp, and you get a smell of leaves like.' It was sharp today. There was a smell of dropped leaves. Peter made a mental resolution to take Mustard a little something extra.

Santa started the story of Alexsis. Gus had heard bits of it, but not that Maxim had definitely refused to let Alexsis go.

'Well,' he said, when they had finished telling him, 'like most arguments there's points both sides.'

Santa, who was sitting in front, looked back at Peter. They both thought it a mean-spirited answer. Everybody ought to take sides.

Gus drove along in silence for a bit. Then he slowed down the car.

'Talking of Alexsis reminds me it's time I had a word with you two. After these three days at Maidstone we've only a fortnight's tenting to go.' He paused and Peter and Santa held their breaths. 'When you first came and were such a couple of ninnies I had planned to send you to those orphanages after we were through on the road. I thought maybe a year or two in one of those places would put guts into you and teach Peter not to argue.'

'And you don't mean to now?' Santa hardly dared ask the question.

'No. You've come on a lot. And you don't like being separated, so I've fixed something different.'

He stopped again. They were coming nearer Maidstone. He had his eyes on the road ahead, looking for the first green stars.

'What are you going to do with us?' said Peter.

'Watch for the stars, you two.' Gus went dead slow for a flock of sheep. 'Well, I've written to that Reverend Stibbings. He speaks well of Mrs Ford. I'm fixing to take two rooms for you in her house. You'll go to school from there. Later there's good technical schools in the neighbourhood. We'll see how you shape. They'll maybe be able to fix you both in offices.'

'Gus, you wouldn't sent us back to Mrs Ford?' Santa's voice had a crack in it.

Gus was hurt.

'What funny kids you are. I thought you'd be pleased. After all, it's that or the orphanages.'

Peter and Santa somehow directed Gus to the ground. It was not easy. All the green stars swam. Both of them had tears in their eyes.

At the ground they did not wait even to fill the kettle. They dashed off in different directions. Santa lay on her face behind the staff wagons. She shook with sobs.

'Back to Mrs Ford. I can't bear it.'

Peter did not cry at first. He stood in a corner of the ground where he could see the stables built up.

No more horses. To go in an office. It couldn't be true. He swallowed. Then tears ran down his cheeks.

17

The End of Tenting

The end of anything you have enjoyed terribly is dreadfully depressing, even when you are going home or somewhere nice. But when you are going somewhere you know you will simply hate it's difficult to be brave about it. Peter and Santa did manage to seem fairly cheerful when they were with people. By themselves they sunk into depths of gloom. They tried to cheer each other up.

'I expect you can be a groom just the same,' Santa said.

But Peter knew it was a false hope.

'What, after just six months with horses? Not likely. If I'd had another year I might have had a chance. Fat chance I've got of even seeing a horse, living with Mrs Ford.'

'It's the same with me. If I'd had a bit longer lessons with Ted I might have been able to train to teach gymnasium. I wouldn't like it much, but I'd like it more than going in an office.'

'Well, you can practise your exercises. That's more than I can my riding.'

Santa shook her head.

'I'm not twelve yet. Over three years of living with Mrs Ford will kill all ambition in me. When I'm fifteen I'll just take the first job I'm offered.'

'We'll be very lucky if we get jobs in offices. I might start as an office-boy, but I shouldn't think I'd ever get any farther. I can't spell.'

'Nor me.' Santa sighed miserably. 'Ours is a very bad outlook.'

'All the same we'll have a try.' Peter looked a bit embarrassed. 'Gus is spending his savings on us.'

'I know. He's giving us a fine start. Everybody says so.'

Peter made a face.

'I do wish he wouldn't. There's one thing, we shan't cost him anything at technical schools. I shouldn't think we'd ever get in. It's a shame he's got such stupid relations.'

'Oh, I wish we could ask him if we couldn't stop with him,' said Santa. 'I'd work my fingers to the bone looking after him.'

'My goodness, how he'd hate that!'

'I know,' Santa agreed. 'Such a pity Gus isn't the sort of man that likes being looked after.'

As the days went by they felt worse and worse. Everybody else seemed to have such nice things to do. The Moulins were off to Paris. They would show the dogs in theaters. Fifi was to work with them over Christmas. Then, when the Moulins and the dogs came back to tent in April, she would stay to train with Mink.

The Schmidts were going to Germany. They would see the relations who were The Flying Mistrals. Fritzi would have some more lessons on the trapeze. Hans would stay with the uncle who had the five lions, three panthers, four bears, and two tigers, with which he would work when he was fifteen. They they would go back to England and spend another lovely six months tenting.

The Petoffs were going to the winter quarters, as were Ben, the Kenets, and Gus. Peter envied them most of all. They were to break some new horses, and work at new acts for the Christmas show.

The only person who was as miserable as Peter and Santa was Alexsis. When the Elgins went to Paris his hopes would go with them. They had finished their contract with Mr Cob. After Paris they were going to America. All his chances of working with them faded the farther away they went. He felt just like Peter and Santa. He was going where he did not want to go, and, like them, could not help himself. It was no good his threatening to run away. He could not go to France with the Elgins without a passport. How could he get a passport without his father knowing?

It is terrible how fast last days go. There had been a fortnight and three days left when Gus told them what was to happen to them. But somehow they did not last as long as a fortnight and three days should. Before you would think even one day had passed they had moved on to Dover. It was too wet and cold there to bathe; besides, time was getting so short they hated to leave the ground. In fact, Peter would not. Every second that he was not in school he spent in the stables. It was awful when they got to Whitstable. Just three days there. Then on the Thursday they moved to Margate. That was the end.

To make it even worse that they were going to live with Mrs Ford, they made big strides in what they were working at. Ted Kenet was really surprised at Santa. On the Friday at Margate he gave her a last lesson after tea.

'Mind you,' he said, speaking rather stuffily through his sweet which he was sucking, 'old Gus is doing right by you. Nothing like education. Never had much of it myself, but I know it's a fine thing to have. All the same, it's a pity you can't keep this up. You've come on wonderful. If I could have had you another year I'd have made a smart little acrobat of you.'

Santa had to turn away and drag on her coat so that he should not see she was crying.

'It's been awfully nice of you to teach me,' she gulped.

Ted looked at her in surprise.

'You got a cold?'

'Just a bit.'

'You come over to my caravan. I'll mix you a glass of peppermint and hot water. Nothing like it in the winter for keeping out the cold.' He looked in her face. Then he gave her arm a squeeze. 'Nor for keeping your spirits up.'

They sat at the table in the caravan and drank their peppermint. Ted told her funny stories about the circus until he made her laugh. Something, either the funny stories or the peppermint, certainly did her good. She went back to her own caravan feeling better.

Ben never was one to say things that would make trouble. He did not say to Peter that he thought it a pity he had to give up riding. It was Gus's decision that they should stay in one place and be educated. Peter was Gus's nephew. If Gus thought it right there was no more to be said. But Peter knew Ben was sorry. He knew he was pleased with the way he had got on. He was doing quite difficult work now: the Spanish walk, all sorts of pirouettes, piaffers; and he was learning to rein back without touching the reins.

On the Friday morning after the lesson Ben came with Peter to feed Mustard.

'Shan't be able to take you tomorrer. It's a lot of work when we finish tentin'. Some of the stuff goes one place, and some another.' He paused while he picked up a straw. 'You work hard where you're going. You try to get into this technical school, because that's what Gus fancies, and 'e's payin' the piper and 'as a right to call the tune. But if you can't make it, then let me know. I'll have a talk with Gus. Maybe we could fix something for you.' Peter's face lit up. Ben put his hand on his arm. 'But mind you, don't you write to me unless you can say honest that you worked all you knew. Neither in a stables nor anywhere else is there room for one as doesn't.'

The Saturday at Margate was a day just in keeping with how Peter and Santa felt. Santa was sleeping in the caravan again as the weather was turning cold. She and Peter woke in the night to a new sensation. The caravan was rocking. They could hear the screaming wail overhead of the wind. They woke in the morning to find grey lowering clouds scudding across the sky. The sea was black and angry. Great waves reared up and hurled across the sea front, scattering pebbles as they went.

Everybody in the circus was anxious. In spite of it being a busy day they had time to stand in knots and watch the sky and stare at the big top. All the morning gossip drifted up from the town. Some tiles had been blown off a church roof. Some bathing huts had been smashed and were drifting out to sea. An old woman had been blown right across a street.

At one o'clock Mr Cob called a committee. The tentmaster, Maxim, the eldest Kenet, and Gus. Was there too much wind? Should they play for safety and pull down the big top?

It was the end of the season. Tents the size used in a circus cost a lot of money. On the whole everyone was in favour of packing up, but Mr Cob was worried. He did not mind about the booked seats. That was easy. He could give their money back. He was thinking of the children who had been looking forward to seeing the circus for weeks, and the poorer of the grown-up people who had perhaps been saving to come.

'Tell you what,' he said, 'we'll risk it. We'll play the matinée and see if we can stand up. Then we'll try the first show. Then all being well we'll risk the last show. My old father used to say: 'A showman's duty is to his public.' Well, pulling down the big top may be safe, but it's not my duty to my public. Put out watchers. If the big top tears, the orchestra plays the people out and we pack up.'

The wind did not get better. It seemed extraordinary hearing it howl by to think a great tent could stand. But stand it did all through the matinée. The house was packed. 'Oohs' and 'Ahs' and roars of laughter came from the audience. Only the people of the circus knew that round the tent in a circle stood watchers staring at the roof. Would the big top beat its worst enemy – wind?

The first evening show too finished safely. The people were battering their way through the gale to the last show.

'Thought maybe it would be too windy for you to keep up,' one man said to Mr Cob, as he hurried his wife and six excited children into their seats.

Mr Cob smiled as if he had not a care in the world and was not a ring-master with one eye glued to the roof.

'It is a bit windy, sir,' he agreed cheerfully, 'but unless it gets worse we hope to get through the show.'

Peter and Santa were too nervous to stay in any one place. The wind made them like that. So it did the artistes and staff. Usually on a last night there are a lot of extra gags and funny make-ups and people congregating in the artistes' entrance to say just one extra 'Good-bye.' So it would have been with Cob's Circus that night. Plenty of jokes had been planned. There were a lot of sad good-byes to say. So many of the artistes were off to other parts of the world. These performers might never see each other again, or they might meet in Buenos Aires or San Francisco; it was a matter of luck. But tonight, with the wind howling and tearing at the canvas, nobody had time for jokes or good-byes. It was 'Hurry, hurry! Shall we get through before the wind blows us down?' Peter and Santa watched part of the show from the entrance and the rest of the time stood with the watchers outside. In a way it was less frightening outside. There you were just banged about with the gale. You could only stare through the night at the roof of the big top. If a ray of light came through, then the canvas was ripped. If the canvas ripped, then there must be the quickest pull-down on record. No ripped canvas could live many minutes; once the wind found a way to get in, it would tear it to pieces.

All the children were running round. The Petoffs and the Schmidts would see each other that summer, but Fifi was not coming back, nor were Peter and Santa. They made wild plans to meet. Fifi said she would come to England for August and stay with her family. Peter and Santa said they would persuade Gus to let them come for the summer holidays. If that happened they would be all together again next year. But even as they made the plan they knew it would not happen. These six months when they had done everything together were finished. It was no good planning to repeat them.

The interval was over. Peter caught hold of Santa's arm.

'Come and see the liberties.'

Glittering and jingling the horses came into the ring. Maxim, looking as cool as usual, gave his orders. He had to raise his voice a little. The side curtains flapped and banged. The tent props creaked. The wind screamed among the guy-ropes. The chestnuts had finished. In came the greys. They stood in a neat ring, all their forelegs on the fence, all their faces looking out over the audience with amused tolerance.

The band played *The Blue Danube*. Juniper and Ferdinand got into position. Then suddenly a man raced up to Mr Cob. Mr Cob nodded. He held up his hand to the orchestra. They stopped playing. The grooms ran in and led out the horses. Mr Cob took off his top-hat. He stood in the middle of the ring.

'My lords, ladies, and gentlemen, the wind has made a rip in the canvas of this tent. If we leave it up it will tear to pieces. I must ask you all to leave as quickly as possible. And please forgive us for disappointing you, but even a showman cannot rule the weather. Thank you.'

Some of the audience grumbled, but they were silenced by others who knew what wind could do to a tent. The orchestra played a cheerful tune. The commissionaires hurried the people out. 'Pass along, please!' They could not say: 'Pass along, please, as quickly as you can, or the tent may blow down on you,' for that would mean a panic.

The moment the show was stopped everybody got to work. The girls dragged at the baskets and flew round throwing the covers off the chairs. Santa, Fifi, Olga, and Fritzi helped. They had seen it done so often they had no need to be told what to do. Peter, Hans, and Sasha helped the men get the seating down.

There was never a pull-down like it. Crash! Bang! Hammer! 'Pass along, please!' Those that had eyes to spare to look could see the rip in the tent now. It was a piece of material torn clean away. It flapped like a banner.

The people were out now, the chair covers packed, part of the seating down, the lorries backed up waiting for their loads. The wagons with the big lamps came and stood by in case the tent should go and the inside wiring snap. Gus and Ted Kenet worked like mad packing their stuff. The Frasconi father and his sons almost tore their trampoline in pieces to get it apart. They were getting the tent-poles out now. Men outside were dragging up the staples. All the ordinary routine of the circus was gone. The quickest way was the best way tonight. Then suddenly Mr Cob was back in the ring. He had a megaphone.

'Everybody outside. There's forty rips in the top. We must drop the canvas.'

It was not a minute too soon. All the wooden tent-props that were left standing were snapping like matches. The wind was tearing through the roof, the whole great tent swaying like a ship in a bad sea.

Everybody ran, the men carrying what they could. The tent-master gave his order. There was no measured lowering of the canvas tonight. Down it came with a rush.

It lay on the ground, a great white patch in the darkness. They turned the lights on it. Then they saw the damage. In falling the tent was pierced and torn in dozens of places by what remained of the seating and structure. As for what the wind had done, it was heartbreaking. There was no strip of the tent left that was worth saving. What they were looking at was a pile of useless fragments of canvas. What had been worth over two thousand pounds would not sell for twopence.

Mr Cob's face showed up in the light as he peered at the damage. They were fond of him. There was no one there who would not have liked to say they were sorry, and no one there who would dare to do it. There was good luck and bad luck and you took it as it came. Mr Cob was not a man who liked pity.

'Get on, boys, and clear up what you can.' He turned to the tent-master: 'Everyone's done fine. Thank 'em for me.'

Peter and Santa had run with the rest. It was difficult to know where to run to. Everything was being packed outside. The lorries were standing close in. They found themselves pressed up against the side of the stables. They just waited to see the big top fall. Then they climbed through a flap and went in.

The horses were being ridden off to the station. Ben was supervising in the other half of the tent. Owing to the show being stopped his system had broken down. The bereiters were not back from the station yet to fetch the liberties. He was getting the greys away, but the chestnuts were still waiting.

Peter and Santa stood looking sadly at the bareness: at the place where the lions had stood; at the stalls that had held President, Rajah, Emperor, King, Rainbow, Whisky, Forrest, Magician, Piecrust, Wisher, Allah, Jupiter, Ferdinand, Biscuit, Halfpenny, Robin, Pennybun, and Masterman. Ben's voice came drifting with the wind:

'Don't hustle 'em. But if you pass the other boys on the road send 'em back as quick as you can. That's right, Alexsis, ride Carter. He'll be easier when you're leadin'.'

It was hard to hear even at that short distance because the wind was driving down to Ben. It was hard to stand up. With the big top down the gale was raging through the stables. Something came with it that for a moment Peter and Santa did not see. Somebody had thrown down a lighted cigarette. It blew in at the door glowing red. It buried itself in the straw in Soda's stall.

With a draught like that it did not take a second for the straw to catch. Nor a second for Peter and Santa to see what was happening. Nor a second for Soda to lose his head. He reared and kicked. Peter could not be afraid of a horse even when he was panicking. He raced into the stall and untied Soda. Santa screamed for help, but her scream was part of the screaming of the wind. Ben outside, seeing off the rosin-backs, never heard it. It was no easy job leading out Soda. The flames were getting a hold on the straw. He did not want to go past them, but Peter saw how quickly the flames could blow into Rice's stall, and so up the line. It was no time to wait for help. Using every ounce of strength and every soothing noise he knew he dragged Soda out.

'Hold him,' he said to Santa, 'then lead him into the other half of the tent. Tell Ben what's happened.' He pulled off his coat.

'What are you doing?' Santa gasped.

'Putting out the fire, of course.'

All the straw in the stall was now flaming or smoking. Santa could see that one boy could not deal with it all. Scared though she was of horses she dragged Soda over to President's stall. She tied him up. As she turned back she saw Peter throw his coat on the blazing straw and roll on it. In a second she had hers off and was doing the same.

Ben came into the other half of the tent with two of the grooms. They stood sniffing. Then they all ran.

There was no need for the hurry. Peter had seen that the danger lay in the straw of the other horses catching, for that was the way the wind was going. It was the straw nearest Rice he put out first. When Santa joined him she rolled on the rest. When Ben and the grooms arrived the fire was out. Peter and Santa were standing holding their charred overcoats stamping on anything that smoked.

Quickly they told Ben what had happened.

'You burnt?' he asked. Peter had a small blister on his thumb. 'Back you go to the caravan,' he said. 'Shove on some tea-leaves. That'll keep out the air.' He went over to soothe Soda. He gave him a pat. 'You're lucky, old man. If there was always people about who could keep their heads, we'd do fine.'

There was almost a party in Gus's caravan that night. Everything which could be saved from the wreckage had been saved. Ted Kenet came along, and Ben, and presently Maxim and Alexsis, and much later the Moulins and the Schmidts. Santa was kept busy. She made bacon and eggs for them all. Everybody said she was a good cook. Then suddenly there was a knock on the door.

'Marrow-bones and gravy, who's that?' said Gus. 'I thought the rest had dossed down.'

Ted Kenet, who was nearest, opened the door. It was Mr Cob.

'I smelt bacon and eggs,' he said. 'Can I come in?'

At once a place was found for him. Santa looked round from the stove.

'How many eggs, Mr Cob?'

'Three, Santa.' He looked at her. Then he looked at Peter. 'What are you doing with these kids, Gus?

I hear they saved what might have been nasty trouble in the stables.'

Gus explained about Mrs Ford, and the technical schools later on. Mr Cobb nodded.

'That's fine. But there's all sorts of education, Gus. It strikes me on the showing of tonight they've learned a good piece travelling with us. Can't you keep 'em with us?'

Gus shook his head.

'I would, but there's no future for them here. You got to think of the future.'

'Who says there's no future?' Ted sucked at a sweet. 'I reckon that by the time she's old enough I'll have Santa better than any of your dancing butterflies. She's got a natural aptitude' – he winked at Santa – 'when she works.'

Ben leant across the table, not to Mr Cob but to Maxim:

'If I can keep this boy, Maxim, you can let your boy go. It'll work right all round. I got Peter coming on nicely. He's born to it. Takes to it natural. Your Alexsis is sore. You're draggin' at 'is mouth. That's liable to spoil any young thing. Peter's fourteen by Christmas year. If you need 'im by then, I'll 'ave 'im ready.'

Mr Cob turned to Gus.

'I'd like it, Gus. I owe the kids something. They can go to the quarters with you and go to school near by. Then Santa can work with Ted and later practise with the girls, and Peter

360

can keep on under Ben. It's a big chance, really.'

'It is a big chance.' Maxim looked at Alexsis. 'You wish to go with the Elgins?'

Alexsis did not need to answer; his face was enough.

Maxim turned to Ben. 'Peter has real talent?'

Ben nodded.

'I said so. I don't make no mistakes about 'osses nor riders.'

Everybody looked at Gus. Gus looked at Peter and Santa.

'Kedgeree and rum! Don't stare at me as if I had to do anything. There's your offer, kids. Will you take it?'

Would they! Peter looked at Santa. They saw the years ahead. Long hours working in the ring for Peter. Long hours of training for Santa. They saw summers spent tenting. The lines of caravans travelling up dusty lanes. They saw green stars pointing the way. They saw flaring posters – THE CIRCUS IS COMING. They were so happy it hurt.

'They don't need to answer,' said Mr Cob. ''Course they're stopping with us. They belong.'